WHEN HEARTS COLLIDE

DANIELLE BAKER

For every girl that has ever felt powerless.
You are NOT powerless, love.

WARNING

Content/Trigger Warnings
DV/Assault/Stalking/Self-Defense
Talk of Alcoholism
PTSD and Trauma
Degradation/Verbal Assault

ONE

"So, you didn't even get to have hot raunchy groomsmen sex? What's the point of being a bridesmaid if you don't get the one perk of being said bridesmaid?"

Punching into the rubberized dummy in front of her, Roxsanna Roberts huffed out a laugh as she turned to look at her friend, who stood off to the side with her arms crossed, one hip pushed out.

"The only groomsmen there were Kasey—"

"Mmm, yeah, I'd tap that."

Roxy glared at her friend and continued, "—who happens to be like my third cousin or something, and the brides two younger brothers, one of them wasn't even over eighteen, so no. No hot raunchy groomsmen sex."

"*Laaaame*," Natalie groaned, dropping her arms from where they were crossed over her chest. "Pleeease tell me Kasey looked drop dead gorgeous in his tux. And Freeman. *Gaawd* that man. Bummer he finally got shackled."

Roxy rolled her eyes and turned back to the rubber dummy, raising her fists and correcting her stance before throwing another punch, making the dummy wobble on its stand. "They both looked very handsome. Jodi is awesome, though," Roxy huffed on an exhale after another solid hit. "And I think Kasey's about to be tied down, too. Sorry for your luck, sis."

"That's alright, I've been trying to get Travis's attention, but the man is like a machine. All he does is train and be all broody and silent," Natalie muttered, leaning against the wall.

"Are you actually going to work out, or are you just going to stand here and bug me while I do?" Roxy snapped, turning to face her again. "Why do you pay for the membership if you don't do anything while you're here?"

"Umm, I get in plenty of cardio elsewhere, thank you very much," Natalie snapped back, though she was grinning. "I'm here for the views."

Following her friend's brown eyes, Roxy turned her head and found what had captured the other woman's attention; former MMA fighter, Travis 'The Reaper' Hayes, known best for his deadly left hook in the cage.

Standing on the other side of the rec center, Travis paid them no attention as he wrapped his hands with red sports tape. Standing in profile, they watched as he wrapped first his right hand, then his left, crossing the roll of tape in an X formation across each hand to protect the knuckles. Light, golden brown hair with streaks of silver throughout hung down past his insanely broad and heavily tattooed shoulders, obscuring his face as he concentrated on his task. A thick but well-maintained beard covered his upper lip, cheeks, and chin. Roxy admired the way his muscles moved across wide shoulders, down massive arms that were nearly as big as her thighs, across an outrageously well-defined chest and abdomen... Also all heavily tattooed. In fact, nearly every visible inch of skin on his body was covered in tattoos, something Roxy had always found undeniably sexy, and the air of danger around the man was intoxicating.

And that was exactly why Roxy had only ever spoken to the man in passing.

Because she didn't do dangerous anymore. No ma'am.

Sexy and intimidating and dark and broody were all things that turned into nightmares later. All that sexy intrigue and the thrill of something dangerous that was so fun and exciting in the beginning… But it doesn't stay that way.

That thrill of danger would turn into the reality of danger. That thrill of risk that was oh-so alluring in the beginning would turn into busted lips, black eyes, bruises on wrists. And then of course the cycle of love bombing would start; the special date nights out, a lavish and unexpected gift, or a blood red rose flower arrangement that would show up on the kitchen counter afterward.

As if that was all it took to make it all go away. Sweep it under the rug. At least until the next time. Until enough was enough.

Never again.

No, she would be perfectly fine with a run of the mill, nice, boring, *predictable* guy… He could wear pleated khakis, eat his turkey sandwich with the crust cut off, and have passively satisfying sex with his socks still on for all she cared. Boring and predictable was A-okay with her. That was *if* she ever decided to date again, which was a *really big* if.

Roxy's attention was brought back to Travis as they watched him bring the roll of sports tape to his mouth and tear it with a set of impeccably straight white teeth. *He must have a killer orthodontist*, Roxy thought hazily, then shook her head and glanced at Natalie when she heard a small moan come from her friend, rolling her eyes to the ceiling.

"You're droolin', doll," Roxy whispered, shoving her friend in the shoulder as she turned back toward the dummy once more.

"I just wanna give him a go," Natalie whispered wistfully as she continued to stare at the man across the room. Tossing her short blonde hair away from her face, she whispered loudly, "You know with moves like that he's got to be great in the sack. Shit, I'll join his class. I don't care. I just want to get closer."

"His kickboxing class?" Roxy asked on a rough laugh. "You'd break a nail in the first five minutes and never go back."

"I'd push through just to spend more time with all that," Natalie murmured, waving her hands in his general direction, pantomiming running them along his body, at the same time that he turned his head toward the two of them. The squeak of abject horror from her friend at being caught ogling him was enough to make Roxy's entire night.

Roxy laughed out loud, though she admittedly felt a flush of heat rise to her cheeks when his eyes rose to meet hers before he turned away as if he hadn't noticed a thing. Almost like they weren't worth being noticed in the first place. *Jerk.*

Bending to pick up her water bottle from the floor, Roxy took a drink before taking a step in the direction of the wide bench that housed several other gym goer's bags, as well as her own. Natalie grabbed her arm, hissing, "Where are you going?"

"I actually did my workout, Nat," Roxy drawled dryly, giving her friend a withering look. "So I'm going home."

"Don't leave me heeere," Natalie whined, trailing after her. Roxy pulled a hooded sweatshirt on over her sports bra and loose fitted tank top. She removed her sneakers, placing them in her bag sitting on the bench, before sliding her feet into Converse low top slip-ons that had seen better days.

"I'm not leaving you. I'm going home."

"Party pooper," Natalie grumbled, but Roxy merely rolled her eyes and hoisted her bag onto her shoulder. "Well, have a good night, you old maid."

"You're older than I am," Roxy reminded her with a wink, making her friend gasp in feigned outrage.

"You take that back."

Roxy laughed, blowing her friend a kiss. "Can't do that. It's the honest truth."

"You're only younger than me by a year!" Roxy heard Natalie hiss to her retreating back, making her laugh harder as she walked out into the early evening air, the sun setting on the horizon. It was a mild evening for January in Melody Hills, Texas, just chilly enough to warrant bundling up in an extra layer.

Roxy shivered, recalling the bitter cold and far too much snow she'd just returned from in the Colorado Rocky Mountains for her best friend Freeman Thorp's wedding the weekend prior. Ugh. So much snow and cold that just seeped into her bones.

Making the short drive from the rec center to the small ranch style cabin she'd taken over the rental lease on when Freeman had moved back to northern Michigan, she pulled into the driveway and stared at the small house for a long time.

She still remembered the night she'd shown up on the doorstep, asking Freeman if it was okay if she stayed there for a few days after she left her boyfriend at the time, Neal Johnson, after he'd put his hands on her one time too many. Free had opened his home to her without a second of hesitation. He'd helped her get a restraining order on him when he began to show up at her work, harassing her for leaving him, accusing her of choosing Free over him, convinced she'd been sleeping with Freeman the entire time.

She couldn't blame him for the assumption; her relationship with Freeman Thorp was unconventional at best. They'd met years ago and had become 'best-friends-with-benefits' or so Kasey had dubbed them ages ago, at least until she'd met Neal. Sex with the rugged and sexy Freeman was always just sex, something to scratch the itch. And when she'd met Neal, that aspect of their relationship had stopped immediately. They'd seamlessly transitioned to simply best friends, something not many people understood. Neal being one of them.

This home was also where Neal had followed her to late one night, knowing she was there alone with Free away in Michigan, and had beaten the hell out of her after she left him. Blind with rage and jealousy that she'd chosen to go to Free's home to escape him, he'd unleashed all his fury on her. She still carried the scar on her lip and her vision was blurry in her left eye from the force he'd used that night.

Neal had fled the area, presumably leaving Texas altogether. The police had not located him, a fact that bothered Freeman and his new wife to no end. They had already started hounding her to consider moving to northern Michigan, to be closer to a bigger and better safety net.

But Roxy didn't mind living alone because he'd never come back. She hadn't seen or heard from Neal Johnson in almost a year and a half. Each day got a little easier, those gray clouds of doom shifting further and further into the distance.

Picking up her duffel bag from the passenger seat, Roxy climbed out of her Toyota 4Runner. She was almost to the front door when she stopped, ice sliding down her spine.

Because there, laying on the doorstep of her front door, was a bouquet of blood red roses.

Two

R oxy sank down into one of the barstools at her kitchen counter, hands trembling violently as she clutched the small white card in her hand. She couldn't stop staring at the roses, which she'd picked up with shaking hands, and carried inside. They sat in front of her on the kitchen counter, the light above the island bar top casting a halo of light around them.

Fingers shaking, she was barely able to manage opening the tiny envelope. She tugged the card out and flipped it over, and her eyes scanned it rapidly and then a frown tugged her brows together.

It was completely blank.

Turning it over again, she shook her head at the blank card. Dropping the card onto the table, she covered her face, her hands still shaking uncontrollably.

The simplicity of it was more terrifying than anything else.

Because it may have been blank… but she knew who had sent the flowers.

Shit. Shit, shit, shit.

She stood, crossing to the blood red blooms with striding steps, where she picked them up and then threw them in the trash.

Her heart was hammering in her chest, fear clogging her throat. She walked through the house, turning on lights and closing blinds, checking every room, making sure every window and both doors were locked securely.

They always were. *Always.*

Panic seized her again and she clawed at the collar of her shirt, pulling it away from her throat and attempting to suck in steadying breaths.

He was back. He had been here. Had he been in the house? She didn't think so, as Free had made sure the locks were changed before he moved to Michigan.

She'd been confident Neal wasn't returning to Fort Worth, to the little community of Melody Hills.

To her.

Until now, at least.

She stripped off her gym clothes in the bathroom with the door cracked open. Every creak and groan of the old cabin made her jump, her heartbeat hammering in her throat, roaring in her ears. Pulling on a pair of jogger sweatpants in a dark, eggplant purple color, and then a matching sweatshirt with the words 'Squat: Because No One Raps About Little Butts' emblazoned on the front. Tying her red curls up in a messy bun on the top of her head, she walked out to the kitchen.

But as she stared at her reflection in the mirror above the sink, she told herself she was just being paranoid. Maybe the roses were from Free and Jodi, as a thank you token for being part of their wedding last week. Maybe they were from Kasey; a thank you for being his 'wing-woman' and helping him get the girl of his dreams.

She snorted and rolled her eyes. That one was farfetched.

But why would Neal return now? After almost a year and a half, why would he come back *now*? Why would he go out of his way to deliver flowers to her doorstep? It made no sense.

Her phone buzzed where she'd set it on the counter next to her purse. Picking it up, she swiped to open the message.

> Natalie: Duuuuude. He's so hot it's not even fair. How do you get anything done with him here at the same time as you? I can't even concentrate on working out. I want to take a bite out of his ass like it's a big ol red delicious apple.

Roxy rolled her eyes and typed a message back to Natalie.

> Roxy: Screenshotting this to put up on the bulletin board in the gym entrance.

The text bubbles immediately appeared, and a moment later, she laughed out loud.

> Natalie: Don't you fucking dare! I would DIEEE!!

A moment later, another message popped through.

> Natalie: Please sign up with me for his kickboxing class! Pleeeeease I will do anything! I CANNOT do this class alone Rox!

Sighing, she stared at the message for a long time. Setting her phone down on the counter, she stepped over to the refrigerator and opened the freezer door, pulling out a single serve Stouffer's frozen lasagna. Tearing the cardboard open, she picked a fork out of the drawer and stabbed the plastic wrap over the top of the container, then popped it into the microwave.

Returning to her phone, she saw several PLEASE, ROX!! text messages and rolled her eyes again. Maybe it wouldn't be such a bad idea to brush up on some self-defense exercises.

Just in case.

That old, familiar chill of dread washed over her spine and

made her shiver, and she glanced around the kitchen. Other than the remnants of the bouquet of flowers that were safely in the trash, everything was remarkably the same.

All except the clawing, chest seizing fear that tightened her throat…

Picking up her phone, she typed up a message back and hit send.

> Roxy: Ok. Count me in.

She could almost hear the squeal of excitement from Nat's end of the phone as her response came in, simply:

> Natalie: !!!!!!!!!!!!!!!!!!!!!!!!!
>
> Thank you!

THREE

*K*eep it movin', ladies. The last thing Travis wanted or needed was more attention. *Unless you're volunteering for a no-strings-attached, hot, raunchy roll in the bedsheets that has absolutely no potential for anything further… Yeah, nope.* Not even the thought of a quick lay was worth the trouble.

Especially the blonde. Way too high maintenance, though her Redbull induced energy could come in handy…

He shook his head, tossing the long strands of hair away from his face as he turned away from the two women across the room. *Nope. Still not worth it.*

The redheaded bombshell paid him little to no attention, but then again, she rarely gave any single person—male or female—any attention other than the blonde that always seemed to tag along with her while actively avoiding doing any kind of work-out. She was polite without inviting anyone into her personal space.

He could respect that. That was how he preferred things, too.

Not that it ever happened.

Travis 'The Reaper' Hayes was the closest thing this gym had to a celebrity. As a retired MMA fighter who had gotten several of his own Pay-Per-View specials, aired from Las Vegas, he had been a household name for a while. His mug was easily recognizable; with the long, sandy brown hair that was now streaked with silver throughout, the full beard that he kept trimmed, also sprinkled with grays now. From his throat all the way down to each fingertip and down to each toe he was covered in black and gray shaded tattoos.

He'd spent a small fortune and a lot of time covering every single inch of skin from curious eyes. Some things were better left unseen.

A giggle to his left perked his ear, but not enough to turn. The gym was overcrowded with New Year's Resolution holders, empty promises to 'do better' and 'be healthier'. Most of them would be gone next week.

Red would still be there, though. Three days a week, she came in and rotated weight training with a light kickboxing routine. He'd wondered about the scar that dissected the left side of her lower lip, the white of the scar a vast contrast to the rosiness of her lips. It was still fairly new, he could tell. Scars were something he was familiar with.

Out of the corner of his eye, he watched as Blondie got Red's attention and pointed toward the neon yellow flyer that had been stapled to the bulletin board at the gym's entrance. He groaned internally. *Fuck.*

Sure enough, he watched as the two women signed their names on the flyer, signing up for his kickboxing class that would start the following week.

The class that he intentionally started *after* all the New Year's Resolution dropouts would call it quits. There would always be the gaggle of women that signed up just to get the chance to ogle him, and on the rare occasion he'd let one gym bunny hop into bed. And there were always men that would sign up in the hopes that they'd get to best him.

Not that they ever won. He was a machine.

A monster.

"Hey, we going to spar or are you just going to stand there looking grumpy all night?" Hector called across the mat, and Travis nodded. Hector was one of his sparring partners, one of the few that stood any kind of chance.

Tapping the Bluetooth earbud in his right ear, music began to play. Disturbed '*Indestructible*' came on and he set his feet, angling his body toward the five-foot, ten-inch Mexican. His hair was cut close to his head, his face shaved except for a small goatee that covered his upper lip and chin. Travis stood three inches taller and outweighed the other man by fifty pounds of pure muscle, but Hector was scrappy as hell, having grown up as the youngest of five brothers.

Travis had been an only child. But it was probably better that way. He'd had a hard enough time keeping himself alive, let alone anyone else.

The mind-numbing rage that used to accompany thoughts of his childhood had dulled over the years. Thousands of fights—some fair, some not so fair—a decade of therapy, and the twentieth anniversary of *that night* meant he'd had a lot of time to work the anger out.

It wasn't gone, of course. He just knew how to harness it better now. And currently, beating the crap out of Hector was going to do just fine to exorcise those demons.

Merv, the fifty-something-year-old gym owner and longtime mentor of Travis's, blew the silver whistle on a string around his neck, and he and Hector were moving.

Ducking, jabbing, landing punches, feinting, circling. They traded punches, one after another. Hector landed a jab to his kidney and Travis grunted, baring his teeth in a grin. Around his mouth guard, Hector grinned back, wiggling his hands in a 'come get me' taunt, and Travis struck fast and hard with a hook that put the smaller, younger man on his back.

Chest heaving with each intake of breath, he grinned down at Hector, flat on his back. Reaching his hand down toward him, Hector hooked his arm around Travis's forearm, and he hauled the other man to his feet. Hector removed the mouth guard and blew out a breath as Travis tapped the earbud in his ear to turn the music off.

"That fuckin' hook, man. You save it for last on purpose, don't you?"

"You should know it's coming by now," Travis chuckled, rolling his neck from left to right. "You're getting soft—"

"Ma'am? Ma'am!"

The anxiety in the male voice across the room was what brought his head around. A heartbeat later he was launching himself over the rubber guardrails surrounding the mat, grabbing hold of the redheaded bombshell's body just as she went limp, and her eyes rolled into the back of her head as she passed out.

FOUR

There was so much noise.

Several raised voices that she didn't recognize talked around her. Another much deeper, rougher voice that seemed to surround her, her entire body humming with it, registered as she came to.

Blinking open her eyes, she squinted against the bright gym light directly above her, and then the light disappeared as a handsome, bearded face came into view.

That was when she realized she was laying across a hard pair of thighs, her back propped up slightly on those legs, her head resting near a bare torso. His deep voice rumbled through her body as he spoke softly. One of his hands shoved up through his long hair, pulling it out of his face, then he cursed crudely and raised his hand to his mouth. Tearing at the black tape that bound his hand with those impossibly straight, white teeth, he unraveled the tape from around his hand until he tossed it aside.

Holy shit. She was laying in Travis Hayes' lap.

"I've got you. You with us, Red?" he asked, his eyes searching hers, his voice gruff. It sent shivers down her entire body. He had long, spiky, dark brown lashes surrounding gentle, honey brown eyes. She nodded dumbly. His lips twitched slightly beneath the beard, and he murmured, "Good girl."

If she hadn't already been lightheaded, those two simple words would have done it. *Good lord.*

"Care to tell us what happened?" he asked roughly, but all she could do was stare up at him, transfixed. He was so much more gorgeous up close, if that was even possible. *And she was laying in his lap.* How was she supposed to form any kind of coherent response with a god this close?

Swallowing hard, she opened her mouth to speak, but what came out was an embarrassing croak. She licked her lips as he looked up, reaching over her to accept the bottle of water someone handed him. He brought it to her lips, and she took several small sips, then finally managed to whisper, "Thank you."

He shifted as he set the water bottle down on the floor beside them, resting his hand, palm flat on the floor so that he was half leaning over her. She could feel the muscles in his arm bunch and shift where it was banded beneath her shoulders, his forearm supporting her head.

"You alright?" he asked, and she nodded. "You passed out. Does this happen often?"

"I have low blood sugar," she said lamely and felt a flush of embarrassment creep up her cheeks. "I have peanut butter crackers and an orange juice in my bag." She pointed to her heather gray Adidas duffel bag across the room, her hand trembling uncontrollably.

A guy with a goatee, who was standing over Travis's shoulder, disappeared and came back a moment later with the package of crackers and the single serve bottle of OJ.

"Can you sit up, Red?" he asked, his voice gentle, a vast contrast to how gruff his exterior looked.

Roxy nodded again, bracing to lift herself off his thighs. The arm behind her shoulders tightened and then she was being lifted into a sitting position… and now her ass was solidly in his lap, her hip pressed tight against the V of his thighs. Blood rushed to her head and pounded in her ears. Though she wasn't sure if it was remnants from the blood sugar crash, or because she could feel *everything* against her hip.

"Take it easy," he murmured low as she shifted. Her fingers shook too much to grasp the plastic wrapped package, so he took it from her hands and opened it swiftly, producing two of the small orange, square crackers. "Where'd your friend go?"

"She left a little while ago," Roxy said, nibbling on a cracker. The crowd around them had dispersed some, leaving her alone with the tattooed god who's lap she was still sitting in.

"Did you drive yourself here?" he asked, uncapping the orange juice and handing it to her.

"Umm… Yes. I drove myself," she said quietly, then shifted again. "I should probably get up—"

With a small squeak of alarm, Roxy found herself being lifted into the air as Travis stood, one arm behind her back and the other hooked under her knees. She was pressed flush against his bare chest, and out of reflex she flung her right arm around his shoulders to hold on. His skin was warm and surprisingly soft against her hand. He walked with her like that to the other side of the room, as if she weighed nothing, then gently deposited her onto her feet next to the bench, where her duffel bag was housed. His hand remained locked on her elbow, though, as if sensing how wobbly she was on her feet. She sank onto the bench seat, and he finally released her elbow.

"I would feel better if you were accompanied home." She looked up at him, taking in more of the up-close view she was being afforded of the man she'd only watched from afar. "Do you think your friend would come back to give you a ride?"

"I can call her," Roxy mumbled, dropping her eyes from his

honey brown ones. Dammit was he hot. Mind addling hotness. Or was that still the blood sugar low?

Glancing up at him from under her lashes, she surmised it was definitely his godlike hotness that was doing the brain addling. All that naked, tattooed skin…

Swiping through her phone to Natalie's contact, she lifted the phone to her ear as he padded over to where his bag had been stowed, bringing it back and setting it down on the floor. He stripped the black athletic tape off his other hand, balling it up and tossing it into a trash bin nearby. Then he plucked a t-shirt out of his bag and pulled it over his head. The sleeves of the shirt had been cut out, revealing large swaths of his tattooed skin on his ribs. She stared at him, her mouth hanging open slightly.

Shaking herself internally, she sighed after several rings went unanswered, then she heard, "You've reached Nat! Sorry I missed you. Leave me a message and I'll call you back!"

Roxy sighed and hung up, there was no point to leaving a voicemail… she wouldn't listen to it anyway. "I'm honestly fine. I'm only about ten minutes away from home. I can drive." Sliding the phone into her bag, she stood, swaying on her feet unsteadily.

"Yeah, that's not going to happen, Red," she heard him mutter as he took hold of her arms again to steady her. She didn't fight when he settled her on her bottom on the bench again before he knelt to zipper her bag closed. "I'll take you home."

Fear at the possibility of being seen with another man bringing her home made panic close her throat. Not to mention Travis was basically a stranger to her. "No, you can't do that."

His head came around and fixed her with that damn pene-trating stare, and she lowered her eyes to her hands, which were shaking more than before. "Alright. At least let me get you some food, I doubt those crackers were enough. Your hands are still shaking."

"I'm totally capable of getting myself home," Roxy snapped,

though it didn't hold the weight she wanted it to. Dammit. She clasped her hands together tightly in her lap to disguise the shaking, both from the low blood sugar and the paralyzing fear of being seen with another man. Because she knew he would be watching… and even if Travis's help was innocent, it wouldn't matter to *him*. Frustrated with herself and the fear this ghost could still induce, she muttered, "You could be some kind of serial killer for all I know. You haven't even introduced yourself properly and I'm just supposed to trust you?"

Travis paused in gathering his own bag, raising his head to pin her with a stare, a guardedness in those golden-brown eyes. Then he blinked, and it was gone. Brushing his long hair away from his face where it had fallen like a curtain on one side, he raised one eyebrow. He rested one elbow on his bent knee, leaning close to her. "You know who I am, Red, so don't pretend you don't know me, because that's bull. I've never once put my hands on a person that didn't know what they were getting into or didn't have it coming, and I always fight fair… mostly. I don't hurt people that don't deserve it, I help them." He fixed her with that golden-brown-eyed stare, and she felt a flush rush up her cheeks again. "Which is why, in good conscience, I cannot let you walk out of this gym and get behind the wheel of a vehicle knowing you're not feeling well, at least until you *are* feeling better."

Then his eyes softened, and he reached out his right hand toward her. She stared at it for a long moment before placing her hand in his, and he shook it gently, then said gruffly, "For the sake of formality, I'm Travis. Nice to meet you, Red."

"Umm, it's Roxsanna, actually," she stammered, fighting the urge to rub her fingers together after they pulled away, her hand tingling at the contact. "Roxy."

Leaning toward her on his elbow which was still braced on his bent knee, foot flat on the floor, he husked, "How about we walk to the sandwich shop next door? I really would feel better letting you leave once that shaking stops."

Oh buddy. If only you knew that the tremors weren't only from the hypoglycemia episode... But she nodded grudgingly, her lips tightening into a line. "Okay. Fine."

He stood in one fluid motion, hiking his bag over his shoulder, then bent at the waist and picked up her bag as well, tossing the strap over his, so both bags were hanging off his right shoulder. With his left hand, he assisted her up off the bench.

"I can carry that," Roxy said, gesturing toward her gym bag, but he fixed her with that golden brown glare and placed his hand at the small of her back, leading her out into the twilit evening.

"You concentrate on walking without falling over; I've got the bags."

Roxy wanted to be offended, but her legs were still shaking enough that she couldn't.

He escorted her down the sidewalk to a nearby sandwich shop, then held the door open for her to enter in front of him. As soon as she cleared the door, his hand returned to that spot on her lower back, making her skin burn with the heat from his hand.

A smattering of silver aluminum tables and matching chairs surrounded the exterior walls of the tiny shop, and a long, glass half-dome covered the stainless-steel prep counter. Stepping forward, Travis ordered a double Tuna Avocado sandwich on wheat bread, then added sprouts, tomatoes, and cucumbers. The tall, gangly thin guy behind the counter started prepping it on a fresh sheet of wax paper, his gloved hands moving over each ingredient. Once his sandwich was assembled and wrapped snugly in the paper, the kid handed it over the domed glass top.

"Thank you," Travis said, his voice rumbling next to her. "What would make you feel better?"

She spied a tall, three-tiered stand with fresh fruit on the opposite end of the counter and stepped over to it, plucking the biggest orange she could find and held it up. "Honestly, just this. Maybe some peanut butter if you have any?" she said, addressing the teen behind the counter.

"No peanut butter, sorry. We have a packet of cashews?" he suggested, pointing to a square plastic container.

"That will work," she said, nodding, and Travis picked up the container, carrying it and his sandwich to the cashier register, after choosing a banana from the same stand she had found the orange. "Travis, I can pay—"

But he was already handing over cash for the sandwich, the banana, her orange, and the packet of cashews before she could finish the sentence. Then he was stuffing cash into the little tip jar next to the register with a deep, "Thank you."

He motioned for her to choose a table, still toting their gym bags and their food. She chose a small two-seater table, sinking down into the hard metal seat opposite him. He tucked their bags under the tiny table between them, then proceeded to tear off the tamper evident seal on her cashews before handing them over to her. His bare arms, tattoos visible from shoulder all the way down to the back of each finger, bunched and rippled with each move he made. Roxy was transfixed by the muscles that shifted in his forearms.

"Thank you," she said softly, taking them from him, digging in and popping several in her mouth. She set a napkin down on the table and started working on peeling the orange.

When her trembling fingers were proving to be ineffective against the tough peel, he reached out and plucked it out of her hands. He dug into the front pocket of his bag and produced a switch blade, which he used to slice the orange clean in half. Slicing it into quarters, he handed each one back to her. He cleaned the blade with a napkin, then shoved it back into his bag.

Taking a massive bite of his sandwich, he nodded toward the orange. After swallowing, he said gruffly, "Eat, please. It will make you feel better, and then I won't feel guilty for letting you talk me out of taking you home."

Biting into the orange, she couldn't help rolling her eyes when he nodded in approval. The air conditioning was on full blast inside the tiny shop, making her shiver. Reaching into her bag beneath the table, she pulled her sweatshirt out and pulled it on over her head, adjusting her hair in the messy bun that was on top of her head. Taking another handful of cashews, she chewed, then swallowed, before pointing to his bare arms and the large swaths of skin on his sides. "Aren't you cold?"

He shook his head. "No. I run like a furnace and I'm always too warm. I hate Texas and the heat. Been throwing around the idea of moving to a cooler state."

"You'd love Michigan, then," she laughed, then shuddered. "My best friend and his wife live up there. Too cold for my blood."

"Have you always lived in Texas?" he asked, then took another bite, and she was transfixed again by how straight and white and *beautiful* his teeth were as they sunk into the soft bread. His hands were large, rough looking, but he moved agilely, like a big predatory cat.

"Uhh," she stammered, moving her gaze away from his mouth up to his eyes, which were just as hypnotizing. Golden brown like rich honey, with darker rings around the irises and lighter flecks of gold near the center. Shaking her head, she asked dumbly, her face flaming, "I'm sorry, what was the question?"

His brown brows pulled low over his eyes as he frowned slightly. Setting his sandwich down, he leaned his elbows on the table. "Are you sure you're feeling okay?"

Blushing furiously, she rolled her eyes and called herself every name she could think of. *He must think I'm a moron!* "I'm fine, I swear. My brain is just a little cloudy still." Biting into another quarter of the orange, she remembered his question and answered, "Yes, I've always lived in Texas. I was born and raised in Fort Worth but moved to Melody Hills about ten years ago. What about you?"

He nodded around another bite. "I was born and raised in Oklahoma. Moved around a lot after high school, then never stuck around any one place for long during my MMA career. Merv—the owner of the rec center—was one of my mentors. He retired years ago and came back here, and when I decided on an early retirement, he asked me to join him and help out at the center, teaching classes. It's been a nice change."

"You don't miss it?" she asked.

He lifted one impossibly wide, tattooed shoulder. His eyes dropped from hers to his hands, which flexed before relaxing. "Sometimes. Most of the time, no." Raising his eyes to hers, he raised one eyebrow. "Look, Red, I'm going to need you to eat, otherwise I will insist on driving you home."

"If you didn't know me, how did you know my nickname is Red?" she asked then, leaning her elbows on the table to fix him with a dubious stare.

His eyes shot up to the bun on top of her head, and she grinned sheepishly. Closing her eyes in a grimace, she laughed to herself, "Wow. My brain must be fried. It's the red hair, huh?"

He laughed quietly and nodded. "Who gave you that nickname?"

Roxy smiled, thinking about Free and the first night they'd met, nearly a decade ago. "My best friend. First night we met, he dubbed me Red, and it just stuck."

Travis crumpled the paper his sandwich had been wrapped in into a ball, setting it aside. He leaned back in his seat, stretching his legs out as far as possible beneath the small table. "This the best friend that lives in Michigan?"

"Mmhmm," she said, taking another handful of cashews and tossing them into her mouth. "He and his wife live there."

"I've been to Detroit a handful of times, and then to Grand Rapids once. Never made it any further north than that."

"The area they live in is beautiful," Roxy said. "They're way up north, right on Lake Michigan. They live way up here—" she said and held up one hand, thumb out, like the shape of Michigan, and pointed with her other hand to the tiny indent where the tip of her ring finger met her middle finger. Travis's eyebrows raised as he smiled. Dropping her hands back to the orange, she continued, "He said they got three feet of snow just before Christmas. Just the thought of all that snow makes me break out in hives. They got married in Colorado two weeks ago, and I hightailed it out of that snowy hell so fast."

"So you're strictly a warm weather state kinda gal," he chuckled, and her heart did a little flutter in her chest when one side of his mouth curved up in a smile. "Got it."

"Oh no, I love Michigan in the summer. Absolutely stunning," she said with a laugh. "But once the temps drop below sixty… get me a pile of winter coats and the thickest, fuzziest blanket you can find. It would take an act of God to get me to leave Texas for somewhere colder."

His chuckle was deep and when he grinned, she could just see the makings of a dimple hidden beneath the beard that covered his cheeks.

"Are you feeling better?" he asked then, rolling on his spine so that he was sitting up straight in his seat. He pulled his legs from where he had stretched them out under the table as he leaned his forearms on the tabletop.

"Yes," she said, holding her hand out to show the trembling had subsided. "Thank you. I should be fine to get home now."

"And you're sure I can't drive you?" he asked again, those honey brown eyes searching hers.

Roxy smiled but shook her head, focusing on keeping her voice steady even as the anxiety of being seen made her chest tighten. "I'll be fine, I promise. Thank you, Travis. I made you miss enough of your workout as it is." She pushed herself up from the seat, grateful her legs didn't wobble. She doubted he would let her leave alone if they had.

Travis leaned under the table to pick up both of their bags by the straps, then stood, easily swinging the duffel bags over one of his shoulders. He motioned for her to walk ahead of him, and she was acutely aware of him following her to the door, then out onto the sidewalk. The sun had set, the sky darkening on the horizon. Light poles along the street cast pools of light beneath them, the shadows between them growing darker.

Roxy extended her hand, and he slid her duffel down his arm and handed it to her. She reached into her sweatshirt pocket and pulled out her car keys, hitting the fob to unlock her doors. The headlights flashed, several parked cars down, and they walked silently toward it.

"Thank you again," she said as she opened the passenger door, setting the duffel inside before closing the door and stepping back up onto the sidewalk at the front of the vehicle. He stepped forward as she did, leaning out to open the driver's side door for her. She climbed in, rolling the window down several inches after he shut the door gently, then tapped the roof of her car. "See you."

He nodded, his eyes sweeping over her once more, and then he turned and walked away. Lights flashed several cars back the opposite direction, and then he disappeared from her sight as she backed out of her parking spot.

FIVE

There was something cathartic about hitting something as hard as physically possible. Feeling the give of whatever surface it was; be it flesh, leather, rubber. The ache and burn of muscles being pushed to their limits. The throbbing in the hands and knuckles with the force of each hit.

Music blasted through the Bluetooth earbuds in his ears, drowning out everything else around him. The nightmares were back, just like he always knew they wouldn't stay away. Not for good, anyway. The only thing that helped was this… or an illegal, underground cage fight, but he'd given those up a while ago. Wouldn't even know where to find one nowadays.

He blamed the time of year, that date on the calendar that he hated with every ounce of his soul. The nightmares always got worse as that date drew nearer. Waking drenched in sweat, bedsheets twisted around his body, reminders of his failure. That he'd been too scared, too weak… too late.

Panting heavily, he let his hands drop to his sides, sweat dripping down his face and neck, slicking his back and shoulders. He'd pushed himself, probably too hard, but he didn't care. His knuckles ached and would be bruised after this workout, but he'd take it as his penance.

The gym was quiet, only a handful of regulars taking up machines. Blondie and Red had been in and left already, he'd seen her flash of red curls from across the room. She had not sought him out, and for that he had been grateful. He knew his mind was in a dark place. That was why he'd stationed himself in the farthest corner away from others, put on his music, and just prayed that he was left alone. He had been thankful that the few glances he took toward her, she appeared to be feeling better than the last time he'd seen her, when she'd passed out. He couldn't seem to keep his gaze from sweeping toward her though, watching for any signs of a repeat incident. His jaw clenched every time he caught himself glancing toward her, annoyance at himself tightening his chest.

He didn't like playing the hero to damsels in distress. Because he would never see himself as a hero, not when *he* was the monster that lurked in the shadows most of the time.

Walking across the mat to the bench along the far wall, he picked up his water bottle and drank half of it in one pull before capping it. He performed a short routine of stretches and then sank onto the bench as he brought one wrist to his mouth, using his teeth to tear at the tape.

Sneaker clad feet appeared in his line of vision and he reached up to tap at the earbud in his ear, silencing the loud music, but he didn't look up from what he was doing. He waited, but as usual, Merv didn't waste time.

"You need a change."

Travis raised his eyes, cutting away from the tape he was unfurling from around his left hand toward the man that had walked up to him. He shrugged his shoulders, noncommitting. Merv harrumphed something unintelligible as he crossed his arms over his chest.

"You're unsettled," he observed gruffly.

"I'm perfectly settled, old man. Maybe you should get your eyes checked, because I'm fine," Travis grunted crossly.

Merv shifted in stance. "Twenty years, Travis."

Travis grunted, his only response. If there was anyone that knew about his life before MMA, other than a handful of police officers and lawyers back in Oklahoma, it was Merv. But they didn't talk about it, and Merv knew that. Travis pinned the older man with a stare that would have quelled a lesser man. Merv wasn't a lesser man and returned the stare with one of his own.

"I know how long it's been, Merv," he muttered on a growl, straightening his spine and resting his elbows on his spread knees. His gaze hardened on the older man. "And I don't need a babysitter."

Merv's graying eyebrows bobbed and he tilted his head in a slight nod, the corners of his lips turning down in thought. "Checking in on a friend isn't babysitting, Travis. It's caring about someone."

Travis shook his head and braced his hands on his knees, pushing himself up to stand. He bent at the waist and grabbed hold of the strap of his gym bag, hoisting it to his shoulder. "I don't need check-ins, either. If I need a check-in, I go to Steve. Someone licensed and bound by confidentiality clauses."

Merv's hand clamped around Travis's bicep and halted him as he made to brush past him. "Travis," he said quietly, though the slight bite in his tone was what brought Travis's eyes around. "Look, I know as men we're taught to be stoic and suffer in silence… but it's okay to talk about things every once in a while. You're a good kid—"

Travis laughed, though it wasn't altogether a pleasant sound. Leaning close to the older man, he muttered quietly, "Merv, I stopped being a kid twenty years ago when I went to jail for beating my old man to death. That doesn't make me a good person. It makes me a monster."

He moved past Merv, who stepped aside to let him pass. Stalking toward the door, he pulled his phone out of his pocket and swiped through the music app, searching for a playlist. Something loud and angry, he didn't care. Anything to drown out his thoughts.

Eyes down, he pushed open the door and took two steps out onto the sidewalk when he heard a sharp gasp and his eyes shot up just as he barreled directly into Roxy.

Grabbing hold of her upper arm with his free hand as they collided roughly, he regained his balance by twisting and pushing her up against the stucco wall that made up the entrance of the rec center, the hand that still held his cell phone pressed against the wall above her shoulder, his bag swinging from his side to thud into the stucco wall near her hip.

His eyes darted across her face, searching for any sign that he'd caused her pain. He had managed to keep his body away from her as they tripped on each other, but somehow one of his thighs ended up between hers, his knee resting against the stucco wall between her legs. He could feel the rough texture of the wall against his bare knee, a sharp contrast to the softness of the athletic leggings she wore as her legs straddled his. Her fingers were fisted tightly in the fabric of his shirt at his sides, the backs of her fingers pressed flush against his ribs as if she'd grabbed hold of him to steady herself. The coolness of her fingers through his thin t-shirt made his heart trip on itself in his chest. Her fingers were like ice.

Her shocked gasp tore through him, and his gaze dropped to her mouth, parted slightly. He stared at the jagged white scar that bisected the left side of her full lower lip before raising his eyes to her hazel ones, and again he wondered where it had come from. She stared up at him, her eyes wide, before she twisted her head to the side, glancing out toward the line of parked cars. When she brought them back to his, they were filled with fear. It was sobering, witnessing that fright as it passed over her features. A reminder of the monster he was, as if that self-preservation instinct in her could sense it in him.

Clearing his throat, he pushed away from the wall, stepping back away from her, giving her space. Her fingers fell away from his sides, releasing the death grip she'd had on his shirt. She shoved her hands into the pockets of her jacket, and her tongue darted out to wet her lips. His eyes tracked every move. Fear and anxiety radiated off of her, making his chest ache.

"I'm sorry," he said roughly, gesturing to the phone in his hand. "I wasn't paying attention. I didn't mean to bowl you over like that."

"It's okay," she said softly, swallowing. "I walked out without my bag, and I wasn't watching where I was going coming back in. I thought I saw something—"

She glanced over her shoulder again, her breath catching slightly, before she turned back to him. His brows drew together as he watched her.

"Nevermind," she laughed lightly, shaking her head. "It was nothing. I'll see you Monday, for the first class."

He nodded then. "Right. You and Blondie signed up."

One of her auburn eyebrows shot up. "Blondie?"

"Your friend," he said. Realization sparked in her hazel eyes, and he sighed, chuckling. "I'm awful with names."

"So you've got Red and Blondie. Anyone else I should know?" she teased lightly.

He laughed out loud then, shifting from one sneaker clad foot to the other as he turned to face the wall of windows. He pointed to a tall, thin guy in the far corner. "The guy in the red tank top and black shorts? String Bean." She laughed out loud and he hated to admit that he loved the husky sound of it. He gestured to the left and said, "Gray sweats, no shirt guy? Princess." When she choked on another laugh, he chuckled. "He's always posing, taking pictures of himself, rarely does anything that actually gets his body moving. There—" he said again, pointing to the right, "—guy all in black, blonde hair and those big gold glasses? Dahmer."

"Oh my god, *Travis*!" she laughed again, raising her eyes to his. A wide grin pulled her mouth, making the white scar show up brightly against the flesh of her lower lip. "You can't call people that!"

"Why not? He looks just like him," he chuckled, shrugging. "Like I said, I'm awful with names. Not that I really get to know anyone that well. If they stick around long enough, then I'll learn their name. Until then, I just make shit up to entertain myself."

A car engine roared to life from down the way, and Roxy jumped, her eyes running up and down the sidewalk nervously. She moved closer to the door of the gym and said, "I should probably go grab my bag. See you Monday, Travis."

And then she slipped inside the door and it swished shut behind her, leaving him out on the sidewalk.

He turned and walked toward his Ford Bronco Badlands, sliding in behind the wheel and pressing the ignition to start. He'd waited until he'd watched her walk back out of the gym with her bag over her shoulder. She glanced up and down the sidewalk, striding quickly over to her vehicle, nearly running the last few steps. She slid inside the driver's door, slamming it shut. He watched as she hastily locked the doors.

His knuckles fisted on the steering wheel. The monster reared its head inside him, awakening. Readying for a fight.

Because the fear in Red's eyes as she stared up at him when he offered to drive her home the other day… the fear in them now as she sat inside her car…he *knew* that look. Knew the way her eyes darted around, searching for some unnamed threat.

It had been the same look of fear he'd seen in the mirror too many times to count as a child. Seen it on his mother's face, until it had been too late.

She was scared of something.

No.

She was scared of *someone*. And he realized then that she hadn't been scared of *him* earlier. But someone else.

Six

"I could have sworn it was right here," Roxy muttered, shifting several bottles of perfume and body spray on the top of her dresser. Her phone was tucked between her ear and shoulder, and she sighed in frustration, turning in a slow circle in her bedroom.

"You still can't find it?" Natalie asked from the other end of the phone. "Are you sure you didn't leave it in your gym bag?"

"I never take that one to the gym," Roxy muttered, half to herself, half to her friend, her eyes scanning over every inch of her room. She padded back to the bathroom, opened and closed all of the vanity drawers to no avail. She slapped one palm to her thigh in aggravation. "That's my favorite. I *know* I just used it the other day. It's almost empty, and I reminded myself to buy more the next time I go to *Sephora*."

"Did you maybe throw it away because it was almost empty, and you just don't remember doing it?" Natalie asked, the ever-helpful devil's advocate.

"No," Roxy said, her tone firm. "It's not *that* close to being empty. I would rather eat slugs than waste that stuff like that."

"Did you take it to work? Maybe put it in your locker?"

Roxy spun in a slow circle, shaking her head. "No, I don't like that one for work. I use the Tornado one for work nights, and I keep it right there in my locker."

Stomping angrily to the kitchen, she flung open random cabinet doors, knowing full well that it wouldn't be in with her baking spices or canned goods, then when of course it didn't pop up amongst the boxes of cereal, she huffed angrily, gripping the phone in her hand as she squeezed her eyes shut.

"It will show up in the last place you look!" Natalie said with forced cheerfulness.

"Not helpful, Nat," Roxy growled in annoyance. "I just don't understand! I'm missing my favorite red panties, too. The one that has the matching bra. I have no idea where they went. I feel like I'm losing my mind."

"I would suggest the gym bag again, but I feel like that would be asking to get tit-punched the next time I see you," Natalie mumbled, and Roxy laughed finally.

"Probably a safe bet," she sighed, then sank down onto one of the backless barstools pulled up to the kitchen island. She let her face fall into her free hand. "Have you recovered from last night's class yet?"

"No!" Natalie whined. "The man is the devil incarnate. There's no way the human body can do that and still function. The only explanation is that he is in fact, *not* human."

Roxy laughed. Travis was a beast. He barely broke a sweat during the kickboxing lessons, but by the end of the hour, Roxy was always flat on her back on the mat and Natalie appeared to be dead. She was surprised that Natalie had stuck with the classes, as adverse she was to perspiration, especially in front of Travis.

"My legs still don't work properly," Natalie continued. The high kicks into the body bags following Travis's instruction had been difficult, the heavy bags impossible to move. But the practice of kicking into the padded mitts on Travis's hands had been brutal in a totally different way. Roxy had maintained leveling her eyes on a spot on the mitt and *absolutely nowhere else* on the man's mind-numbingly hot body. She also refused to look him in the eyes. Those whiskey and honey-colored eyes were too intoxicating, especially up close. "Trying to sit on the toilet to pee and get back up is its own special form of torture that the CIA should look into utilizing."

Roxy laughed again, brought back from her reverie of all of that tanned, tattooed, insanely muscled skin that was always so distractingly on display every class. He wore a pair of tight exercise shorts—the material as they clung to his heavily muscled thighs reminded her of a sexy pair of boxer briefs—which she assumed were to keep the family jewels from being on full display beneath a slightly shorter pair of loose gym shorts. The only other thing that adorned his body was the colored athletic tape that crisscrossed his large hands, protecting his knuckles.

Roxy didn't bother with the tape, just a pair of kickboxing gloves she'd purchased off *Amazon*— Prime shipping had saved her life after the first class and her knuckles had been beyond tender. He'd noticed the way she was pulling punches and had startled her by asking to take a look at her hands.

He'd taken them, one at a time, into his large ones. One hand encircled her wrist, his fingers pressing into the pulse point on the inside of her wrist, and she was terrified he could feel her heartbeat as it skyrocketed at his touch. His other hand curled and uncurled her hands into fists several times, then the pad of his thumb ran over the tender skin across her knuckles.

She had felt it all the way in her belly.

Nope. No. No no.

He had been talking to her in that low, gentle tone that he seemed to reserve for her and her alone. He never spoke that way to Natalie... or any of the other women. *Not* that she had noticed. Definitely hadn't noticed... or secretly swooned because he seemed to pay closer attention to her than others...

"You're going to want to bandage these, or find some gloves to protect the knuckles, Red," he'd murmured quietly, his thumb still stroking over the ridge of knuckles on her left hand. His hazel eyes were searching hers. "I can tape them if you'd like. Or I can show you how."

"Uhh," she'd stammered like an idiot, caught irretrievably in the golden brown of his eyes. She tugged her hand out of his grasp and shook her head. "That's not necessary. I'll get some gloves."

She'd damn near tripped on her own feet as she'd turned and bolted away from him. Her heart was in her throat. Touching her wrist shouldn't have been so…so *erotic*. What was this, *Bridgerton*? An ankle exposed, a wrist touched, and suddenly there was a herd of elephants stampeding through her midsection? *Not good.*

Little warning bells had started going off in her head, as if warning of danger ahead.

She'd studiously avoided eye contact or any kind of physical touching in the three weeks since, unless absolutely necessary for the class.

"Ugh, maybe I'm just losing my mind…" Wracking her brain, she sank down onto the foot of her bed.

"Well, what do you need that perfume for right now anyway?" Natalie asked. Roxy could hear her vehicle's blinker through the phone. "And you're going to be late for work if you don't leave in the next like, five seconds."

Roxy growled. "I know. I just, I feel like I'm losing my mind. It was right there, I swear… And I'm trying to find my cutoffs. My *good* cutoffs."

"Ooh. The ones that make your ass look—" Natalie made the sound for a chef's kiss and Roxy laughed, rolling her eyes as Nat continued, "—mmm. Fucking divine. I'd tap that ass in those jean shorts."

"You're a hussy," Roxy laughed, finally giving up on the missing perfume and spotting the cutoffs buried in the laundry she'd piled in the corner. She hiked them up her thighs and over her ass, buttoning them, then secured her belt around her waist, shoving her feet into her boots.

She checked her reflection in the full-length mirror in the corner of her room one more time. The short, cutoff jean shorts hit high on her thighs, the pockets hanging out of the bottom slightly. Over the knee brown cowgirl boots adorned her feet, and a tightly fitted, plain black t-shirt was tucked into the waist of the shorts. Her signature silver and turquoise embellished belt buckle was strapped around her waist, and her curls had been piled on top of her head into an artfully messy topknot. Chunky turquoise earrings dangled from her ears and a wide silver bangle bracelet twisted on her wrist.

Her make-up was far less done up than several of the other girls that worked with her at *Lawless*, the line dancing bar that was a hot spot just outside of Fort Worth. Though it had gained traction with the tourists visiting Fort Worth, it was still a favorite spot for the locals, a little hidden gem that she hoped stayed that way.

"Are you in the fucking car yet? You're going to be late," Natalie groused, and then the sound of a car door closing hit her ears. Natalie must have just gotten to work. She really was running late if Natalie was there already. "And I am not taking that Matty bullet for you again, sis."

"Matty can eat me," Roxy muttered, pulling a black jean jacket on her arms and slinging her purse over her shoulder. Double checking the door was locked on her way out, she pulled it closed and hustled to her car. Though sixty-five degrees could be considered warm weather up in the frozen tundra that Freeman had moved to, it was frigid for her warm-blooded bones, and she shivered. Damn Matty and his insistence that they wear shorts in place of full jeans. At least on busy weekend nights.

Adjusting the thermostat to turn the heat to high, she buckled, then backed out of the driveway. Placing her phone in the cupholder, still on speaker, she mumbled, "I'm on my way, don't get your bedazzled panties in a twist."

"Excuse you, my panties are not bedazzled," Natalie protested, and she laughed. "My shorts are, but not my fucking underwear, you psycho. God, can you imagine one of those falling off and getting stuck all up in—"

"You're so fucking weird," Roxy laughed, cutting Natalie off. "I'll see you in a few."

Ending the call, she turned the radio up as she made the short ten-minute drive to work. Pulling in, she spotted a dark head of hair walking toward the front door of the bar and froze, her heart rocketing in her chest. The man turned and she sighed, swallowing hard.

It's not him. You're fine.

Parking, she clambered out of the car and raced across the parking lot, unlocking the employee entrance with her key and hurrying inside. Tossing her things into her locker, she stripped the leather jacket down her arms and shoved it in, not even bothering to hang it on the hook.

Skidding to a halt at the computer, she punched in just in time, then looked at Natalie, who was grinning and shaking her blonde head. Roxy headed toward the bar, where she would be tending all evening and called over her shoulder, "Let's go, girl."

SEVEN

"Ohmygod," Natalie groaned as she sank down onto a barstool at the end of the night. "Remind me to throw these boots away."

Roxy made a face of commiseration. "I thought these were comfortable?"

"Nothing is comfortable when you're hauling ass for nine hours straight, especially anything with a heel."

Spreading the cash tips she'd made out with her fingers like a fan, Roxy bobbled her eyebrows at Natalie. "But it's so worth it…"

"Not if I have to replace my damn feet by the time I'm done working," Natalie complained, though she was grinning. Then she groaned again. "We have kickboxing with Travis tomorrow. I'm going to die. My legs are going to fall off."

"You're so dramatic," Roxy mumbled, rolling her eyes. "C'mon. I wanna go home."

It had been a busy night, busier than usual, which meant they were late getting their closing duties done. They ran with two bartenders at each of the two bars in the building, along with a dozen servers for weekends. It had been a hectic evening, and Roxy knew as soon as she stopped moving her thighs would start to ache, along with the arches of her feet. Epsom salt baths were her savior most nights.

The bouncers escorted them out—Matty may have been a hard ass but the safety of his employees was always top priority, something Roxy had admired about the guy—and they said good night as Roxy, Natalie, and several other employees headed out to their vehicles in the dark parking lot.

"See you tomorrow in Hell," Natalie called over to her before sliding into her car, parked several spots down from Roxy. Roxy waved, then climbed into her Toyota 4Runner, immediately turning the heat up.

The drive home was quiet, at three am the roads between Fort Worth and Melody Hills were mostly deserted. Climbing out of her car, she groaned, her legs screaming in protest. She quickly walked to the front door, unlocking it and slipping inside, before relocking it.

Walking into the kitchen, she took a wine glass down and opened the fridge, pulling out the bottle of Reisling and pouring a hefty glass. She carried it with her to the bathroom, setting it down on the rim of the bathtub before turning the water on. The tub began to fill, steam rising from the hot water, and she ladled a large scoop of citrus scented Epsom salt into the water, along with a dash of bubble bath.

Stepping into the bedroom, Roxy stripped, piling her boots in the closet and tossing the jean shorts and black shirt haphazardly on the foot of the bed, along with her bra and underwear. Picking up her Bluetooth earbuds, she padded back into the bathroom. Lighting several candles throughout the room before turning off the overhead light, she then climbed into the now nearly full bathtub. Sinking into the hot water, she sighed and stretched her legs all the way to her toes several times beneath the water, loosening the sore muscles.

Swiping through her phone, she queued up her audiobook app and pressed play. Setting the phone back on the edge of the tub, she took a swallow of her wine before settling her back against the sloped edge, resting her head on the bath pillow Natalie had gifted her for Christmas last year.

As *Teddy Hamilton's* voice growled at her through the earbuds, she closed her eyes, letting herself get swept away into another world.

Jerking upright and splashing water wildly as her limbs flailed, she panted in the dimly lit bathroom, her eyes wide in panic.

Fuck, did I fall asleep?

The water had cooled drastically, the bubbles were long gone, and her audiobook was several chapters beyond where she'd started it. Snatching her phone off the ledge of the tub, she groaned, then stood, shivering.

"Fucking four thirty," she mumbled to herself, pulling the earbuds out of her ears and tossing them onto the counter by the sink. She wrapped herself in a fluffy towel and hastily dried off. Her fingers and toes were pruny, but at least her legs and feet didn't ache anymore.

She blew the candles out and exited the bathroom, padding down to the kitchen to dump out the half empty glass of wine before rinsing the glass and setting it in the sink. The house was dark and quiet, and no moonlight filtered in through the windows.

Yawning broadly, she rolled her head across her shoulders and walked back down the hallway to the bedroom and dropped the towel. A pair of skimpy sleep shorts were hastily pulled up her legs, and then she yanked on an extra-large sweatshirt, shoving her arms into the sleeves.

Turning, she reached for the clothes that she'd left scattered on the bed before her bath, but stopped, her gaze flicking from each item, her brows drawing into a deep V as her breathing accelerated.

Her clothes were neatly folded on the end of the bed, and the red lacy bra she'd worn was nowhere to be found.

EIGHT

"Alright, stop."

Those hazel eyes that had been so far away all evening returned to his and his lips thinned. The rest of the group had stopped as well, and he turned to everyone and grunted, "You all can keep going. I'm talking to Hot Mess over here."

Her hair fairly bristled as her spine straightened, her head cocking to one side with indignation. Wrapping his fingers around her elbow, he pulled her off the mat and to the side. She yanked her arm away from him as soon as they were away from the group, and he sighed heavily. "I don't know where your head is at tonight, but if you don't pay attention and focus, you're going to hurt someone, or yourself, Red."

He'd been watching her all class, but she was jumpy, her eyes flicking every direction or she simply stared off into the distance. Deep purple shadows hung beneath her eyes, as if she hadn't slept in days. Something was wrong, he was sure of it.

"If you can't pull your focus back to the task at hand, I'm going to have to ask you to leave the class for the night. I can't have you not paying attention and take the chance of hurting your sparring partner or yourself."

"I'm fine," she snapped, her eyes regaining a little of that fire he was so used to.

"Are you? Because it doesn't seem like it," he snapped right back, crossing his arms over his chest. He watched as her eyes tracked the movement, her gaze lingering on his biceps, forearms, and pecks, and his male vanity stirred, hoping she liked what she saw. But then her gaze returned to his and she wet her lips, and he had to think very hard about not getting an erection. *Not the time, buddy*, he warned himself. *Not the time, definitely not this woman.*

"You don't know me," she muttered sourly, shaking her head. "So please don't pretend to. I'm fine."

"Those carry-ons you're lugging around under your eyes say otherwise," he grunted, notching his chin toward her face. Her lips thinned, eyes narrowing on him. "And your strikes look like shit. You're pulling punches, not extending, and your frame is fucked. You're better than this. So what's going on?"

"None of your fucking business," she hissed, that fire he was used to returning in full force. "We're not friends, Travis. You teach a class I'm taking. We see each other two to three times a week, and sometimes just in passing."

"Only because you avoid me like the plague," he muttered darkly, keeping his gaze focused on hers. She blinked, stunned, and he nodded once, lowering his eyebrows. "Don't think I didn't notice, Red. I spent my entire life making sure I know how to read a room, how to read an opponent; it's a conditioned survival instinct. So when I tell you I can fucking tell that something is wrong, it's because I can read you like a goddamn book, baby girl."

Roxy shook her head, her hazel eyes burning into his. "Then I guess you'd better get some fucking glasses, because there's nothing to see. Are we done?"

"Not even close," he growled, leaning down closer to her. "But I'll let it go for now."

"You'll let it go, *hard stop*, because I'm fine, Travis. *Leave it alone.*"

With that, she spun on her sneakered heel and strode off, bypassing the others completely and heading straight toward her gym bag. He watched as she snatched up her belongings, stuffing them into the gym bag. She took her gym shoes off and shoved them into the bag, zipping it closed, and then she yanked a hoodie on over her head, knocking the messy bun on the top of her head askew as she did so. A second later, the glass door swung shut behind her as she left.

Tearing his gaze away from her as she crossed in front of the bank of windows toward her car, he whistled low to the group and called, "Good job everyone." Blondie looked between himself and the windows, where Roxy had disappeared out of sight, before heading off the mat and toward her own gym bag.

Christ, what was wrong with him? He never got involved with anyone's personal issues. No matter what. So why was he so goddamn invested in finding out what had caused those shadows under her eyes and why she's so fucking jumpy all the time?

She's right, it's none of his damn business.

Was that going to stop him from obsessing over it? *Probably not.*

NINE

Running the sanitizer cloth along the bar top, Roxy looked up when the door to the bar opened, letting in a stream of sunlight across the polished wood floor. Peanut shells littered the floor and crunched beneath the booted feet of the man that had just entered.

"You lost?" she asked, straightening. Fidgeting with the cloth between her fingers, she watched as he moved forward, sinking into one of the wooden barstools along the bar.

Tuesday afternoons were boring as hell, but each bartender and server was mandated to work one of the slower shifts in order to work the busy weekend shifts. Matty said it was to ensure that no one was accused of favoritism, but Roxy didn't mind. And it meant she could wear full jeans instead of shorts. Her black jeans were well fitted, and her usual black t-shirt was tucked in at the waist. Her hair was piled up on the top of her head, though curls had escaped, grazing her cheeks.

Only a handful of the barstools were occupied at this time of day, still too early for the usual local crowd that would be popping in for their happy hour beer and complimentary peanuts in another hour or so. They blocked off the main part of the dance-hall, so just one of the two long bars was open for customers.

"Christ, you're the prickliest damn woman I've ever met," Travis muttered as he rested his forearms against the edge of the bar. She stepped toward him, setting a beverage napkin down in front of him and raising one brow at him in question. "Dos Equis please. Just a pint."

Roxy sighed and reached down into the cooler in front of her, plucking out a chilled pint glass before pouring the draft expertly.

She set the beer in front of him, then slid a red plastic food basket filled with peanuts across the bar to him, and he nodded. "Thanks."

Roxy swallowed hard, grabbing up the sanitizer towel again and wringing it between her hands. He looked different than she was used to seeing him. Faded, well-worn jeans that fit far too well and fell over dark cowboy boots. A thin flannel shirt was buttoned over his broad chest and shoulders, though it did little to hide the muscles she knew were hiding beneath. Several buttons were left undone, leaving his throat exposed. The arms of his shirt were rolled to his elbows, and all that exposed skin showed off his myriad tattoos. His hair was left down today and it fell over his shoulders. It looked clean and soft, and she wondered if it felt as soft as it looked.

But it was the hat that was making it hard for her to concentrate… A black felt cowboy hat sat low on his head, the brim shadowing the upper portion of his face. As if sensing her avid stare, he reached up with one heavily tattooed hand and took it off, setting it carefully on the bar beside his beer. Gym Travis—wearing nothing but those damn gym shorts and athletic tape on his hands, long hair tied up—was enough to make any woman forget her own name. But street clothes Travis with a damn cowboy hat… Roxy forgot how to *breathe*. He was magnificent.

He plucked several peanuts out of the basket, his fingers

deftly shelling them. She was transfixed. The shells were tossed onto the floor—the oils in the shells were beneficial to the wood floors—and popped the peanuts into his mouth.

"You're staring."

She startled, then narrowed her eyes on him. "Am not."

His grin was quick, and the low chuckle that rumbled out of his chest made her belly do strange flipflops that she was altogether not a fan of. *Dammit to hell.*

Busying herself behind the bar, she peered at him out of the corner of her eye, before Rudy got her attention for another beer several seats down. She wandered back closer to Travis, who was shelling peanuts and tossing them back between drinks of his own beer. He had somehow produced a pen and was doodling on the edge of the napkin idly, the pen nearly swallowed by the size of his hand. Moe requested a dollar in quarters for the jukebox, and a few moments later the first bars of *Chris Stapleton's* 'Tennessee Whiskey' floated through the bar on the hidden speakers around the place.

"I'm sorry for snapping at you," she said quietly to him several minutes later, pulling glasses out of the bar dishwasher below the counter and setting them aside to dry. She glanced up at him. "Last week. It was… it was a bad day and it was wrong of me to take it out on you."

He nodded, the only concession to having heard her. He wrapped his fingers around the pint glass—his hand was so large his fingers nearly wrapped around the entire glass—and brought it to his lips before setting it back down. Pushing the basket of peanuts away, he leaned his forearms against the edge of the bar again and leaned forward, his upper body leaning over the bar slightly. His eyes met hers and she stilled, the golden-honey brown of his eyes riveting even in the low light of the bar.

"Bad days I understand better than you could possibly know, Red," he said quietly. She swallowed again, and nodded, though she wondered what he meant by that, curiosity peaking at what demons this man could possibly be hiding. He cleared his throat, his eyes never leaving hers, and continued gently, "I'm sorry I pressed. You're right; it's none of my business what's going on in your life. However, I will step in when it puts you or anyone else at risk if you're incapable of focusing during a class. Inattention can cause accidents, and I don't like those. Too much paperwork."

Roxy couldn't stop the scoffing laugh that escaped her, and she shook her head, sighing in defeat. She braced her hands on the edge of the bar, leaning against her outstretched arms. "I promise I won't cause you any extra paperwork, Travis. And you're right, too; I wasn't paying proper attention. I didn't mean to cause you any alarm."

He reached out across the bar and covered the back of her hand with one of his, squeezing lightly. "It's a bad habit of mine, a reflex I can't shake. I once didn't do anything about warning signs I saw, and it cost me. Ever since then…" he shrugged, pulling his hand back and gripping the beer again. "Let's just say if I have a gut feeling, I'm not usually incorrect."

Roxy's heart hammered in her chest. The touch of his fingers along the back of her hand had sent a zing of electricity up her arm and straight to her middle, and it had nothing to do with static or science. And then his words caught up to her. *Shit.* "You have a gut feeling about me? Why?"

He stared into her eyes for what felt like an eternity before he simply said, "If you need anything, don't hesitate to reach out. I mean that. *Anything,* Roxy. Day or night."

Then he pushed himself back from the bar and stood lithely. He finished the last of his beer and set the empty glass down, then fished in his back pocket, pulling out his wallet. He tossed a twenty down and she reached for it, mumbling, "I'll just grab your change—"

He shook his head and said, "That's all set."

She gaped at him and stammered, "Travis. It's a three-dollar beer—"

He shrugged as he picked up the cowboy hat by the cap and placed it on his head. Those honey-colored eyes came back to hers again and she had to remind her lungs how to work properly. "See you, Red."

She nodded, staring after him as he made his way across the wooden floor toward the door. As he pushed the door open, light flooded the dim room again, the sunlight catching on his light brown hair, turning the strands into a kaleidoscope of golds, ambers, blondes, and silvers as it danced around his shoulders. As the door closed behind him, a low whistle sounded and she whipped her head around to the far side of the bar. "*Oooowee, doll.*"

Rudy and Moe, both well into their fifties, were watching her with grins on their faces. "What?"

"That boy didn't come here for beer or peanuts, doll," Moe chuckled, bobbing his graying eyebrows. Their words were heavily accented, that Texas twang lilting as they spoke.

"No, sir, he sure didn't," Rudy laughed, taking another drink of his beer. "That boy got it bad."

Roxy glared at them both. "Got what bad, Rudy?"

Rudy and Moe shared a glance and then Rudy pointed toward the napkin still tucked beneath Travis's empty beer glass in front of her on the bar.

"Ten songs that napkin has his number on it."

Lowell, another regular, chimed in then, saying, "That boy's fixin' to marry you, honey."

Roxy turned back toward the glass and napkin before pinning them all with a stare. "You're all fucking knocked in the head. Rudy, no dice."

"Only cuz you know I'm right," he chuckled. She snatched up the empty glass and the napkin, spinning it so that she could make out what he'd been doodling in the bottom corner. Sure enough, his phone number was scrawled across the bottom.

"So? How's about them songs, doll?" Rudy called over, still chuckling.

Stuffing the napkin into her back pocket, she muttered sourly, "Rudy. You're cut off."

"Aww hell, Roxy, we were just playin!"

Ten

I'm sorry I took the perfume.
Forgive me. It just makes me
feel better having it close.
I miss you so much, Rox

She hadn't noticed the note at first and was unsure how long it had actually sat there on top of her dresser, while she undressed from work. Until she stepped up to it to place her earrings in the jewelry dish that sat next to her selection of perfumes, and it had caught her attention in the dim shadows of her bedroom. The moonlight falling on it as if to say *'Hello, I'm here'*.

In the place where her favorite perfume usually sat, the one that had been missing for weeks, sat a bright, neon orange post it.

With shaking fingers, she picked the handwritten note up, reading it over and over again before crumpling it in her hand and tossing it into the garbage.

He was back. It was him; she knew now. And he'd been inside her house.

Inside her house.

Probably more than once.

He'd stolen her perfume. Her favorite red bra and matching panties, too, she guessed, the night she'd fallen asleep in the bathtub. The roses. It was all him. It had to be.

How many times had he been inside? How many times had he rifled through her things, stolen from her, watched her?

She glanced around, eyes wide. He wasn't threatening her, she reasoned with herself, trying for calming breaths. He wasn't hurting her, wasn't trying to hurt her. He was leaving her love notes, as he'd see them.

Did she dare call the police? Would they even take this seriously? He wasn't hurting her. But this was harassment, stalking at the least, right?

Crossing the room, she reached for an inconspicuous cloth bound book between several others that sat atop her nightstand. Opening the front cover revealed a small secret safe. She twisted the dial to the combination and it opened, revealing her small handgun hidden there. Roxy replaced the book, sliding it between a worn, faded linen copy of *Pride and Prejudice* and an old, frayed copy of Bram Stokers *Dracula*. She sat on the edge of the bed, letting the weight of the handgun become familiar again after so long. She'd gotten it after Free had brought her home, after Neal had beaten her bloody and then hightailed it out of town. It was registered, legal, and she knew her way around it well enough and was a decent shot, at least at the range she had frequented in the months after the attack. It had lived in her purse for over a year, carrying it with her everywhere she went, just in case he came back.

She had retired it to its hiding place in the book safe, after she was sure Neal wasn't coming back. It was a terrifying, welcome weight in her hand now. Because he *was* back.

And she wouldn't go down without a fight. Not this time.

ELEVEN

"Hips closed, knees open, feet planted, shoulders dropped. Make sure you brace for impact."

Roxy chanted the words back to herself in her head after he called them out. Repeating them over and over again in her head, trying—and utterly failing—to concentrate on the drill they were working on, and not the sculpted, bronzed, half naked man that was prowling through the paired off duos spaced across the gym floor.

"Strike."

She struck the mitt on Natalie's right hand and her friend stumbled backward with the force, having not prepared for the hit. Roxy fought the urge to roll her eyes. To Natalie, this was just an hour of ogling Travis… but to her, it was vital.

He was back.

In the days since she'd found Neal's note, she'd hardly slept, could hardly eat for the fear coursing through her veins every waking moment. So she'd thrown herself into training. Listening to every single word Travis taught them. Because she knew… she knew she would need it.

Maybe not right now, but she would.

He was back, he had sent those flowers, and he had been *in* her house, multiple times it seemed. He'd stolen her perfume, had taken her clothes…had come back to leave a fucking note, asking for *forgiveness*. She nearly snarled with the memory of that note.

She'd fallen asleep in the bathtub and he'd crept through her house without her even knowing it, while she was there, totally unaware. Had he spied on her in the bathtub? Had he watched her, naked and completely vulnerable? Her breath quickened as anxiety spiraled through her, making her chest seize, but she shoved it down. Focusing on her stance; her every muscle straining with how tense she was.

He could have stood over her, doing God only knows what, could have harmed her… and she had been totally oblivious of his presence. He had come back, after that. To leave that note. To tell her he was here, and he was watching.

She had called Bobby, her landlord, and he had come out to replace the locks on the doors, installed a new chain bolt, as well as to check all the windows. She hadn't told him why; just said she'd thought she'd seen someone lurking and wanted to make sure everything was up to snuff. But still, she felt on edge and hated being home alone at night, terrified to sleep in case he was able to get in again.

Shivers ran up and down her spine as she adjusted her stance and waited for Natalie to return to her position. Natalie's eyes flicked toward Travis just as Roxy struck again, and Natalie stumbled back a second time. Travis's head swiveled toward them, and then Natalie groaned when he made his way through the sparring partners over to them.

"Focus," he grunted at Natalie, who flushed crimson beneath her blonde hair. He stepped back, crossing his arms over his chest. His honey-colored eyes bounced between them before returning to Natalie's. He tipped his chin and said, "Show me your stance.

Learning how to take *and* deflect a hit is just as important as learning how to strike properly."

Roxy straightened out of her stance while Travis worked with Natalie one-on-one, positioning her feet, knees, hips, and shoulders properly. Natalie's face was burning with a blush, and Roxy couldn't help the smirk that tugged at her own lips watching her friend struggle with having Travis so close. It effectively pulled her out of the dark spiral her mind had been in.

When he was satisfied with Natalie's posture, he stepped into Roxy's bubble, forcing her backward a step, and demonstrated a strike; though with a fraction of the speed and power that she was sure he could produce. Natalie nodded, concentrating as he repeated it.

Roxy took the moment to fully appreciate the man's form while he wasn't watching her. His sculpted back that rippled with muscle, covered in more black shaded tattoos. His waist was trim but thick, and she didn't doubt for a second that this man's core strength was impeccable with a tree trunk like that for a waist. The athletic shorts he had on accentuated the narrowness of his hips, and the muscles in the backs of his thighs and calves bunched and shifted with each move he made on the balls of his feet. It really truly was unfair how attractive he was.

As he straightened, she tore her attention away from his beautiful form, hoping it wasn't mortifyingly obvious she'd been shamelessly checking him out as he turned to face her. He smirked at her, his golden eyes sparkling with humor at having caught her. One brow arched high, teasing her silently, and her belly did that annoying flipflop thing again. *Damn him.*

"You're turn, Red. Show me what you've got."

He widened his stance, taking over where Natalie had left off, those honey-gold eyes of his shining tauntingly. She gritted her teeth and shifted into position; her own eyes locked on his in a silent challenge.

She struck the mitt on his right hand and he grunted in approval. The sound ricocheted through her mind and scattered every coherent thought from her brain. He nodded once, shifting. The muscles in his chest, shoulders, and arms rippled. Her eyes tracked the motion and his quick smirk told her he'd caught her in the act. *Fucker.*

"Again, Red," he taunted low.

She focused her gaze on the mitt on his hand, refusing to meet those teasing eyes, and did as he said, striking hard.

"Good," he rumbled and she forced her face to remain impassive.

Her muscles were already screaming at her, tensed as she was with anticipation and adrenaline, as well as burning from the hour of work they'd already done. Her shoulders were going to ache after today's class, she just knew it.

"Can you give me one more?" he asked gruffly, and she thought she just might die from the eroticism of that simple question. Her eyes snapped to his, her mouth parting. His lips tilted up in another almost imperceptible smirk as he tracked her response to the question.

She nodded stiffly, then took a deep breath in, focusing intently on the mitt that covered his hand. She struck again, annoyed with herself at just how much his approving rumble affected her, how much she realized she sought his approval. She was *Roxsanna fucking Roberts.* She didn't need any man's approval.

But oh that sound that rumbled out of his chest was music to her ears, every damn time. He let that corner of his mouth lift in that teasing smirk again, before turning his attention back to the rest of the class. "That's enough for today. You all did well. See you in a few days."

And then he sauntered off toward the corner of the room, where his gym bag was situated on one of the many benches that lined the walls. Roxy and Natalie walked off in the opposite direction toward their own bags. Natalie was quiet, for once, probably still embarrassed at having Travis so close in her space and correcting her on her form, but Roxy didn't mind the quiet. The thoughts roiling through her head were loud enough.

Ever since he'd stopped in at the bar, it felt like things had shifted between them. Were Moe, Lowell, and Rudy right? *Was* he interested?

She mentally shook her head. Even if he was—which she highly doubted, because, look at the guy—*she* wasn't.

She *wasn't.*

Not totally, anyway.

Fuck. Okay, maybe a little. But only enough to *look*, not to do anything about it.

Only because when he looked at her with those damn honey-golden eyes, she could feel it all the way to the very center of her. Like he could see everything, even the broken and ugly parts of her that she fought to keep hidden. And she hadn't felt attraction to another man in so long… men weren't worth the trouble that came along with the more enjoyable parts, so she'd kept her distance and stocked up on *eh-hem*… toys.

Toys that had gotten an obnoxious amount of use since he'd shown up at the bar, in those jeans and that cowboy hat… A flash of lightheadedness swept through her.

Natalie called a quiet, "Good night," to her and Roxy waved as her friend exited the gym doors, heading down the sidewalk to her vehicle. Roxy sat down on the bench, taking several deep, slow breaths, eyes closed.

"I swear to God if you pass out on me again—"

Roxy let out a scoffing laugh and opened her eyes to find Travis standing in front of her, about four feet away. He'd pulled on a hoodie that had the sleeves cut off—*did the man not own anything with sleeves still attached?*—and the colorful athletic tape had been removed from his hands. His gym bag was slung over one shoulder.

"I'm fine," she said, softening her tone. "I just need a quick snack."

"You need to start preparing a pre-workout snack *before* class, especially if you're going to insist on working yourself as hard as you did today," he grumbled roughly, and she narrowed her gaze on him in irritation. Before she could open her mouth to offer a scathing retort, he slid the bag down his arm until it thumped to the floor and he knelt by it, deftly unzipping a side pocket. He produced two small Tupperware containers, one filled with sliced orange wedges, and the other, filled with mixed nuts. He pried the lid off the one with the sliced orange, passing it to her.

She stared at the little plastic container in his hand for a long time before raising her eyes to his in shock.

He shrugged one shoulder, still holding out the container of cut fruit. His eyes never left hers. "I make sure to have some in my bag, just in case. Any night you don't need it, I eat it on the way home." He shrugged again. "And it's easier to have it precut than have to use my switchblade all the time."

Her head fell to the side just slightly, shaking in awe. Tears stung her nose sharply at the thoughtfulness of the gesture. She reached out and took the container from him, their fingers grazing. "Travis…"

"You promised me no extra paperwork. If you pass out again, that promise is then null and void, and we're going to have a problem. Eat, please." His eyes were shining with humor, but he nodded toward her hands anyway, indicating for her to start eating. He grinned then, resting his elbow on his bent knee, leaning toward her slightly as he murmured huskily, "Unless you're just looking for an excuse to get me to take you out for dinner again. All you have to do is tell me, baby girl."

Her mouth dropped open in astonishment, a startled laugh

bubbling out of her. He winked, and Roxy felt more of that barbed wire fence wrapped around her heart giving way. *Shit I'm in so much trouble*. He's just so goddamn *charming*.

She sat up straighter then, as if being yanked upright, as warning bells blared in her head a moment later. *Charming*. Charming was dangerous. Charming was a façade for narcissistic behavior. Neal had been charming once, too. And she'd told herself never again would she be wooed by a pretty face or dashing smile. Men didn't do things out of the goodness of their hearts without expecting something in return. And she had nothing to give. Nothing she was willing to give.

Dropping her gaze from his to the pieces of sliced fruit in her lap, she tried to tell herself that Travis wasn't like Neal. He wasn't trying to hurt her; he was trying to *help* her.

Anger bubbled up then, and she shoved the container back at him. He took it, more out of surprise, his light brows furrowing over his honey-gold eyes. "I don't need your pity oranges, or a pity date, Travis."

"*Pity oranges?*" he growled, and she felt his eyes as they bored into the side of her face, which she kept resolutely turned away from him.

"I don't need your help, either."

"What the fuck are *pity oranges*, Roxy?" he asked, his voice low and lethal.

She gestured toward the Tupperware still in his hand, while stuffing her things into her own bag. Her hands shook. Fuck. Maybe she should have eaten at least a few of those before shoving them away. No. She wouldn't let him see her tremble. Raising her defiant stare to his, she said, "I'm not your problem to deal with, Travis. Again, nothing about me is any of your business. So leave me alone."

"It is my business if you pass out in my class because you're too stubborn to accept help when you need it—"

"I don't need your help!" she exclaimed, surging to her feet. Lights flashed like stars on the outsides of her vision, but she steeled her shoulders. "I don't need help from any man, Travis. So back off."

Hoisting her gym bag over her shoulder, she marched across the now empty mat toward the door. Pushing open the door, she sucked in the cool evening air, taking long, deep breaths, before heading down to her car. She sank into the driver's seat, fumbling with the zipper of her bag and pulling out a package of peanut butter crackers. She managed to tear the plastic open despite how badly her hands were shaking, and took a bite of the cracker.

Resting her head against the head rest, she sighed, closing her eyes as she chewed through three of the six crackers. The trembling lightened, but it wasn't completely gone, her heart still racing slightly.

Eyes still closed, she heard his footsteps on the sidewalk, and then next to her car, before a light knock sounded on her window. She opened her eyes, glancing at him, before sighing and rolling the window down. He leaned his forearms against the windowsill, his face appearing as he ducked to look in at her.

"Are you done?" he asked, his tone droll.

She rolled her lips in between her teeth and took another long, deep breath in, letting it out just as slowly. She knew he wasn't referring to the blood sugar attack… but rather the temper tantrum she'd just thrown. She nodded grudgingly.

"So, you get ornery when your blood sugar dips, that's good to know," he murmured gently, teasing lightly. She rolled her eyes. "Dinner or a drive home, what's it going to be, baby girl?"

Admitting defeat, she caught his gaze and whispered, "Dinner, please."

He grinned, a quick flash of his beautifully straight white teeth, and winked again. "I told you all you had to do was ask, Roxy."

TWELVE

"This isn't a date," Roxy muttered over to him from the passenger seat of his Bronco.

He grinned again, glancing over at her from the driver's side. He had his left hand draped loosely over the steering wheel, his right hand resting on the shifter between them. She was so cute when she was prickly.

"Of course not," he agreed, though the grin stayed in place, tipping the corners of his mouth up slightly. He could practically hear her rolling her eyes at him and chuckled.

"And I could have driven myself," she continued, crossing her left leg over her right, as if trying to angle her body away from his. He knew she wasn't as unaffected as she tried to portray. Christ, his entire body was on fire knowing she was close enough for him to touch. He wouldn't, of course. But this little spitfire did things to him that he hadn't expected. Felt a vicious tug in his chest that he had thought was long dead.

He glanced over at her with a baleful glare and she huffed, crossing her arms over her middle. "Your hands are still shaking; you weren't driving anywhere, Red."

"Where are we going?" she asked, watching out the passenger

window as he turned them onto the highway headed toward North Fort Worth.

"Salty's Steakhouse." He glanced over at her again as they merged onto the interstate. "You can google their menu. It only takes a few minutes to get there."

"I've been to Salty's," she muttered sourly, though he watched as she dug her cell phone out of her pocket and opened the browser. She scrolled through the menu, her right hand tapping at her mouth idly, and then she pulled her bottom lip through her teeth and he had to bite back a groan. "Ooh, they have grilled salmon." Turning her head to look at him, she said, "Let me guess; you're a strictly lean chicken and raw veggies kinda guy. No carbs, no sweets, no fun foods."

He laughed out loud, flipping his blinker on as he moved them onto the exit ramp behind a lifted F-250. "When I'm training, sure. But I don't fight professionally anymore, so I'm not as strict on myself as I used to be." He patted his stomach for emphasis, covered in the material of the hoodie. "This isn't what it used to be."

He took pleasure in watching her mouth drop open in shock, a grin tugging at his mouth again. He couldn't remember a time he'd smiled as much as he did when she was around. It was both concerning and somehow freeing. Her mouth worked, and then she squeaked, "What do you mean? Like, you used to be *more* in shape than *this*?"

Travis laughed again, nodding, as he turned into the parking lot of Salty's Steakhouse. "My only job was to train hard, fight hard, and win."

She shuddered lightly in her seat and he chuckled, shaking his head. He unbuckled, climbing out of the Bronco. He rounded the hood of the car just as she was sliding out of the seat, and he took her elbow lightly, just to make sure she wasn't still wobbly on her feet, and shut the passenger door. His fingers felt electrified where he had made contact with her, even through the material of the thin jacket covering her arms.

They made their way toward the doors, and Travis made sure to open it before she could, allowing her to pass in front of him. They both still wore their gym clothes; her skin-tight, ass hugging athletic leggings delineating every curve of her backside and thighs. The leggings she wore were a dark teal color, the same color as the matching sports bra she had on—now covered by a fitted zippered athletic jacket in a lighter teal—and it complimented her coloring in a way that had made it damn difficult for him to concentrate during class earlier. He'd found his eyes roving toward her every chance he could. Her wild curls were piled on top of her head, a few stray strands falling out to frame her face. He had pulled on a pair of sweatpants over the gym shorts from earlier, and the hoodie he had pulled on had the sleeves cut off of it. Part of why he'd chosen Salty's was because it was low key and casual. Their attire didn't attract too many strange glances as they were seated by a harried looking server.

It was decently busy inside, loud enough with the music playing overhead and the din of other customer voices that they would be able to talk and not be overheard, but not too loud that they would have to shout at each other from across the table. The booth they were directed to was along one wall toward the back, and Travis gestured for Roxy to slide in before he took the bench opposite her. Laminated menus were set down in front of both of them, but the server that had sat them disappeared quickly.

He watched Roxy over the top of his menu, cataloguing her face and pleased to see that some of the color had returned to her cheeks; was no longer ashen and pale, and the trembling in her hands had eased. Her hazel eyes drifted over the menu held in her hands, and in the dim lighting they looked more brown than green.

He knew how they shone with the prettiest shade of jade

green when the sunlight hit them, such a gorgeous contrast to the dark auburn eyelashes that framed them. She glanced up at him, catching him staring, though he didn't drop his gaze. He watched as her throat constricted as she swallowed, her tongue darting out to flick across her bottom lip and that damn white scar that he wanted to run his tongue over. He wanted to know where it had come from…who had given it to her.

A different server stopped at the edge of their table; a black t-shirt stretched across his chest. A black apron was tied around his waist, and he wore jeans and black sneakers. A small notepad was flipped open, and a pen was poised in his fingers. "What can I getchya?"

"Roxy?" Travis prompted, turning his gaze back to her. She set the menu down in front of her and tapped a fingernail on an item listed. "The grilled salmon, please. Can I get double vegetable and no potato?" The server nodded, writing down her request. Travis watched as the guy—who couldn't have been older than twenty-three or twenty-four—stared at Roxy, his cheeks heating as he took her in. Even dressed down in athletic clothes fresh out of a workout, she was the kind of stunning that made men pay attention. "I'll take a sweet tea, too. And a water, please." She smiled and handed her menu over, and the poor schmuck tucked it under his arm, still dazzled by the small smile she graced him with. "Thank you."

Travis cleared his throat and the server turned toward him. Travis handed over his menu, leaning back against the back of the booth as he said gruffly, "I'll take the ribeye, medium, with sauteed mushrooms. Baked potato and whatever the house vegetable is, please." The kid jotted everything down, his eyes flicking over Travis's face and then down his tattooed arms, which he'd crossed over his chest. "And I'll take a tall Lone Star, please."

The kid disappeared after a mumbled, "Sure, I'll be right back with those."

Roxy glared at him over the scuffed wood tabletop. "You didn't need to intimidate the poor kid. He's just doing his job."

He leaned forward, leaving his arms crossed, and braced them on the table. He raised his eyebrows at Roxy and murmured, "He didn't realize I was even here; he was so dazzled by your smile."

She laughed out loud—a scoffing, self-deprecatory laugh—and shook her head. "Yeah, okay, buddy. I don't dazzle."

He cocked an eyebrow at her. "You don't believe me?"

She rolled her eyes and glanced around the busy restaurant floor, ignoring his question. The waiter was back then, placing her sweet tea and water in front of her, and his tall beer in front of him. They each said thank you, but the server was off again, and she hadn't paid one lick of attention to the way the kid's eyes had tracked over her face.

Travis let it go, instead fully enjoying the flush of heat that crept up her neck to stain her face whenever she caught him staring at her. He couldn't help it. He could say it was because he was watching her to make sure she didn't pass out again, but in reality, it was simply because he wanted to. She was fire and light and sunshine… and dynamite. All rolled into one. He'd kill to watch her go off. All fireworks and heat.

She folded her arms on the marred and scuffed wood table top, leaning on them as she returned his stare. "You can look at me like that all you want, Travis. I'm not going to pass out."

"Can't blame me for making sure," he answered drolly, reaching out and wrapping his hand around his beer, bringing it to his lips. He watched her eyes dart from his to his mouth, and fought the urge to smile knowingly. He couldn't keep the laughter out of his eyes, though, and when she brought her gaze back to his, she scowled. "You have a bad habit of not taking care of yourself."

That scowl deepened. She was fun to rile up. "I don't need to be taken care of."

"I didn't say you did." He set his beer down and leaned closer again. "I said what I said; you don't take care of yourself, Red."

"I take care of myself just fine. It's just been a rough few weeks." She leaned back as the waiter arrived with their food, setting first the salmon in front of her, and then his steak in front of him. They both said thank you to the waiter, who disappeared again quickly. She unrolled her silverware, placing the paper napkin in her lap. "I've been on my own since I was sixteen. I know how to take care of myself."

"Is that why you're scared all the time? Because you can take care of yourself?"

Her hand froze, fork poised to stab into the grilled salmon, and he knew he'd hit the nail on the head. She was afraid of something.

"You can talk to me, Roxy," he said gently, quietly. Beseechingly.

"I'm not scared of anything," she countered, not raising her eyes to his as she stabbed her fork into the salmon, breaking off several pieces of the flaky fish. She placed the bite in her mouth, chewing, her eyes trained on her plate. "And yes, I can take care of myself, Travis. I don't need some hulking macho man to swoop in and play the hero." She swallowed, then continued, almost as an afterthought, "Because there's nothing wrong."

Prickly thing.

He nodded, digging into his own plate of food, though he continued to watch her closely. The color was returning to her face fully now, no longer pale, and her hands had stopped trembling finally. She polished off most of her meal, the salmon had disappeared quickly, and only a few heads of broccoli remained on her plate as she pushed it away. He reached over the table with his fork, stabbing the remaining florets with the tines and bringing them to his mouth. She just shook her head, a half-smile tugging at her mouth as she watched him clean his plate.

The waiter returned, clearing their plates. "Did y'all save room for dessert?"

Roxy groaned, shaking her head with another smile. Travis plucked the drink and dessert menu from where it was stashed close to the wall of the booth and flipped it over to glance over it. "Rox, wanna split a slice of pecan pie?"

If he hadn't looked up at her at the same time he'd asked the question, he would have missed the fear that clouded her eyes, the way they darted around them in sheer panic. And then her face shuttered, the fear gone, but so was the warmth, the easy banter. She shook her head no. He replaced the menu in its spot on the far edge of the table and turned to the waiter. "No, I think we're good. Thanks, though. Just the check."

As the waiter retreated again, Roxy raised her eyes to his, and the blankness in them couldn't completely mask the fear buried deep. His chest ached. "Don't ever call me that."

He nodded gravely, his eyes tracking every nuance of her face, her expression. "Roxy."

She swallowed hard, dropping her eyes from his, her arms banding around her waist tightly.

"Roxy." Still, she kept her eyes averted, returning to sweeping across the still crowded restaurant. He lowered his voice into a gruff murmur. "*Red.*"

Her eyes came back to his finally, and he kept her stare, holding her gaze.

"I'm sorry. I didn't know."

She nodded, just once, the movement stiff. She offered no other explanation, and he didn't press for one. He dug into his back pocket, pulling out his wallet, and placed several bills into the black book that the waiter came back with moments later. The poor kid was still watching Roxy avidly, his tongue damn near hanging out of his skull. Travis glowered at the kid, who finally got the hint and shuffled off quickly.

Wanting—needing—to touch her, he offered his hand to her after he stood from his side of the booth. She stared at it for a long time, as if weighing the decision, but then she slid her fingers across his palm. His fingers curled around hers, and the shock that grazed his skin had nothing to do with static energy.

She stood, keeping her fingers entwined with his as he led them back through the crowded restaurant and out the front door. The night air was crisp, cooler than when they'd entered, and he watched as goosebumps flashed across her exposed skin. It felt wonderful to him, the coolness of the air combatting the inferno that was raging under his skin, radiating from where her hand was tucked safely into his. He released it as they approached his Bronco, opening the passenger door for her to climb in.

He took several deep, steadying breaths as he rounded the hood of the car before climbing in behind the wheel.

They drove in silence, the only sound in the cab of the vehicle the thrum of the tires on the road as it flew beneath them, and the country music that was playing quietly in the background.

When he pulled into a parking space several cars down from where her car was still parked outside of the gym, he turned the car off and exited. She climbed out as he rounded the hood again, and then he walked her toward her car in the darkness. The lights from the gym were still on, casting light to dancing across the sidewalk as they approached her car.

"Red."

She stopped, her hands tucked into the pockets of her light teal jacket, and looked up at him. She had the stretchy athletic jacket zippered clear up to her chin against the slight chill, the collar brushing beneath her chin and sides of her jaw. Her hair, still piled on top of her head in that adorably messy topknot, begged to be let down. He wanted to feel those curls wrapped around his fingers. Those mesmerizing green and gold flecked eyes met his.

She was so fucking beautiful it hurt.

Hands shoved into the pockets of his sweats; he took a step toward her. She retreated, her back coming into contact with the side of her car. Her head tipped up, eyes remaining laser focused on his, but her lips had parted slightly, and he could see the rapid fluttering of her heart in her throat. He was desperate to feel that wild fluttering with his tongue.

"You want to know how I know that kid at the restaurant was dazzled by you?" She stared up at him, her eyes wide, as he moved in one step closer. He ached to press his lips to the smattering of freckles that ran across each cheek and bridged her nose. Lazily, slowly, he let his gaze track over her face before murmuring gruffly, "Because I'm dazzled by you, too."

He could have sworn she stopped breathing as she stared up at him, and he smirked, just the corner of his lips tilting up. He tilted at the waist, hands still shoved in his pockets—to keep from touching her—until he leaned down close enough to let his lip trail over the corner of her mouth, flitting over her cheek lightly. Fuck she smelled good.

Her breath drew in on a sharp gasp, and the sound did awful, wonderful things to his cock, but neither of them moved an inch. He didn't come any closer, and she didn't shove him away. Slowly, so slowly, he straightened. His gaze found those wide, hazel eyes once more.

"Good night, Roxy."

Thirteen

He waited until she'd scrambled into her car, starting it, before he turned away to walk back toward his. Her heart was a jackhammer in her chest, sending debris and shards of herself flying throughout her body, her soul, making one helluva mess at the very center of her being.

She didn't dare look his direction as she put her car in gear and backed out of the parking spot, though out of her peripheral she could see him as he climbed in behind the wheel of his Bronco. Roxy kept her gaze fixed straight ahead as she drove away, only daring to look in the rearview mirror afterward. She could see the red glow of his brake lights, and then the flash of white as he reversed out of his parking spot, too. He turned in the opposite direction, and as she turned the corner, his taillights disappeared out of sight.

Her mind was a maelstrom; every thought whirling too fast to process before the next was nearly suffocating her.

The feel of Travis's mouth, his lips brushing over the corner of her mouth, her cheek… heat coursed through her at the memory and she blew out a steadying breath in the darkness of the car.

"Ohmygod," she whispered into the void. The softness of his beard as it tickled her cheek, she had wanted to reach up and grab hold of either side of his face, just to finally know what it felt like beneath her fingers, her palms. Her nails had dug craters into her palms where she'd squeezed them inside the pockets of her jacket, just to keep from reaching for him, from touching. She had wanted to twist his head so that his mouth—that had been so dangerously close to her own—could connect with hers. She wanted to know what his lips felt like against her own, wanted to know what he tasted like, what his tongue would do as it entered her mouth.

She was home minutes later, pulling into the driveway. The headlights shone on the front of the house briefly before she turned the car off, climbing out.

Now that she was home, her body felt weary, exhaustion weighing her down heavily. She hadn't been sleeping or eating well, instead throwing herself headfirst into work, workouts and classes. The physical toll of working herself as hard as she had earlier, along with the hypoglycemia attack had left her drained.

She dragged her gym bag out of the backseat and walked on weary legs to the front door, unlocking it and stepping inside, locking it again as soon as she was inside the darkened house. Her gun was tucked into her gym bag, easily accessible if needed, but the house was quiet, nothing out of place—that she could see anyway.

Flipping lights on as she went, she checked every room. Once satisfied that the house was empty, she trudged into the bedroom, dropping the gym bag onto the foot of the bed with a groan. Roxy untucked the gun from the inside pocket of the bag, hiding it beneath her pillow before stripping the athletic jacket down her arms. Peeling the obnoxiously tight leggings down her legs, she tossed them both onto the pile of clothes overflowing the laundry basket in the corner of the room. Struggling, she wriggled free of the skintight sports bra, breathing out a sigh when the spandex material landed on top of the pile of clothes with the rest of her outfit.

Shimmying out of her panties, those too followed into the pile. Padding into the bathroom, she turned the shower on and waited for only a few minutes before stepping in beneath the warm spray, just long enough to wash the sweat off her skin. Toweling dry and wrapping the fluffy towel around her body, she retreated to the bedroom. Pulling on a pair of waffle weaved lounge pants, she shoved her arms into a matching cropped sweatshirt, the buttery material soft on her skin.

As she climbed into bed, Roxy's thoughts turned once again to Travis. Whatever this was, she was struggling to continue fighting it.

And by the sounds of things, he was, too.

He was dazzled by her?

Her?

She grabbed the tv remote from her nightstand and flipped the tv on. A rerun of *How I Met Your Mother* started, and she settled in beneath the covers as Ted started another tall tale.

FOURTEEN

Headphones on, angry metal music blasting in his ears, he climbed out of the old, rusted Ford F-150, the hinges groaning as he shut the door as quietly as he could. Slinging his gym bag over his shoulder, he sighed as he stared up at the dilapidated two-story house that had been his home for as long as he could remember. He was running late getting home, something he didn't do often; as much as he could help it, anyway. Turning off the hand-me-down I-Pod, he tugged the headphones off his head, letting them rest around his neck as he jogged up the cracked concrete walkway toward the back door. Dad's car was parked in the driveway already, which meant he was home early. He swore, hustling toward the back.

At nineteen, it was probably time to find his own apartment, but the thought of leaving her alone with him... No. He could tough it out for a while longer. If it meant keeping her safe, he'd do anything.

Pushing the back door open, he entered the mudroom and took off his work boots, setting them in the corner, then dropped his gym bag next to them. He knew better than to call out to announce his homecoming, that would just piss him off. And depending on the mood he was in...

Padding through the mud room into the living room, he made note of the baseball game on the old tv across the room, the volume up louder than normal. The smell of dinner wafted from the kitchen, though his nose perked at the slight burnt notes in the air.

"Fuck," he muttered, grimacing. That was sure to piss him off, too. He hated it when Mom burned dinner, even if it wasn't on purpose.

Stepping toward the kitchen, he stopped in his tracks, his eyes not fully processing the scene in front of him.

Her face was beet red, eyes bugging out of her head, arms hanging limp at her sides. The pretty, floral dishtowel a noose that was wound tightly around her neck, held by big, beefy hands. And when those dead, dark eyes raised to his, those hands slackened, dropping her lifeless form to the worn tile floor in a heap.

Rage. Rage the kind that he had never felt before welled inside him and he roared in agony and grief and fury as he launched himself at the monster in front of him, the monster that alcoholism had turned his father into. A gruff shout, and the flash of silver glinted only a second before razor sharp pain sliced through him, but he didn't stop moving forward. Again and again, that flash of silver in his vision, and he realized it was a butcher knife from the counter. The fucker was stabbing him, repeatedly. Blood poured from him, over the floor, splattering the cabinets and her too-still, lifeless body, but he managed to wrestle the knife out of the bastards' hands, sending it clattering to the floor.

His hands curled into fists and then he was swinging, over and over again. The crunch of bone, the spray of blood, none of it registered through the haze of blind hatred, rage, and bloodlust that fueled him. Until the monster beneath him didn't move, until his face was completely unrecognizable... until there was nothing *left of him to salvage. He turned away. This monster deserved not one more second of his time.*

Ignoring the pain that slashed through him everywhere, he dropped to his knees next to her, lifting her lifeless body into his arms as tears made his vision swim. Grief tore through him in agonized screams as he tucked her gray streaked hair behind her ears, hating the blood that he was spreading over her, but he couldn't stop. Blood poured out of him, out of the wounds he'd attained, but still he didn't let her go. Wouldn't let go even after the county sheriff came in through the door, and he fought like a madman to get back to her as he was torn from her, even as the bite of metal cut into his wrists.

From his stomach on the kitchen floor, he let the tears roll down his face as he stared at her. His mother. His beautiful and lovely and kind mother. Taken from him by that monster that now lay in a bloody mess across the room, his life snuffed out as surely as he'd snuffed out hers.

TRAVIS WASN'T SURPRISED WHEN HE WOKE UP FROM THE nightmare.

Drenched in sweat and breathing raggedly into the darkness of his bedroom, he sat up, throwing his legs over the side of the bed, and settled his bare feet against the hardwood flooring. He let the coolness of the floor against the soles of his feet anchor him as he took long, deep breaths in, then let them out slowly again. The sheet was twisted around his waist. He clenched and unclenched his fists in the sheet beneath his hands on either side of his hips until the tension ebbed away.

He'd known the nightmare was coming. It always did.

The chest tightening, throat closing, mind numbing knowledge that he'd been too scared, too weak, *too late* to save her. Every goddamn time.

He blamed Roxy for the nightmares return. It wasn't fair, and he certainly wouldn't take it out on her… but regardless, he still blamed her for bringing those old feelings up. Of being too late to help. Seeing that same fear in her eyes was doing things to him, bringing up all those old demons that he fought so hard to keep at bay.

Resting his elbows on his knees, he scrubbed his hands over his face, shoving his unbound hair back and took long, deep breaths in, letting them out just as slowly.

Twenty years. It felt like a mere heartbeat and an eternity had passed at once.

In their tiny town in Oklahoma, justice was a joke; it was more about who you knew and who could pad pockets than who was actually guilty or not. His family had lived in poverty most of his life, especially after his dad had lost his long-time job as a bailiff in the tiny one room courthouse due to his drinking. But he was still buddies with several of the deputies, including the sheriff, and when Jenkins had shown up that night… it hadn't mattered that his dad had been the one to kill his mother, or that Travis had been stabbed sixteen times with that butcher knife. Jenkins spun a tale in retribution for Travis killing his old man, and he'd sat in that county jail for three months before a court appointed lawyer had come to get him out. He'd told him that the charges were being dropped on account of several neighbors coming forward about what they'd heard that night, and some fancy investigating that had proven Travis's story after all.

They hadn't let him out to attend his mother's funeral; not that there was one, anyway. They'd cremated her and put her ashes in a shoe box. He had to pay to have her ashes released to him. He didn't know what had happened to his dad's body, or where he'd been buried, or if he'd been cremated, too. He didn't give a shit. He hoped he rotted on that kitchen floor. Hoped he was burning in

Hell. He'd see him again; he was sure of it. That's where he was headed, too, when it was time. If he were to believe in all that.

He was just as much of a monster as his old man was. It didn't matter the reason. Blood was on his hands, and always would be.

Pushing to his feet, Travis strode out of the darkened bedroom and down the short hallway to the kitchen, naked except for the boxer briefs he wore. Swiping a bottled water out of the fridge, he drank it down in one long swallow.

Bracing his hands on the counter, he leaned against them and hung his head between his arms, his chin nearly touching his chest. The faint glow of the light over the stove cast the thin, narrow scars across his arms and chest into sharp relief. Most of the time, they were barely visible, but when the light hit them just right... They'd hurt like a bitch when he'd had every single one covered in a tattoo, until ninety percent of his body was covered in the ink. Scar tissue wasn't pleasant to tattoo over. Most of the scars peppered the left side of his ribcage and stomach, though several long gashes had sliced up his forearms, as well as his thighs as his father had swung that knife wildly.

Shoving away from the counter, he treaded back down the hallway and began to dress, pulling on a pair of gym shorts and an old t-shirt with the arms cut off. He pulled socks on and then slid his feet into a pair of sneakers. Strapping his cellphone to his bicep, he queued up a playlist and then headed outside.

The moon was still up, but on the horizon, he could see the first signs of dawn; the inky blackness giving way to gray skies in the distance. Travis stretched, loosening his tight muscles, and then set off at a brisk jog. His feet pounded the pavement as he ran, his strides eating up the miles beneath him as he pushed himself. By the time he made it back home, his legs ached and sweat had drenched the front and back of his t-shirt.

But his head was clearer, and he headed to the bathroom to shower. Turning the water on to warm, he stripped, tossing his sweaty clothes into the hamper, and then climbed in beneath the spray. He let his mind wander to Roxy. She had somehow burrowed under his fucking skin. He hadn't let himself get attached to anyone in decades, but somehow this fiery redhead had weaseled her way in, and he was powerless to fight against her draw. He felt an overwhelming urge to protect her, to shield her from whatever was causing that fear in her.

He scrubbed the sweat away and washed his hair, lathering the long strands with shampoo, and then a conditioning treatment. He thought back to their not-a-date last week, and how badly he'd wanted to kiss her smart and sassy mouth afterward. How he hadn't wanted to let her leave without tasting her, just once. Remembering what those leggings did to her thighs and ass, he groaned lightly when his dick responded to the memory, hardening even as he fisted himself in his hand.

Stroking from root to tip, he braced one forearm against the shower wall as he imagined everything he wanted to do to Roxy, what he wanted to do to that sassy mouth of hers, what he wanted her to do to him. It wasn't long before his balls tightened, and he grunted low as he came, painting the shower wall with it, and her name fell off his lips.

FIFTEEN

"Motherfucker!"

"You kiss your momma with that mouth?" Natalie asked drolly from the other end of the phone.

"I haven't seen my momma since I was sixteen and you know it," Roxy muttered sourly, her phone set to speaker. "I just feel like I'm losing my goddamn mind lately. My shampoo is gone, and I can't find my teal sports bra or leggings either."

Wracking her brain, she sank down onto the foot of her bed. She couldn't remember putting them in the wash after she'd gotten home from the not-a-date with Travis, but knew for a fact that she'd tossed them into the basket in the corner of the bedroom because she'd had to wrestle the damn sports bra off. And the way he'd stared at her all evening in them… they were her new favorites.

Which was why she wanted to wear them to the gym tonight, just on the off chance that Travis would be there, too… since he hadn't been able to keep his eyes off her the last time. She groaned.

"Actually, the entire outfit is gone. Leggings, sports bra, the jacket. I know I put them—" she stood, going through the motions to recreate it, tossing the invisible clothes onto the hamper. She stepped over to it, digging behind it, but there was nothing there. Turning back to the bed, she dumped the clean laundry out of the basket and into the middle of the mattress. Rifling through, she shook her head in frustration. There was no other laundry in the wash; this was all she had. And they most definitely were not in the pile of clean clothes.

Ice filled her veins then. Had he come back? Had he gotten inside again, and taken her clothes?

Striding around the small house, she checked every window and both doors, but everything was secure. Bobby had replaced the locks and double checked all the window locks, and she had the only copy of the key. There was no way he was getting into her house, not now. So those clothes had to be here *somewhere*.

"—do you want to go to Waylon's tonight?"

"Huh?" Roxy asked, shaking herself back to the present at the sound of Natalie's annoyed voice through the phone.

"*Welcome back to Earth*," Natalie intoned sourly, and Roxy wondered how many times Natalie had asked that question already. "I was asking if you wanted to go to Waylon's tonight? That new country band is playing tonight, go with meeee. We haven't been out for a girl's night in months. You always bail on me."

Natalie was right. Roxy hadn't joined her for a girls' night out since the roses had shown up in her kitchen. Paranoia had made her overly cautious, and with the note from two weeks ago…

But… she thought wistfully, chewing on the inside of her cheek, *things had been uneventful the last two weeks*. Maybe the roses hadn't been from Neal after all. It could have been her imagination, the paranoia making her see him watching her from across the street at the gym. She hadn't actually seen him, just a flash of that dark hair across the street... The note was admittedly slightly alarming, but altogether not threatening, exactly. She could go out, just for a few hours. She would be in a highly public place, with Natalie, surrounded by people. Bouncers, even. It would be fine. He wasn't trying to hurt her. Even if it was creepy.

"You know what, why not? I think a night out at Waylon's sounds perfect," Roxy said into the phone still tucked under her ear. "I'm going to get a quick workout in, but I'll see you there at nine?"

"Yesss!" Natalie whooped and Roxy rolled her eyes, then chewed on her bottom lip, her heart doing a little nervous flutter in her chest.

Because just one night out couldn't hurt, right?

SIXTEEN

He knew the second she walked into the gym, as if his entire being was somehow attuned to her presence. The air got thicker, heavier, time seemed to slow and speed up all at once until all he could seem to focus on was the woman that was crossing the gym floor to the opposite side of the room, toward one of the hanging body bags.

Sage green leggings encased her thighs and her bottom, delineating each curve. A darker sage green jacket was zipped up and over her breasts, but she removed it as soon as she made it over to the other wall, where she'd set down her gym bag. A matching sports bra was all that covered her upper body, and even from this distance he could see the muscles that had developed on her shoulders and arms in the last months. Her back was defined, her waist trim, and flared into wide hips. He ached to know what those hips felt like beneath his hands, gripping them as he pulled her back onto him—

Travis averted his gaze quickly, willing his mind away from imagining her the way he'd imagined her in the shower. He thought of dead locusts crunching beneath his sneakers on the road as he ran, sorting and folding socks, and sang the states song in his head to will away the erection that had begun tenting his gym shorts. *Not a good time, buddy.*

But it wasn't long before his eyes returned to her, and he watched her out of the corner of his eye as she sank onto one of the benches and laced on her sneakers, then pulled out her sparring gloves and pulled them on her hands, velcroing them in place. She stretched her fingers wide, opening and closing her hands several times to work the gloves into place.

She tucked a pair of headphones into her ears and flipped through the screen on her cellphone, before tucking it into the side pocket of her leggings. Roxy stretched for several minutes, and then she began.

He stopped what he was doing to watch. Her stance was good, solid, and strong. Her jabs and hooks were precise, and he couldn't help the pride that settled into his chest as he watched. She'd learned a lot in his class, and was happy to see that she was taking that information and not only using it, but applying it properly.

But she was lost in whatever world her mind had taken her to, and she never once glanced over at him. She punched and struck and jabbed until he could see sweat rolling down her forehead, her neck, her chest.

When she finally slowed, her arms dropped to her sides and she simply stood in front of the bag, watching it sway from the last strikes she'd given it, her back heaving with labored, heavy breaths. She reached up and yanked the headphones out of her ears, letting them hang around her neck.

Travis roused himself from simply staring at her, walking the thirty feet or so over toward her. She didn't react when he stepped up beside her, her eyes still staring at the slowly swinging bag suspended on its thick chains. Emotion rolled off her in waves, and though he ached to reach out a hand to touch her, he refrained, letting her have the moment.

"You don't have to do this alone. Whatever it is…*Roxy*," he murmured low, his voice coming out huskier than he intended. Beseeching, almost. "Let me help you."

She looked up at him then, her face flushed and glistening with sweat, lips parted slightly between shallow, quick breaths. Her words were quiet, resigned, when she finally whispered back, "I don't need saving, Travis."

She ducked her head, dropping her eyes from his, and he felt the loss like a physical blow. What kind of witchcraft did this woman possess over him?

Roxy had taken several steps away, toward the bench and her gym bag when he surged forward. "Come to dinner with me."

Her mouth twitched up in one corner in a wry smile. "I can't."

"Why not?" he asked, his eyes scanning her face again. Those freckles were killing him, and being this close to her, he could see there were hundreds of them smattered across her mostly bare shoulders, too.

"Because I have plans tonight."

He swallowed hard as his chest seized painfully. A date? With another guy? *Fuck that*.

"Break them."

She laughed then, her lips pulling into a wide smile, and she shook her head. "Oh no. I'm not facing Natalie's wrath by bailing on her."

That tightness in his chest eased a little. He crossed his arms over his chest. "What are you girls up to?"

"Line dancing. At Waylon's." Her head tipped to the side slightly, a teasing smile on her lips, and her eyes sparkled with far more green than gold tonight. "You line dance, big guy?"

"Maybe. You asking me out?" he asked, taking a step forward, until they stood nearly toe to toe, and she had to tilt her head back to continue looking up at him.

"Not a chance."

Her eyes were dancing with mischief, and fuck if it didn't excite the hell out of him. He couldn't stop the grin that tugged at his own mouth, and dammit did he like the way his chest felt lighter when he was around her. A lightness that he hadn't believed still lived inside him after all these years. He leaned down slightly, ducking his head closer to her own, his lips grazing the shell of her ear. "Come on, Red. Ask me out."

"No," she whispered breathily and he groaned low, dragging his bottom lip between his teeth as he straightened just enough to look down into her face. He didn't miss the way her eyes tracked his mouth, her eyes pinging back and forth from his lips to his eyes. *Fucking hell.*

The nearly silent buzzing of the cellphone in her pocket roused them, and she backed up a step as she slid the phone out of her pocket. Swiping at it, she raised it to her ear. "Hey. Yeah, just finishing up. I'm gonna go home to shower and change, then I'll head over there." He waited while he could hear Blondie's voice on the other end of the line, muffled. Her eyes never left his. "See you at nine."

She hung up the call, sliding the phone back into her pocket as she backed away another couple steps. He didn't say anything as she gathered her things, peeled the gloves off her hands, and changed shoes. She was just pulling the jacket up her arms when he stepped forward, grabbing hold of the two sides of it. His knuckles grazed the flat plane of her stomach as he lined up the two halves of the zipper, and she gasped. The sound cut through him, rocketing straight to his dick.

His own breath was unsteady as he pulled the zipper up, so slowly it was nearly torture, allowing his knuckles to drag along the bare skin of her midriff. Up and over the swell of her breasts, stopping in the middle of her sternum. Travis could feel the hammering of her heart beneath the backs of his knuckles where they remained pressed against her chest for several seconds too long. Her tongue darted out to lick her lips, her breaths coming out in short, quick pants. Fuck he wanted to cover her mouth with his, to taste those breaths, to know just how much his simple touches had affected her. He could see it in her eyes, pupils blown wide.

He dragged his knuckles across the still exposed skin of her chest, tracking along another smattering of freckles that dotted her skin, before letting those knuckles trail up the side of her neck.

Fuck, he needed to stop before he did something else, something she may not be interested in, or ready for. Travis curled one stray curl around his index finger, tugging on it gently as he grinned down at her.

"Maybe I'll see you later, Red."

And then he turned and walked away, praying to God no one noticed the way his dick was tenting his gym shorts. Again.

This damn woman was going to be the death of him.

SEVENTEEN

The teal leggings, matching sports bra, and the athletic jacket were sitting on the welcome mat in front of her front door, the neon orange post it note sitting on top. She knelt, picking up the note with trembling hands as she scanned it quickly, before her eyes dropped to the workout clothes. A small, despairing moan left her mouth as she picked them up; the shredded and tattered pieces falling through her fingers back to the welcome mat they'd been left on.

She wanted to scream, to cry, to fall apart; but she just stood there, frozen. Her heart was a jackhammer in her chest, fear and anxiety making her dizzy.

He had seen her with Travis. She was unsure what part of the evening he had been witness to, but he had seen her with Travis. Wearing this outfit. An outfit that was exceedingly formfitting and showed off her body in ways that most clothes didn't.

Had Neal been witness to their dinner? To them returning from dinner, before she'd clambered into her car? When Travis had almost kissed her?

When she had nearly begged Travis to kiss her?

Her stomach roiled, heart hammering in her chest. Was he still watching her? Even now?

Travis had kept his hands stuffed into his pockets, as had she. He hadn't touched her, other than to assist her out of the booth at the restaurant… other than to lean in dangerously close and let his mouth drag across the skin of her cheek…

Anger boiled through her then and she swiped up the tattered remains of her workout clothes and the note, crumpling it in her fist as she strode into the house. Dumping the shredded mess onto the counter, she dropped the gym bag to the floor and unzipped it. Rifling through, she let her fingers curl around the handle of her gun, and it was a welcome weight as she pulled it out. She'd taken to carrying it with her again, and she was glad. Though Neal had not done anything threatening, she still felt better with it close by. He was escalating. Tucking it back in place, she sighed.

A stress headache was forming behind her eyes, and although she had been looking forward to going out tonight, she wasn't sure she had the energy now. Taking her phone out of her pocket, she messaged Natalie:

> Roxy: Hey, I hate to bail, but I'm not going to go out tonight. I have a headache. Raincheck!

The three typing dots showed up and disappeared repeatedly. She grimaced. Ooooh, Natalie was going to skin her alive.

> Natalie: Unacceptable. Take some Tylenol, you big baby. Be there in ten. You better be dressed.

Roxy rolled her eyes and headed down the hall to take a quick shower to rinse the sweat off after her workout, then ran, naked and wet, back to the kitchen to shove the tattered pieces of the workout clothes into a random drawer in the kitchen island. She wasn't ready to explain that to Natalie yet. Streaking naked back to the bedroom, she was just pulling on a pair of lounge pants and a t-shirt when the pounding on the door started. It was quickly followed by Natalie calling through the house, "Like fucking hell you're bailing on me, you twat!"

Roxy exited her bedroom, padding down the hallway quickly. Natalie stood in her kitchen, hands on her hips, one cowboy booted foot tapping in annoyance on the polished brick floor.

Natalie pointed toward the hallway. "Get your ass back in that bedroom and get dressed. You promised you'd go out, I did not just do all this—" she hissed, gesturing to her scantily clothed body, made up face, and done up hair, "—to not go out with my bestie. No."

Roxy rolled her eyes. "Natalie, I have a headache. I don't want to go out to a loud bar."

"No. Take some damn Tylenol and put your fucking big girl panties on. *You promised.* You're not sitting in here on another beautiful fucking Saturday night to do what?" Natalie's eyes nearly bugged out of her head when she glanced over toward the living room. "Are you fucking *knitting?!*"

"Hey, Jodi and Free are having a baby and I wanted to make a baby blanket—" Roxy protested, gesturing to the start of a slightly crooked baby blanket, but Natalie whirled on her.

"Absolutely not on a Saturday night when I look this hot. Let's go." Natalie grabbed Roxy's hand and yanked her down the hallway. Roxy laughed, stumbling behind her friend as she dragged her into the bedroom, shoving her toward the closet. "If you don't pick something to wear in the next ten seconds, I will. Move it! Our Uber is waiting!"

Roxy laughed again, but said gently, "Nat, I know I promised, but I really shouldn't go. I can't explain why. I just... tonight's not a good night for me."

"What, do you have a hot date with Travis instead?"

"God no," Roxy muttered, but her cheeks heated as she turned toward the closet. She didn't need to know that Travis had in fact asked her to ask him out, though…

"Get dressed, I'm gonna go raid your liquor cabinet for shots. You can wash down the Tylenol with tequila."

"Oh, good God," Roxy laughed on a snort. Blowing out her breath, she sighed heavily and nodded in defeat. "Fine. You win."

Natalie clapped her hands excitedly and disappeared out the bedroom door, off to find them something suitable for pre-game shooters.

Ten minutes later, Roxy clicked the light off in the bathroom and walked down the hall to find Natalie sitting at the counter on one of the barstools, several shots lined up waiting for them. When her friend turned to look at her, her mouth dropped open in a pout and she stood.

"Bitch, how am I supposed to catch anyone's attention when you're dressed like that? It's not *fair*."

Roxy rolled her eyes. Her jean jacket was hanging over her forearm. Roxy eyed her friend up and down pointedly and muttered, "Like you're one to talk. I'll bet you don't pay for a single drink all night."

Natalie tossed her blonde hair over her bare shoulder and shrugged. A Brooks & Dunn band tee was tucked into the front of her short cutoff jean skirt, and a pair of red knee-high cowboy boots covered her feet and calves. Her lips were painted a shocking red.

"You're just flawless," Natalie moaned, gesturing to Roxy again. "Those jeans should be illegal."

The black jeans were tightly fitted to her body and she knew they did great things for her ass and legs. The bootcut hem flared slightly over the turquoise blue cowboy ankle boots she had on. A wide silver and turquoise embellished belt buckle on a black leather belt cinched in her waist.

She'd gotten ballsy though, choosing to tie on a black and

white paisley bandana as her top. It was tied in the center of her back, leaving her shoulders and most of her back completely bare, as well as her sides where the overlapped corners of the bandana dipped down toward her belt buckle. Chunky silver and turquoise earrings dangled from her pierced ears, and her fiery red hair had been left down to riot around her shoulders in haphazard curls.

Neal would have lost his mind if she'd tried to wear such an outfit. Actually, if he saw her in it, he *would* lose his mind. It was probably unwise to wear something this risqué in light of his most recent note… it was probably unwise for her to be out at all, honestly. But it was a highly public place, with lots of other people around, including bar employees as well as bouncers. She would be fine.

Hopefully.

Tossing her hair over her bare shoulders, she grinned. She was going out, for the first time in months it felt like. "Give me one of those shots."

"Yes, bestie!"

EIGHTEEN

er partner's hands were light on her as they circled the dance floor, and he was good, practiced. His sandy blonde hair was curly and had that Morgan Wallen mullet look to it, which made her laugh every time she caught sight of it peaking beneath the brim of his cowboy hat. He looked young, maybe twenty-four or twenty-five and way too innocent, like a puppy dog. But, he was a good dancer and kept up with her, even if his hands were bravely resting on the low curve of her bare back, nearly at her ass.

The song ended and the group of them applauded just as the next song began. His hands came back to rest low on her back, leading her around the dancefloor. But halfway through the song, she stumbled, her eyes widening as she searched the crowd for what she'd just seen. *Was that—*

Roxy swung her eyes left and right on a continuous loop, her feet never faltering in the practiced steps, but she knew... she knew he was out there, somewhere. He was watching her. It was cloying, like he was physically touching her. It made her skin crawl.

That same chest tightening, breath stealing sense of being

watched made the hairs on the back of her neck stand up, but she shook herself mentally. The honky-tonk was crowded for a Friday night, the dance floor jam packed and the standing room only that surrounded the fenced in dance floor was elbow to elbow, too. The bar was two deep. She could just see Natalie's blonde hair as it shone in the blue and red stage lights that bloomed over the bar.

Lainey Wilson's *Watermelon Moonshine* began and they settled into a slower moving dance, and she let her focus leave the crowd beyond the dancefloor, convincing herself she was just paranoid, especially after that note earlier. She was fine. She was having fun. She was out for the first time in what felt like forever.

When the song ended, she excused herself from the guy she'd been dancing with and weaved her way across the dance floor through the throng of bodies gearing up for the next dance to begin, heading toward the door. It was stifling hot in the crowded room. While Natalie was busy getting them drinks, she stepped outside to get some fresh air and cool her fevered body. Gathering her heavy curls off her neck and shoulders, she secured it on top of her head with a hair tie that was around her wrist, arranging it into an artfully messy knot. She passed a group of men and women as they entered the building, and she was blissfully alone outside. The loud thumping of the bass from the song *'Freight Train'* drowned out everything, until the door slammed shut, muffling it slightly. Roxy wandered down the side of the building, tilting her chin up toward the night sky and reveling in the stars that were visible above her. The breeze that drifted around her cooled her bare shoulders and back, causing light goosebumps to rise along her skin.

Boots crunched on the gravel to her left and she dropped her chin, whipping her head around to the person that had just stepped up close beside her. Roxy's throat closed and fear skittered over her when Neal's face loomed over her, his own lips pulled into a grimace of a smile, his eyes zeroed in on her.

Roxy stumbled back a step as he murmured to her, that slow, calculated drawl sending goosebumps over her flesh. "You're in a lot of trouble, darlin'."

She shook her head as he stepped forward again, bringing them within inches of each other, and he reached for her. Shoving the heels of her hands into his chest, she pushed with all of her strength, sending him stumbling back several steps as she turned and fled.

She ran, pumping her legs as fast as she could. She had wandered too far away from the door, and she had taken off in the wrong direction as she ran. She had nowhere to go, no doors to enter, no way to get back into the building unless she doubled back, which wasn't an option. She would never make it past him.

So she put on a burst of speed, pumping her legs as fast as she could as she crossed into the rows of parked cars in the parking lot beyond on the backside of the building. Maybe if she could weave her way through them and hide from him long enough, she could make it back to the doors, to the safety of the inside of the building. She could find Natalie, or a security guard, anyone that could help her. Because out here in the deserted and dark parking lot, she was at his mercy.

Dodging between a row of vehicles, she let out a scream of terror when she heard gravel beneath his boots, the grunting of his breaths as he chased after her. He was too close. She wasn't going to make it back to the doors

Racing around a different row of cars, she backtracked and ducked behind one, clamping her hand over her mouth to stifle her panting breaths. She heard his feet on the gravel as he passed her, racing forward. Barely daring to breathe, she remained hunkered down behind a car, her body hidden by the tire. If he decided to look under the rows of vehicles, she wouldn't be visible. She was angry with herself for putting the gun back in her bag instead of in her purse like she should have.

She hadn't even thought of it before she left. Lot of good it was doing her where it was, safely tucked into the gym bag... at home.

There was no moonlight, the sky cloud-filled and dark. The only light was that of the streetlight poles stationed throughout the expansive parking lot, but she was too far away from any of them for the light to reach her.

"Come on, baby," she heard him croon on a call throughout the darkness. She trembled violently. He was only a few rows away from her, stationed between herself and the doors now. He knew her plan and was cutting off her only escape. Panic seized her throat. She could hear the crunch of gravel beneath his feet as he walked, slowly now, around vehicles and down row by row. His voice was chilling, and how she had ever found him to be attractive eluded her now. He was terrifying. "Come out, Rox, and I won't hurt you. If I have to find you..." He let the threat drift off, but she knew what it meant. "You let that guy touch you, put his hands on you while you were dancing. You know what happens when someone else touches what's mine." Chills went down her spine. "It's probably my fault, doll, I've been gone for so long you forgot what the consequences are. But now I have to remind you, and I'm sorry for it."

Shifting as quietly as she could on the balls of her feet, using her hands on the car she was using as a shield to balance, she crawled around the backside of the car. The sound of the gravel shifting beneath her cowboy booted feet may have been nearly silent, but it sounded like a goddamn bomb going off in her head.

"Rox..." he called again, that chilling tone in his voice lilting and squeezing her throat closed again in panic. She knew if he found her, if he got his hands on her, he would hurt her. Knew it with every fiber of her being. But he was still between her and the doors... and she had left Natalie inside... "Don't make me have to find you, Rox. I love you. I don't want to have to hurt you, but you do need to learn your lesson. You've been disobedient in my absence."

Skirting around another car, a tear slid down her cheek when she saw his shadow pass where she'd been minutes before. He was too close now to safely move, he would hear her for sure. Clamping her teeth tightly over her lips from the inside, she attempted to steady her breathing through her nose, but she felt like she was suffocating. She should have known after that note had shown up. She should have known better than to tempt his wrath.

Natalie had to realize she was missing, right? Had to realize that she wasn't on the dance floor anymore…

A fist thumped into the hood of the car she was hiding behind and she nearly screamed, jumping in terror. Fear tasted metallic in her mouth and she shook violently. "Rox… I'm giving you one more chance, baby. Come out. I didn't want to have to hurt you…"

He was so close. Standing just on the other side of the car now. Any second he was going to round the hood and he would be able to see her. She needed to run, but she was frozen in fear. He was too fast. There was no getting away from him now.

His footsteps faded in the opposite direction, the gravel crunching beneath his feet and she sucked in a lungful of air, letting it out shakily. Shifting, she was poised and ready to make a mad dash toward the doors when her head was suddenly snapped back by her hair and she screamed a heartbeat before a hand was slapped over her mouth. Dragged backward off the balls of her feet, she landed on her bottom in the gravel as his fingers fisted around the topknot of her hair, yanking so sharply that tears sprang to her eyes and a muffled cry escaped her.

Instinctively, her hands came up and wrapped around the forearm that had a hold of her hair, attempting to take some of her weight off the hair being pulled from her scalp. When that didn't do anything, she reached up and dragged her fingernails down his arm, at the same time attempting to sink her teeth into the hand still covering her mouth. He grunted in pain, but it did little to help. Instead, he shook her violently by her hair, making her cry out again behind his palm.

"You stupid fucking bitch," he snarled into her ear, dragging her kicking and screaming against his chest. Her heels dragged in the gravel as he pulled her backward. She sobbed, the pain in her scalp overpowering everything.

He stopped, using the hand in her hair to spin her around, her knees hitting the gravel agonizingly, and she could feel the jeans tearing on the sharp rocks beneath her knees. His other hand left her mouth, but it was a heartbeat later that pain ricocheted through her as he backhanded her across the face, his knuckles connecting sickeningly with her cheekbone.

She stopped fighting, her body sagging as he leaned down, panting as he snarled, "I told you, Rox. I told you what would happen… you only have yourself to blame." Yanking her head back with his fingers still fisted in her hair, he caressed her unbattered cheek and she flinched violently, sobbing silently. His voice softened then and he whispered beseechingly, "I don't like having to do this, Rox. *Why do you make me do this?*"

"P-please—" she whimpered, her lower lip wobbling. "Neal—"

He hummed in the back of his throat and she squeezed her eyes shut. "Say it again, Rox. Say my name again. I haven't heard you call me by my name in so long…"

She shook her head, as much as she could with her hair still fisted in his fingers. He snarled and shook her.

"*Say it,*" he snarled, leaning down into her face again.

"No," she gritted out, bracing herself. Another blow to her face knocked her off her knees, her palms hitting the ground, the gravel digging into the tender flesh through the jeans. "*Fuck you.*"

Neal growled in outrage and she knew whatever was coming next was going to hurt. Where the hell was everyone? How was there not a single soul walking through the parking lot? Not one person to see, to help her. She was completely at his mercy.

The sound of gravel beneath feet sounded to her left and she snapped her eyes open just in time to see a huge, looming figure dart around the back of the vehicle he had her against. Her hair was released and she fell to the ground, landing on her rear as Neal was lifted away from her by a hand at his throat. Tossed against the vehicle parked next to them, Neal gasped for breath against the fingers squeezing his trachea.

"So, you like feeling like a big tough guy, putting your hands on women? Does it make you feel like a man?"

Roxy gasped out a broken sob. *Travis*. It was Travis.

Neal struggled futilely against Travis's superior strength, his toes barely scraping the ground where Travis had him lifted off of his feet, pinned to the side of the lifted truck. He gasped for breath, his hands scrabbling uselessly against Travis's arm.

"Pieces of shit like you make me fucking sick," Travis growled low, his voice deep and menacing. "I'm going to let you go, buddy. You want to hit someone, you fucking hit me, and I'll even let you."

She watched as Travis let Neal go, and he dropped back onto his feet with a wheezing gasp as he sucked air back into his lungs. Travis stepped so that he was fully between herself and Neal. She attempted to stand, but her legs shook too badly. Travis's hand splayed wide, as if to tell her to stay where she was, so she did. Her face ached, her cheek on fire, and she felt loose tendrils of hair falling out of the abused topknot.

Travis splayed his feet wide, angling his body slightly toward Neal, who had regained some of his composure and was looking absolutely furious at being humiliated. Travis pointed to his own right cheek and taunted, "Come on, buddy. You wanna hit someone? You get one shot at me before I lay your ass out, so make it count."

Panic flooded Roxy again. What if Neal did do enough damage to Travis to take him down? She'd be at Neal's mercy again. "Travis—"

Neal's face went a mottled red with rage as his eyes bounced from hers back to Travis, and he was shaking with fury. Roaring, he took a wild swing at Travis, who dodged it effortlessly. A quick jab into Neal's kidney knocked him back before a deadly right hook connected with Neal's cheek, snapping his head back. And then he was flat on his back in the gravel, too dazed to even move.

Travis stepped over him, grabbing him roughly by the front of his shirt, and he leaned down to snarl into his face, "You will *never* go near Roxy again, do you hear me? I beat a man to death with my bare hands once; I have no problem doing it again if you so much as even *breathe* in her goddamn direction. *Are we clear?*"

Neal's head lolled in the gravel; his torso half lifted off the ground by his shirt still fisted in Travis's hands. He nodded dazedly, and Travis released him, shoving him back to the ground as he straightened. Stepping over him, he turned and reached for her where she still huddled against the side of the vehicle.

She stared up into his face, the fury from moments before gone, his sandy brown brows pulled low over his eyes in concern. *Where had he even come from?* she thought shakily. *Had he been here the whole night?*

His large hands spanned around her waist, pulling her into a standing position. She swayed slightly and one of his hands slid around to her back, pressing lightly to steady her as her hands came up to fist into the fabric of the t-shirt that stretched across his impressive upper body. He was so warm. She trembled from cold and shock.

"*I've got you*," he murmured quietly at her temple, and she nodded mutely, staring down at a groaning Neal. "I've got you, Red."

He sidestepped them around the end of the car, though his hands and arms never released her. He moved them toward the doors and she panicked, twisting slightly in his hold. "Travis—"

"We need to go find Blondie while we wait for the police to show up. They should be here any minute, I called them when I couldn't find you or this piece of shit inside."

"But what are you doing here?" she asked slowly. Her head was pounding, her stomach roiling with the pain.

He stopped, turning toward her. "I couldn't pass up the chance to dance with you, Roxy, even if you were too stubborn to ask me out." She let out a halfhearted, scoffing laugh, more an expulsion of breath than anything. His hands trailed up her arms and then she sighed, letting her eyes drift closed when the warmth of his hands cupped her jaw on either side. "I had just gotten here when I saw you dancing with that puppy. I was about to come cut in when I saw this guy watching you the way he was… I just had a bad feeling, but then someone recognized me and I got caught up signing autographs for a few minutes. I lost sight of you both and when I couldn't find you inside and realized you weren't with Blondie, I came looking for you. I'm sorry I didn't get here in time."

She opened her eyes as his thumb tracked over her battered cheek ever so gently, but just the faintest touch made her wince. His thumb grazed over her lower lip, touching the jagged white scar that bisected the left side. She swallowed hard, pulling her face away from his touch and lowering her gaze to the ground.

"This isn't the first time, is it? He did this, too?" he asked quietly and she took a deep breath in before letting it out slowly. She nodded. "How long?"

"It's… complicated," she whispered, lifting her hands so that they bracketed her temples, pressing in and closing her eyes against the pain that reverberated through her skull. Her cheek was still on fire, but she was grateful that the skin hadn't split this time.

Blue and red lights began to flash in the distance, and the sound of a siren could be heard as it drew near. She looked up at him just as the door burst open and then she heard Natalie's angry voice, "Fuck, Roxy! You couldn't have told me you were coming outside? I've been looking for you for like ten minutes! Oh! Uhh… hey, Travis…"

Natalie stumbled as she rushed forward, and when Roxy turned to look at her friend as she approached, Natalie's eyes widened in alarm when she saw the angry mark on her face, the mess she was sure her hair was. Glaring up at Travis, she snapped, "What the fuck did you do?"

Roxy shook her head slightly, wincing. "It wasn't Travis, Nat. It was… it was Neal."

"*Neal?*" Natalie gasped, her mouth dropping open in shock. Roxy nodded. "I thought you said he was gone?!"

Roxy hung her head in shame and shook it slightly. "I don't want to talk about it right now—"

"*Is he back?* You didn't tell me he was back!" Natalie screeched, her arms ramrod straight at her sides. Travis's hands settled on Roxy's back and shoulder as she swayed slightly, clutching her head tighter. "How long has he been back, Roxy?"

Roxy swallowed and mumbled, "Since I got home from Colorado."

"*Since January?*" Natalie seethed. "What has he done?"

She didn't want to do this, not in front of Travis. She was already embarrassed to all hell; he'd been giving her kickboxing lessons for months and what good had any of it done? She'd been as helpless as before. "Natalie, I don't want to talk about it—"

"Oh no, you don't get to get out of this," Natalie fumed,

crossing her arms over her chest as the sirens cut off as they got closer. Two squad cars pulled into the parking lot, coming to a halt in front of the doors. "What haven't you told me? Is it the flowers again? And all that stuff you keep finding going missing?"

Roxy sighed heavily as four uniformed officers stepped out of the two police cars. Travis waved at them and they started their way over toward them. Roxy was spared having to say anything more to Natalie in front of Travis, as he shook all four of their hands and then led two of the officers away, toward where they'd left Neal laying in the dirt over by the cars. The other two officers remained with her and Natalie. She answered their questions, denied the suggestion of going to the ER, and then they waited. She shivered, despite the warmth of the evening.

Travis and the other two officers returned, but Neal wasn't with them. Travis shook his head as they approached, and Roxy's panic came back. He had managed to sneak away before the police showed up. Which meant he was out there. She hung her head when the realization hit of just what she would have to do.

Tomorrow she would have to make a phone call to Freeman… and tell him she was coming north, for good.

Nineteen

Travis kept his eyes on Roxy as she spoke with the officers. She looked as though she had folded in on herself, her arms wrapped tightly around her middle as if to shrink into her own body. Her head remained down, staring listlessly at the ground as the officers spoke to her. She looked scared and defeated in a way that he hated. She was always so fiery… and now it seemed that all that fire had been snuffed out.

He flexed his hand, the knuckles aching in the best way possible. It had felt so damn good to lay that bastard out. The fury that had coursed through him at finding Roxy in the clutches of that animal… he'd seen red. Only by pure willpower had he stopped at one solid punch. He wanted to keep hitting him, over and over again, until he was a bloody mess on the ground. Until he was physically incapable of hurting Roxy ever again.

Roxy shivered and he moved on instinct, stepping around her. He settled his hands on her bare shoulders and then smoothed them down her arms, the skimpy bandana top doing nothing against the evening chill. She sighed and leaned her back against his chest and he felt her body shudder with another shiver. This damn top was little more than a fucking handkerchief. He turned to Blondie. "Did she bring a jacket?"

Blondie snapped her eyes up to his and nodded dazedly. "It's inside. I can go get it."

He nodded once and shifted his gaze back to the officers standing in front of him and Roxy. "Are we almost done here?"

"Yes," one officer said, his hands settling on his utility belt. He looked down at Roxy. "You really should go to the ER. Have them check you out."

"I don't want to," she whispered. "I just want to go home."

"We'll have an officer do periodic drive throughs, since Mr. Johnson has disappeared. You'll need someone to drive you, or we can give you a ride home," the other officer said.

"I'll take her," Travis said, his hands spanning wide across her biceps. He expected some kind of reaction from her, but there was none. Which worried him even more. Leaning down, he spoke quietly in her ear, "I'm going to take you home, okay, Red?"

Blondie returned and held out Roxy's jacket, which he took and draped over her shoulders. He could feel the blonde's stare drilling into the side of his head, but didn't bother to acknowledge it, instead stepping back several paces. She stepped in front of Roxy and took her hands in her own. "Roxy. Do you want me to come over?"

Roxy shook her head, and he saw her squeeze her friends' hands gently. "No, Nat. It's okay. I'll be fine, I promise."

"I can take you home," she said quietly.

"I'll get her home," he said gruffly. Blondie's eyes widened and she stared at him.

"Oh…I didn't realize you two were…" her friend whispered, shooting a glance over Roxy's shoulder toward him. He leaned to one side and shook both the officer's hands as they said their good-byes, but kept his body angled toward Roxy, as if she had some gravitational pull that he couldn't break free of.

"We're not," Roxy said dully. "He stopped Neal. That's all. I just want to go home."

Her friend nodded and squeezed Roxy's hands once more. "Call me tomorrow, okay?"

Roxy nodded and Blondie stepped back before heading back into the bar. A group of curious onlookers had congregated outside the doors a while ago, but the officers had ushered them back inside to give Roxy privacy while recounting the events of the night. As he'd listened, he'd gotten more and more angry at the motherfucker. All those times he'd witnessed Roxy being jumpy, the constant looking over her shoulder… his gut had been right after all. She was scared of someone. And that someone had hurt her, on more than one occasion. A monster.

Again, he flexed his fingers wide at his side, letting the ache in his hand anchor him. He was a monster, too. A different kind of monster.

I may be a monster, he admitted, *but I'll fight like hell to protect her*.

Stepping forward, he settled his hand at the small of her back. "Ready?"

She glanced up at him finally, those hazel eyes far away until they connected with his, and she seemed to come back into herself a little. "Thank you, Travis."

His eyes swept over her face; the battered cheek that already had a bruise blooming beneath her eye, the smudges of mascara beneath her lashes, that jagged white scar that bisected her bottom lip. "You don't thank me for this, Red. I've got you, okay?"

She nodded, taking a deep, shuddering breath in and letting it out in a slow exhale. "My head hurts."

"I wish you would let me take you to get checked out," he murmured gently, pressing with his hand at her back to urge her to move forward. He guided her toward his vehicle. "You could have a concussion."

She shook her head as he opened the passenger door of his Bronco and assisted her up into the seat. He reached over her and buckled her in, since she was still trembling slightly. "I doubt it. He didn't hit me as hard as he has before. I just need some Tylenol."

His back molars ground together as he clenched his jaw so tightly together it ached. "He's lucky I didn't kill him tonight."

He closed the passenger door and rounded the hood, climbing in behind the wheel and starting the vehicle. He adjusted the heat inside the car—the late May evening air was chilly, and he knew from experience she hated the cold—and sighed in relief when moments later she stopped shaking, settling into the seat.

"You… you said something to Neal…" she started, and he tightened his fingers around the steering wheel as he steered them out of the parking lot.

"Which way?" he asked gruffly, and she pointed toward the left. She told him her address and he nodded, heading that direction.

"You told Neal you'd killed someone… Was that true?" she asked quietly, and he could feel her stare through the dark interior of the car. He sighed again, running a hand over his mouth and chin, scratching at the beard that covered his lower face.

"Yes," he said simply, his voice low. "Yes, I killed a man with my bare hands once." Turning to look at her, he said earnestly, "You have no reason to be afraid of me though, Red. I may be a monster, but I won't ever hurt you. I promise."

He heard her swallow hard in the quiet between them. "I'm not afraid of you, Travis. I can see that you're a good man. If you did that to someone… I'm sure that it was deserved."

He stared ahead at the lines of the road that blurred in the headlights and flexed his fingers around the steering wheel again. He had never talked about this with anyone, other than the police, his lawyer, and his therapist. Regular people didn't understand. "It was deserved. But that doesn't make me a good man, Red."

TWENTY

"You don't have to come inside," she said quietly, too quietly. Travis hated the defeat in her tone, in every muscle in her body. As if all the fire and fight had been leeched out of her at the hands of that asshole. Travis flexed his hand again, relishing the ache that still burned in his knuckles. He would have caved the man's skull in if it meant she would never have to look at him with that soul wrenching fear again. It gutted him.

"I'm not leaving you alone tonight, so you're stuck with me, Red," he murmured gently through the darkness of the vehicle as he put it in park in her driveway, next to her Toyota 4Runner. She stared at him for a long moment, the moonlight luminous in her eyes, and then she nodded. "Good girl. Wait for me."

She did as he asked, surprisingly, and waited for him to round the hood of the Bronco and open the passenger door. He witnessed the wince of pain as she reached across herself to unbuckle and fought back the growl of fury that roiled through him at the sight of it. He stepped forward, placing his hands on either side of her waist to help her out of the seat and down to the ground. Her hands rested on his chest, lightly, her fingers curled slightly in on the fabric of his shirt.

"Would you like me to carry you?" he asked quietly, though he already knew the answer. She shook her head no and he nodded, stepping back enough for her to lead the way. She shocked him when she reached for his hand, curling her fingers into his and squeezing lightly. He squeezed back.

Her house was small, a dim porch light illuminating the pathway up to the stone front porch. She unlocked the door, flipping a light on as soon as she entered. Fingers still entwined around hers, he felt her stiffen and then begin to tremble as the light revealed the quaint kitchen, and a bouquet of roses situated in the center of the kitchen counter.

Her breathing accelerated at the sight of those flowers, and he drew her behind him on instinct, his gaze scanning the still darkened living room and hallway beyond. He stepped forward, his eyes lighting on a scrap of neon orange shoved between heads of the blood red roses. Roxy reached for it, her hand trembling violently, plucking the neon post it note out of the bouquet. His eyes scanned it as hers did, his blood boiling in his veins and heart pounding in his ears at the words written there.

I can't keep apologizing for the things you do that make me mad. I don't know what you expected to happen tonight. You know how to fix this, how to fix us. We both make mistakes, I forgive you, Rox.

"DO YOU THINK HE'S STILL HERE?" HE COULD BARELY FORM THE words past the fury in him. She shook her head.

"I doubt it. I've never seen him in here, after the notes show up. This is what he does. Sends flowers in lieu of an apology, when he knows he's fucked up. He's probably watching, though." She shivered. "I'm sure he knows you're here with me, which is just going to make it worse."

Travis planted his hands on her shoulders and spun her to look at him. "Please tell me you're joking." He watched as her throat worked with the swallow she took. He squeezed his eyes shut and took a long, steadying breath in before releasing it slowly, and then opened his eyes. "How many times has this happened?"

She shrugged, her shoulders bobbing up and down beneath his hands. Gesturing to her face, she admitted quietly, "This? Three times, though this one wasn't as bad as the second time. Since he's been back, I'd have to guess that he's been here five or six times. Possibly more. I don't know. I changed the locks, but he's still getting in, somehow."

"He's been inside?" Travis growled, rage boiling inside him like a fucking battering ram. "Why haven't you called the police, Roxy?"

"He's never been caught. I filed a restraining order against him after the last time he… but he took off and they weren't ever able to arrest him or give him the order. I'm sure they'll add tonight's incident to the order, but they still have to find him to serve him." She shrugged, then winced at the movement. God, he wanted to crush her to him and hold her, never let go. Never let this animal close to her again. But he didn't, simply stood before her, hands on her shoulders. She lowered her head then, dropping her eyes from his. "I found a note from him earlier tonight, after I got back from the gym. It was out on the porch. I knew he was already upset with me; I shouldn't have gone out tonight."

Travis's hands tightened on her shoulders slightly, though he tempered his grip enough to not be rough or bruising. "If you hadn't gone out, he would have found you here, Roxy. And I wouldn't have been here." Her eyes misted. "What makes you think he was already upset?"

She sucked in a deep breath and then let it out. "He saw us, Travis. I don't know if he was at the restaurant, or if it was just when you dropped me back off at my car. Neal has always been… insanely jealous and incredibly volatile when that jealousy comes out…" she breathed almost silently, and then turned to open a drawer in the island. She pulled out scraps of fabric and another neon orange post it note, setting them on the counter next to the roses. He recognized the color, then realized he was staring at the shredded remains of the teal leggings, sports bra, and jacket she'd worn to dinner with him last week. He let his eyes scan the post it, his rage returning full force. "I know he's been watching me. I knew he would be enraged if I went out and I tried to cancel on Natalie, after I found it, but she showed up and dragged me out anyway. And then I convinced myself that it was fine, that I was out in public and he wouldn't do anything to me in a bar. I was wrong. He knew I was there. Chased me outside. He was so mad because I danced with some guy."

"The puppy."

Roxy made another scoffing laugh, but then she clutched her head in between her hands. "That's what I had named him in my head, too. He reminded me of a puppy dog."

"Where's the Tylenol?" he asked, stepping around her.

"In the bathroom cabinet." She pointed down the darkened hallway, and he set off in that direction, flipping the light on as he went. Travis did a quick walk-through of each of the bedrooms along the hallway, checking the closets and under the beds, just to be sure this prick was truly gone.

He was back a minute later with the bottle of Tylenol in his hand. He opened it, shaking out two of the extra strength capsules and held them out to her. She cupped her hand and he set them in her palm, before turning to the sink and filling a glass with tap water. He crossed his arms over his chest as he watched her swallow them down, his gaze tracking over the myriad bruises and scrapes that were coloring her face. Rage surged through him again.

"Thank you."

"I checked the other rooms while I was back there, the house is clear." His voice was gruffer than intended, but the anger simmering just below the surface as he watched her was taking all of his considerable willpower to maintain. She swallowed hard, but nodded. Fear clouded her eyes briefly, and he fucking hated it. He would gladly kill this sonofabitch for putting that fear in her, for putting his hands on her. "Come on. Let's get you into bed."

"You don't have to stay, Travis," she said quietly, though she didn't fight him when he stepped forward, placing his hand at her lower back and leading her down the hall. By checking the other rooms, he knew which one was hers and directed her toward it.

"I'm not leaving you alone tonight, Red. I think you have a concussion; I'm not comfortable leaving you here by yourself. And if he decides to come back, I'll be waiting. I'm staying."

She sank down onto the foot of the bed and held her head in her hands gingerly, cautious of the right side of her face. "The guest bed is comfortable, and has clean sheets on it."

Travis nodded. "Pajamas?"

"I'll get them."

"You just sit there. Where are they?"

She lowered her hands, glaring at him with all the ferocity of a bunny rabbit, but he didn't let the smile show on his face. "I don't want you rifling through my drawers, Travis. That's inappropriate."

"Do you have inappropriate things in your drawers, Red?" he teased gently.

"Well I don't want your giant hands pawing through my panty drawer. What if I have vibrators in there?"

His lips twitched with the need to smile. "Do you have vibrators hiding in your unmentionables, Roxy?"

"You'll never know," she mumbled, standing. She stepped toward the dresser and opened several drawers in succession, pulling out a set of pajamas, and then a set of clean underwear, which he glanced away from. She was still shaky on her feet.

"Do you want to change, brush your teeth, anything before you get into bed?" he asked.

"I probably should," she said quietly, closing her eyes where she stood. She was still so pale, and those bruises that were rapidly forming seemed garish against her pale skin.

"Come on," he murmured, placing his hand at her back again. She let him lead her back toward the bathroom, where he flipped the light on.

"I really want to wash my face, but it hurts."

He forced down another surge of rage. As gently as he could manage, he murmured, "You change, brush your teeth, and then open the door when you're done."

She nodded, and he exited, pulling the door closed behind him. He walked down the hallway to the kitchen, helping himself to a glass of water. He had just finished it when he heard the door open and saw the light spilling into the hallway. Travis returned, stepping into the small bathroom with her. She had changed out of the tattered and dirty jeans and bandana top, both laying on the floor in the corner, and into a set of waffle weaved lounge shorts and an oversized Reba McIntire band tee. Her breasts were unrestrained beneath the material of the shirt, and the hem had been cut shorter, so that it hit just below her bellybutton. Her hair had been released from its topknot, though the curls were a tangled mess around her shoulders. Her knees were scraped up and raw, the gravel having torn through the knees of her jeans when that piece of shit had dragged her through the gravel of the parking lot. Fury at the bastard for hurting her tore through him all over again.

Turning on the tap in the sink to hot, he let it warm and pulled a washcloth off the little shelf over the commode. Wetting it thoroughly, he wrung out the excess water, and then turned the water off. Tipping her chin up with his fingers beneath her jaw, he stared at her for a long moment, his eyes spearing into her own. He swallowed hard, then lifted the washcloth to her face. She sucked in her breath sharply at the heat of the washcloth. He made sure his touch was gentle, carefully washing away the make-up that was tear streaked down her face, until her skin was clear and the only thing marring it was the bruises. He wanted to press his lips to every mark, every discoloration, to erase the memory of the last thing that had touched her there. To replace it with his own touch. But he didn't.

They didn't speak. Fuck, Travis was barely breathing. He set the washcloth on the counter before placing his hands on her shoulders, letting his palms slide down the outsides of her arms. "Come on. To bed, baby girl."

Roxy's eyes bounced between his, but she nodded, lowering her gaze as he led her back into the bedroom. She climbed into the bed and he could see the cautious way she moved. She was in more pain than she had let on earlier. Lowering herself to the pillows, she lay on her side, her right arm tucked under the pillow beneath her head. He watched her wince, and wished he had the guts to touch her, to help her as she rolled to her other side, so that she was laying on the unmarred side of her face. Her back to him now, he tucked the comforter around her and leaned down to kiss her temple gently, and her eyes fluttered closed at the contact. He watched as a tear escaped her eye, rolling down her battered cheek and into her hairline.

"I'll be in the next room, Roxy. If you need anything, just call, okay?" he whispered, and she nodded, though she didn't turn her head. "Good night, baby girl."

She didn't say anything more as he backed out of the room, shutting off the light as he went. Though he did leave the bedroom door cracked open just the slightest, so he could hear her if she needed him.

TWENTY-ONE

Pacing through her kitchen, morning sunlight streaming through the window, she stared down at her cellphone in her hand. Freeman's contact was pulled up, but her finger hovered over the call button, hesitating. She'd had her finger hovering over that call button for fifteen minutes, working on the courage to begin what was going to be a difficult conversation.

Sighing heavily, she squeezed her eyes shut, letting her head roll to the back of her neck so that her face pointed up toward the ceiling. Her head still ached, and her entire body hurt like hell. Standing naked in front of the full-length mirror in her bedroom this morning, she'd catalogued every bruise and mark on her body. Her face was an abysmal sight to behold.

Glancing at the screen again, she leaned her hips against the counter and looked around her small home. Birds chirped outside, the open window allowing a warm breeze to enter. She didn't want to go. She didn't want to leave her home. She loved Texas, loved Melody Hills. She would miss Natalie, her job, her friends. Travis.

And she was angry that Neal had brought her to this. To running away, scared for her safety, if not her life. She knew she couldn't stay; last night had made it clear he wasn't going to back off. She knew the statistics; he was only going to get more volatile until it came to a head... whether it ended with him in jail, or her potentially in a body bag.

Chills rushed over her at the thought. The look in his eyes last night had been pure evil, sinister and cold. He wasn't going to stop until he had her... or until he killed her. She was sure of it.

So what choice did she have? He had already made it obvious he could get in and out of her house without being detected, her locks did little to deter him. And if he was deranged enough to attack her in a public parking lot... what else was he willing to do?

She would have to be careful though, since he was still out there. She had to assume he was watching her, always watching her. If she made it obvious that she was planning on leaving, he would stop her, or follow her. She could have a go bag packed in an hour. Should she leave everything else behind, or take the chance of him catching wind of her plan by renting a U-Haul? Her entire life was in this small house, not that it mattered when it was her life that was in danger. Should she fly? Or drive? She would need a vehicle once she got to northern Michigan, so driving was the obvious choice... but also dangerous. She'd be utterly alone and vulnerable, on the road, for days at a time...

Fear skittered across her and she leaned against the countertop on her hands, phone still clutched in one hand. If she wasn't careful enough, and he did follow her... traveling across the country alone was already unfairly dangerous for a woman, but with Neal on the loose, if he found her alone...she was as good as dead.

Because she would never go back to him, that was for sure. And if Neal couldn't get what he wanted from her, she had no doubts of what lengths he would go to keep her from anyone else.

Panic clogged her throat. Even if she did manage to sneak

away, get across the country and start over in Petoskey close to Freeman and Jodi, what was stopping Neal from tracking her there? Resuming the stalking and breaking and entering, just in a different location? He already hated Freeman with a passion… would he try to hurt him or Jodi just to get to her? She conceded that she wouldn't put it past him.

The police had documented everything from the night before. Photographs were taken of her battered face, her statement was taken down, and everything was added to the current Restraining Order she had against him… if they could ever find him to serve him the order. Not that it did any good. It was just a flimsy piece of paper. It hadn't stopped him so far.

Taking a deep, restorative breath in, she exhaled and picked up the phone again, hitting the call button before she could talk herself out of it. Setting it to speaker, she held it in her hand in front of her mouth, about chest level. It rang several times and then she nearly burst into tears when Freeman's heavy Texas twang greeted her through the line. "Hiya, Red. What's got you callin' so early?"

Tears clogged her throat, but she swallowed around them and said quietly, "Free. Is that offer still open?"

She could sense the change in him even over the phone. She could hear Jodi's soft voice and then Free growled, "Is he back?"

"Yes," she whispered miserably. He swore on the other end of the line, crudely. Jodi's panicked voice met her ears, and he murmured to her gently. "Free, I don't want to put you and Jodi in danger—"

"You get here as quickly and quietly as you can, you hear me?" he said firmly. "*Fuck.* Red, do I need to come down there and get you?"

"No," Roxy said, shaking her head. "You need to stay there with Jodi, in her condition… I just have to figure out how to get out without him realizing I'm leaving."

"Roxy," she heard Jodi's soft voice, as if she'd taken the phone from Free's hands, though it sounded like they too had their phone on speaker. "I'm okay. I would much rather Free come get you than to let you travel alone—"

"And I won't take your husband away from you while you're pregnant, Jodi," Roxy said gently, smiling. It had taken a while, but she and Jodi had a solid friendship now. She was fortunate to have them both. "I'm a big girl, I can make it there. I just needed to know if that offer was still on the table."

"Always," Jodi said softly, and Roxy could sense the sincerity in her voice. "You're family, now. We take care of our own. So you just do what you need to do and get up here, we'll have everything ready when you get here. Are you driving or flying?"

"I don't know," Roxy said and shook her head, leaning her head back to stare at the ceiling again. "Flying would be faster, but I need a car once I get there. And driving is risky, too…"

Footsteps sounded and she turned, swallowing hard when Travis appeared in the doorway to the kitchen, looking sleep rumpled and far too attractive for so early in the morning. He wore the same clothes as he'd been in the night before, and his long, light brown hair that was streaked with silver fell around his face and shoulders in slight waves.

Free spoke. "Red, I'm gonna send Bobby over—"

"No," Roxy said, tearing her gaze away from Travis. She nodded in greeting and gestured toward the coffee pot that was filled with strong black coffee. Travis moved into the kitchen, his hulking frame seeming to shrink the already small space. It was strange to have him in her home, but she'd admittedly slept better than she had in months knowing he was just a room away. He plucked a coffee mug off the mug carousel on the counter and poured himself a steaming cup, leaning his hips against the counter across from her. She lowered her eyes from his intense gaze, returning her attention to the conversation at hand. "No, if

Neal is watching and sees Bobby, he will know something is going on. I already had the locks changed. Bobby can't know until after—"

"Dammit, Red, I can't just fucking sit here and let you do this alone," Free bit out, and she hated the fear she could hear in his voice. It almost made it worse, because if he was scared… it drove home that the fear she was feeling was really and truly justified. *Shit.*

"She's not alone," Travis said then, his deep, sleep husky voice cutting through the quiet.

Roxy groaned internally as Jodi's gasp cut through the air with a curious, *"Ooooh,"* at the same time Free grumbled darkly, "Uhh, who the hell are you, buddy?"

Roxy wanted to laugh out loud when she heard a light *thwack,* a low grunt, and then Jodi's hushed, *"Freeman! Be nice!"*

"Well who the fuck is this guy—"

"Guys—"

"—*oooh, maybe he's her boyfriend,"* she heard Jodi whisper and mortification flushed over her hotly. She glanced up at Travis, who was smirking down at her.

Roxy flushed darker red when she heard Free mutter sourly, "—*oh, like hell he is—"*

"Oh my god, you guys, stop!" Roxy called loudly over them. Holding the phone close to her face and turning away from Travis slightly, she whisper shouted, "He's *not* my boyfriend!"

Travis plucked the phone out of her hand from over her shoulder and she attempted to snatch it back, but he chuckled lightly and spoke directly into it, "Name's Travis. Roxy is in my kickboxing class. I stayed to keep an eye on her after last night."

Roxy waved her hands frantically, silently begging him to stop, but it was too late. She groaned out loud and buried her face in her hands when Free's angry voice boomed, *"What the fuck happened last night, Red?"*

"Thanks for that," Roxy muttered sourly to Travis, who just smirked and refused to hand the phone back to her. "Free, I'm fine—"

"She has a fresh black eye and potentially a concussion," Travis said over her. Free's colorful expletives sounded from the phone and she groaned again.

"Let me guess, she wouldn't go get checked out?" Free asked sourly.

"You may know her well," Travis said with a light chuckle, leaning his hips against the counter and crossing his arms over his chest. She stood in front of him, her foot tapping out a beat in annoyance, her eyes narrowed on his face.

"How bad?" Free asked.

"*It's fine—*"

"It's not pretty," Travis interrupted, glaring down at her. Speaking directly to her, he muttered, "You're not going to play this off like you're not in pain, Roxy. As someone who's made a living off being hit and doing the hitting, I know for a fact how much pain you're in. Don't lie to us."

Jodi's quiet gasp sounded through the phone and Roxy could hear her whispering to Free. "Who did you say you are?" Free asked, wariness coming through his voice.

"My name is Travis Hayes," Travis said softly, his eyes never leaving hers as she stared up at him. "I'm a former MMA fighter. I teach a kickboxing class at the gym that Roxy goes to. She's in my class."

"What happened last night?" Free asked gruffly.

Travis stared down at her. "Can I trust you to tell the truth or do I need to recap?" Roxy glared up at him.

"You're a bully," she whisper hissed, but he just smirked again, handing her the phone. "You don't get to yell at me, Free."

"Not a good way to start, Red," she heard his grumble through the phone. She sighed wearily, and he murmured, "I promise not to yell at you. What happened, Red?"

"Neal sent me flowers the week after I got home from Colorado. That's when it started again." She recounted the events from the last few months, leading up to the night before, skimming some details and earning a disgruntled interruption from Travis. By the time she'd reached the end of the night, her head was pounding. She pressed her fingers into her right temple and squeezed her eyes shut.

"You'll let me know when you're hitting the road?" Free asked. She hated the fear she could hear in his voice. She'd thought she was free of Neal. It was laughable now. "I really hate the idea of you traveling alone, Red."

She sighed quietly. "I'll be fine, Free—"

"I'll drive her."

Her eyes snapped open, her gaze flying to meet Travis's, her mouth slack in shock. Roxy shook her head and said, "No, that's not necessary—"

"I like that idea," Free said, the damned traitor. She glared down at the phone screen and then raised her eyes back to Travis's. "Travis, take my phone number down."

Travis pulled his own phone out of his pocket, typing in the numbers as Free rattled them off. He saved the contact, then slid the phone back into his pocket.

"You're all bullies," Roxy muttered grumpily. "I don't need—"

"Bullies who care," Jodi called softly, interrupting her, and Roxy inhaled deeply to try and restore some semblance of calm to her system at being railroaded by all three of them. "We just want to make sure you're okay."

"She's with me, I won't let this coward near her," Travis said thickly, his brows dipping low over his eyes intensely. "You have my word."

"I'll call you later, Free," Roxy snapped, hanging up the phone and slamming it down onto the counter next to them. Fire lit through her as she glared up at him. "Look, Travis, I appreciate your help last night, but I don't need you to drive me to Michigan." He simply stared at her, silent in that way of his that unnerved her. "I have been on my own since I was sixteen, okay? I don't need a babysitter; I don't need you swooping in and trying out that newly fitted superhero cape. I'm not a damsel in distress—"

"I beg to differ," Travis muttered darkly, crossing his thickly muscled arms over his chest. She pulled her lips in through her teeth and closed her eyes, counting to ten in her head and letting out a long, heavy exhale in an attempt to keep herself calm. When she opened her eyes, he nodded toward her face, indicating her cheek, and said, "I'm no hero, Red, and I'm not here to save you. But I've seen firsthand what men like Neal are capable of when they get it in their minds, and I'll be damned if I sit back and watch it happen again. Until I get you to Petoskey safely, baby girl, you're fucking stuck with me, so you better get over this temper tantrum quick."

Twenty-Two

The fire in the hazel eyes that glared up at him gave him a perverse sense of pleasure. It was a relief to see that fire return to her after the emptiness he'd witnessed the night before. He understood her frustration, but this was one fight he wasn't willing to lose.

His chest had seized when he'd pieced the conversation together, realizing she was leaving. He knew it was best, she would be safer up north, but still… it ached. He'd gotten used to having her around, enjoyed having her at the gym, liked the banter that they shared, the fiery nature that had come out to tempt him on more than one occasion. He'd miss that spark in her, those gold and jade green eyes that haunted him at night when he was home alone. The fiery curls that bounced when she moved that he ached to touch with his fingers, to have those strands wrapped around his fists…

He'd miss *her*.

Dammit, he'd fucked up.

Travis admitted to himself—even if he would never admit it out loud—that he had gone and caught feelings for the fiery bombshell standing before him.

He sighed. Maybe… maybe if they'd had more time, something could have come from all of the flirting, the banter, the electrically charged glances and heat-filled exchanges between them.

He hadn't wanted that anyway, he reminded himself. This was for the best, for both of them.

He took a sip of his coffee, raising one eyebrow at her as he stared down into those hazel eyes. After swallowing, he asked, "So what do you need to do first? Put me to work."

Roxy shook her head slightly, her lips pursed into a thin line, her eyes bouncing back and forth between his own. "You don't need to do this, Travis."

He took another drink of coffee, nodding. "But you're stuck with me nonetheless. So put me to work. What all are you taking? Do we need a U-Haul?"

She sighed deeply, a long, slow expulsion of breath that rounded her cheeks. "I don't know," she admitted almost dejectedly, her shoulders slumping. "I hate the idea of leaving all of my furniture, but the time that it's going to take to get the U-Haul, pack everything into boxes, and then load the big pieces into the trailer… It leaves a lot of time for him to figure out what's happening." She shrugged. "Whereas if I just pack what I need to get there, I can always hire a moving service to come back in and move the rest…" Pinching the bridge of her nose between her forefinger and thumb, she shook her head. He hated seeing her so dejected. He preferred the fire from before. "What do I do?"

Fuck if he knew. What *he* wanted to do was track down the son of a bitch and pummel him into oblivion so that he couldn't terrorize her anymore… but he'd been to jail before and didn't relish the idea of going back for pre-meditated murder.

"Pack the necessities and anything you can't leave behind. We should be able to fit everything into the back of the 4Runner, provided you don't deem half the house necessary—" she glowered at him and he smirked, continuing, "—and we can hit the road before he's any the wiser. But you're right, a U-Haul would attract too much attention, and it would slow us down." He scrubbed a hand over his face and down over his beard, scratching under his chin lightly. "When do you want to leave? I just have to tell Merv and postpone classes until I can get back."

She groaned, then swiveled her head so that she was staring up at the ceiling. "I need to contact work and tell them I'm leaving. Ugh, I hate leaving them like this. And Natalie is going to hate me."

"If she's a true friend, she will understand that you need to go for your own safety," he said gently. "It's a helluva lot easier to contact someone a few thousand miles away than it is to talk to a gravestone."

He watched as she blinked several times, and then a tear tracked down her cheek as she remained staring unseeing at the ceiling. She nodded sadly, her lips pinching tightly together, though he could see the trembling in that full lower lip. "I hate this. I hate him so much for running me away from my home."

"I know."

She brought her head back down until she could look at him again, and he wasn't sure what he saw in her eyes as she stared at him.

"Thank you."

Setting his coffee down, his brows drew together. "For what?"

She shrugged. "For everything. For teaching me. For last night. For being willing to take a stranger on a road trip halfway across the country purely out of the goodness of your heart."

Stepping forward, he backed her against the opposite counter, then braced his hands on either side of her hips on the edge. Leaning closer, he dragged his lips across her cheek, inhaling the jasmine and gardenia scent of her. "You're no stranger to me,

Red. And believe me, I'm not doing this to be selfless. If this is all the time I have left with you, I'm not going to miss one second of it."

Twenty-Three

Oh fuck.

Every nerve ending was on fire, where his lips had grazed her cheek… and down. Straight to the very core of her. She ached. *Why did she have to find him now? Now, when she was leaving?*

Life was so unfair.

His breath misted over her cheek, the corner of her mouth. "I'm going to kiss you, Roxy." She gasped, a soft inhalation, and she felt his smile against her cheek. His words were quiet, just breaths, as he spoke to her. "Not right now. Not with that bastard's marks all over your face and that memory in your head… but I am going to kiss you, baby girl."

She was a puddle of frayed nerves and needy desire when he finally pulled back, her breaths coming in quick, ragged puffs. He grinned, but then his gaze fell on the bruise on her face and his eyes grew dark, sad. He raised one hand and trailed it along her marked-up face, gently, so gently his fingers were mere whispers against her flesh. And then he was ducking his head, pressing tender kisses to the bruises along her temple, below her eye, across her nose, and then to that jagged white scar that bisected her bottom lip. A healed memento of the last time Neal had struck her.

"I'll never let him put his hands on you again, Roxy," he murmured gently, a quiet promise. She licked her lips, swallowing hard. "You have my word."

She could do nothing but stare up at him, a long way up, as he hadn't moved more than a foot away from her. Then he smiled gently. "Now, put me to work. What do you need?"

Her mind was blank except for screaming for more. *I need more.*

He grinned then, his beautiful, straight white teeth flashing in a knowing smile. "I already told you; not right now. Get your head out of the gutter."

Glaring up at him, she shoved against his chest, and he grinned again, allowing himself to be moved backward. "My head is *not* in the gutter. Your giant male ego is showing."

Closing his hands over the backs of hers where they were still pressed to his chest, he ducked his head. "My ego isn't the only thing that's giant about me, Red."

She rolled her eyes, though her heart was hammering in her chest. She could feel his own heart beating beneath her hands, still pressed to his chest. "You're ridiculous," she whispered faintly, though a smile tugged at the corner of her mouth.

His thumb was stroking the back of her hand, making it hard for her to concentrate, and then he leaned forward and rasped, "If I put my hand in your panties right now, would I find you wet?"

Oh Jesus fuck. "No." *Because I'm soaked.*

"*Liar,*" he breathed tauntingly, then pecked a chaste, closed mouthed kiss to her lips before dropping his hands from hers and stepping away.

She was stunned into silence, the feel of his lips against hers —even in the totally chaste kiss—sending her entire being into a spiral. How was she supposed to concentrate on anything with him so close? With the memory of those lips on hers? With the memory of what he'd just *said* to her?

"Put me to work, Red. Want me to go pack your unmentionables?"

She glared at him again. She was over here fighting for her damn life after that kiss—could that even be called a kiss?— and he was unruffled enough to be *teasing her*?

"Why don't you go home and pack your own stuff—"

But he was already shaking his head, all levity leaving his face, those honey-gold eyes serious as he stared down at her. "I'm not leaving you alone. I don't trust him, and I would never forgive myself if you got hurt again because I wasn't with you." He smirked then, crossing his arms over his heavily muscles chest, making his biceps bulge. Her mouth went dry. "That, and I don't trust you not to take off without me."

She sighed heavily. She had thought about it, the bastard. "Okay. So how are you supposed to get your things? It's going to be probably two or three days to drive north, and then another day or two for you to get a flight back. Which I'll pay for, by the way. But I'm sure you'll need a travel bag."

"Let me worry about how I get home. We'll get you packed up and then drive over to my place to get my stuff. I don't need much, just a couple changes of clothes and my toiletries."

"What if he sees us leaving together? What are the chances that he follows us?"

"We're not going to take an obvious route north. I'll make sure we get there safely, Roxy. I told you; I'm not going to let anything happen to you."

"You're really not going to let me go alone, are you."

"Not a chance in hell, baby girl," he murmured, shaking his head.

She nodded in defeat, sighing again. Looking around the kitchen, she let her eyes linger on everything, just for a moment.

"Even if I'm not taking much, it's going to take me most of the day to pull everything that I do want to take with me together. I have to say good-bye to Natalie, I have to call work, and Bobby—"

His hands came out and clasped her shoulders firmly, grounding her. "Put me to work, Roxy. Let me help you."

"I don't even know where to start," she whispered forlornly, her shoulders drooping beneath his hands.

"You know what, why don't we start with breakfast. I'm starving, and can't think on an empty stomach. Let's get some food, sit down, we'll compile a list for each room, and go from there."

Licking her lips, she gazed around the kitchen again, analyzing everything. Categorizing items into necessity, want, and not needed. Then, as if in answer, her stomach growled nosily. He grinned down at her. "I guess I'm hungry, too."

Swiping his phone out of his back pocket, he scrolled while she poured herself another cup of coffee, then went to the fridge to take stock on what she had to make breakfast with. He tucked his phone back into his pocket and grinned. "Uber Eats is the best invention."

"Did you just order us breakfast in?" she asked, laughing, as she closed the fridge door.

"Denny's breakfast will be here in twenty minutes. The whole works. We've got a lot of work to do, and I'm not doing it on an empty stomach." When she raised her eyebrows knowingly, he rolled his eyes at her. "Mind out of the gutter, Red." She couldn't help the smirk or laugh that escaped her. He notched his chin toward the barstools at the counter. "Why don't you grab a paper and pen and we'll get started on listing what we need to do today."

Half an hour later, the two of them were sitting shoulder to shoulder at the kitchen counter, to go containers of fluffy scrambled eggs, crispy sausage links, perfectly browned pancakes, crunchy hashbrowns, and an entire container of fresh fruit sitting open in front of them. Travis lifted a tall glass of orange juice to his lips, and Roxy had to force her eyes away from the way his Adam's Apple bobbed with each swallow, her pulse thrumming through her entire body straight down her middle. A notepad and pen were situated between them, listing each room and what items would need to be packed to take with them on this trip. The back of her 4Runner was big, but looking at the growing list between them, she knew it was going to be full by the time they were done.

Travis ate twice as much as she did, polishing off the sausage links and the final pancake, as well as the hashbrowns, which he slathered in ketchup. Roxy stabbed a piece of pineapple from the to go container, bringing it to her mouth. It was tangy and sweet. She went to stab another piece, but he reached out and took hold of her wrist, guiding the fork to his own mouth. He bit it between his straight, beautiful white teeth, tearing the fruit before closing his lips around the fork entirely.

He winked. "For later."

Oh god. She was in *so much trouble*.

Twenty-Four

Natalie showed up around eleven that morning, face tear streaked and eyes red from crying. "I can't believe you're leaving. I don't want you to go!"

Travis had excused himself to the guest bedroom while she and Natalie embraced, giving them privacy for their good-byes, which she was grateful for. When he emerged from down the hallway, they both turned to look at him. He hitched his thumb over his shoulder, back down the hallway. "Bed is stripped and all the sheets are in the wash. Was that last bin in the bathroom ready to go?"

She nodded, and then Blondie swiped her face free of tears, before huffing out a breath and setting her hands on her hips. "Okay. Put me to work. I can't cry anymore or I'm going to get a bitch of a headache. What else needs to be done?"

"Honestly, we got a lot banged out already," Roxy said, gesturing toward the two suitcases piled by the door, and a large storage tote filled with other necessities. Piled on top were her pillows and a soft blanket that she would be taking for the road trip. It was all she was taking with her. Travis ignored the choice of words, though he did rather enjoy the telltale flush of red that flashed across her face when she realized what she'd said. Natalie's eyes ping-ponged between them. Roxy vaulted toward the kitchen, raiding the fridge for bottles of water. She handed one to him, not meeting his eyes, and then strode over and handed another to Natalie. She wrung her hands in front of her. She wished she had a garage that she could pull her vehicle into to hide it away from prying eyes. "I'm worried about how to get all of that into the car without him seeing, if he's watching. He'll know what I'm doing. And I don't want him to know where you live, Travis, if he follows when we go to get your things. What about your car? It's still in the driveway."

"It can stay here for now."

"What if Neal does something to it?" she asked, wringing her hands. She'd feel terrible if Neal did something to damage Travis's car.

"It's just a vehicle, Roxy," he said gently. "My concern is you, not my car."

Natalie pursed her lips. Roxy had explained everything to her over the phone, when she'd called to tell her she was leaving. Now, Natalie twisted the cap of the water bottle repeatedly. "What if you come with me for like a coffee run? Get you out of the house, if he's really out there like you think, he'll follow *us*, right? If he's as possessive as we think, he's not going to let you out of his sight, and he'd never be ballsy enough to try and do anything to Travis after the beat down he got last night. You'll be with me, we'll be in public… he can't be stupid enough to attack you in a fucking Starbucks, for god's sake. While we're gone Travis can get the car packed up, maybe even sneak over to his place and get his things?" Roxy bobbled her head, considering the idea. Natalie gestured to Travis. "He can lock up on his way out, and then we can meet somewhere with a back exit, and we'll sneak you out. You guys can be on the road before he knows you're gone."

"That's actually a really good idea," Travis said gruffly, nodding.

Natalie laughed and shrugged. "True Crime Podcasts are my jam. He's easy to figure out." Turning to Travis, she said, "We'll be super careful while we're out. We won't go anywhere secluded; we will stay in busy public areas until you call to let us know you're ready." She looked at Roxy then. "And you're bringing your gun, just in case."

"You have a gun?" Travis asked, turning those honey gold eyes on her. She nodded, and his eyebrows shot up in surprise. "Good. I'll have mine with me as well, after I get it from home. Take my number down, both of you." They did as he said, entering his phone number into their contacts, just in case. Then he gestured around to the house. They had tidied up and boxed as much as possible that she would be having the moving company come back for later. Natalie would be in charge of making sure that happened, in another couple weeks. "Is there anything else we need?"

Roxy shook her head, looking around her small house. "No, I don't think so."

"Why don't you two head out then, and try not to cry into your coffees?" he teased, though she saw the gentleness in those eyes. Giving her the time to say a proper 'see you later' to her best friend.

"No promises," Roxy murmured softly, smiling over at Natalie.

"If you cry, I cry."

"Oh, I'll definitely cry," Roxy laughed then, shaking her head. "I just need to grab my purse; my gun is already in it, don't worry. Oh, and my sunglasses."

She had been loathe to put make-up on her battered face, knowing even just the pressure of her make-up sponge would be painful. Travis still hadn't been able to keep his eyes off of her all morning, though she wasn't sure if he was staring at *her*, or the bruising marring her face. She'd pulled on a pair of soft biker shorts in a bright teal color, and they hit high on her thighs. A loose fitted Jelly Roll band tee that she had cropped hung at her waist. Her hair was pulled up into a high topknot. So, with no make-up to hide the state of her face, big, chunky sunglasses would have to do. She picked them up off the counter and placed them on the top of her head before sliding her feet into a pair of comfortable sneakers. Settling her purse—weighed down with the gun nestled inside—across her chest, the strap dug in between her breasts.

Glancing around the house again, she blinked away the tears that stung her nose and eyes. This was the last time she would be here. It had been her home for so long. She turned to Travis, then gasped and dug into her purse, pulling her keys out. "You might want these," she laughed, placing them in his palm. "You're sure you're okay to stay here and load up?"

He rolled his eyes. "You have two small suitcases and a tote bin. I think I can handle that."

"Don't forget the blanket and pillows," she teased, heading toward the door with Natalie.

"My little Passenger Princess, your carriage will be awaiting you," Travis teased back, chuckling. He stopped her by taking hold of her hand before she got to the door, and when she looked up at him, he said earnestly, "I'll probably be an hour or so, is that okay? You call me if you see him, if he gets anywhere near you."

"Okay, Travis," she said softly, nodding. His eyes tracked over her entire face again, his lips thinning, those brows furrowing.

"I'll see you in an hour, baby girl," he murmured quietly, and she sighed, knowing the first thing Natalie was going to grill her about once they got into the privacy of her car.

"See you in an hour," she agreed, and then he squeezed her fingers lightly before they left.

Twenty-Five

Travis watched out the window as the girls climbed into Blondie's car, parked behind Roxy's in the narrow driveway, and continued watching until they backed out and disappeared down the street. He swiped through his phone for a few minutes, killing time, just to make sure Neal followed them if he was out there, and then got to work.

It only took two trips, but he got the back of Roxy's 4Runner loaded up with her two small suitcases, the bin of other necessities and items she didn't want to leave behind—including two customized, branded cowgirl hats and several pair of expensive looking cowgirl boots—and her pillows and blankets. He set the pillows and blankets in the back seat, along with a small tote bag that had essentials like chargers, the bottle of Tylenol, and several bottled waters so that it was easily accessible once they got on the road.

He didn't want to have to stop for as long as possible. He would fill the gas tank on his way to pick her up, and then they would hit the freeway north. He wanted to get as far north as Des Moines in this first leg of the trip. Put as much distance between them and Neal as possible. It would be a ten-hour stint, getting them into Des Moines late that night, but he didn't mind. She could nap in the passenger seat, if she needed to.

Glancing around her small house, he double checked everything before locking the front door and pulling it closed behind him. They wouldn't be returning.

He had to push the driver's seat all the way back to accommodate for his long legs, and then he was off, backing out of the driveway and heading down the street. It took fifteen minutes to get home, and he used that drive time to call Merv, filling him in on what had happened and what the plan was and letting him know his car was going to remain at Roxy's until he could get back.

"You actually coming back?" Merv asked through the phone, and Travis scoffed.

"Yes, I'm coming back. I'm not staying. Just getting her there safely and settled in."

The older man's only response was a gruff harumph, filled with suspicion, which made Travis roll his eyes.

"It's not like that, Merv."

He harumphed again. "Alright. If you say so."

"I do say so," Travis muttered, pulling Roxy's car into his driveway and turning off the engine. He groaned out loud when he glanced down, noticing she was overdue for an oil change. There was no way they could make the trip without getting that done, first. "I gotta go, old man. This woman is going to be the death of my sanity."

"The good ones usually are. Be careful, Travis."

Travis climbed out of the car, assuring Merv he would be cautious. Though he wasn't sure if the old man was referring to the trip, or to Roxy herself.

It didn't take long to throw a travel bag together, a few changes of clothes, underwear, his bathroom toiletries, and a hooded sweatshirt. A couple changes of workout clothes and his sneakers went into the bag next, because after being cooped up in a car for twenty hours he was going to need to loosen his muscles.

He changed out of the clothes he still had on from the night before, pulling on a pair of soft, well-worn jeans and a clean t-shirt, as usual the arms cut out of it. He grabbed his phone charger and then set out to pack his Glock, checking to make sure the magazines were full and then tucked all the pieces into his duffel.

Locking up on his way out, he situated his duffel in the far back of the 4Runner, and shoved the hoodie in the backseat, in case Roxy got cold. Climbing in behind the wheel, he started it, but took his phone out and shot a text to Roxy.

> Travis: Hey, it's me. Leaving my house, but your car is miserably overdue for an oil change. I'll stop through a Take-5 on my way to get you.

It wasn't long before the message bubbles showed up, his heart doing a little flip-flop in his chest, and she responded.

> Roxy: Sorry. I was meaning to do that, it's been a chaotic couple weeks. I'll give you cash when you pick me up. Thank you, Travis.

Typing out another message, he asked:

> Travis: I'm not worried about it, Red. Are you alright? No sign of him?

She messaged back seconds later.

> Roxy: We're fine. Sitting at one of the patio tables at Arcadia on Bryan. There's a back entrance I can use to sneak out of when you get here. We're okay, I promise. See you soon.

He liked the sound of that. Possibly too much.

Twenty-Six

Setting the phone down on the wrought iron patio table, a bright orange umbrella offering them shade from the afternoon sun, Roxy picked up her iced coffee, taking a sip. Natalie had already grilled her on what was going on between her and Travis, which Roxy had maintained was *nothing*. Nothing was going on between them. She was leaving, she was a hot mess, and that was that.

"That stupid fucking grin on your face says otherwise, I hope you know that," Natalie muttered drolly, gesturing to her face.

Roxy pulled her lips in between her teeth to force the smile down. She had liked seeing his name pop up on her phone. Even through the device, she could practically envision the intense, serious expression on his face as he would have been staring down at the phone in his own hands, worry for her etched in every line and plane of his stupidly handsome mug.

Natalie waved her hand in dismissal with an exaggerated, morose sigh. "It's fine, whatever. He was never going to be interested in me anyway. You just have to promise to tell me that the sex is terrible, so I can pretend he's not worth my time."

Roxy laughed out loud, shaking her head. Her sunglasses

were still in place on her face, shielding the worst of her bruises from curious eyes, though no one paid them any attention where they'd tucked themselves into a back corner of the patio. They'd ordered panini's and split a bag of crisps, too.

"I can't tell you that, because nothing has happened. And it's not going to," Roxy muttered dryly. Natalie bobbed her blonde eyebrows.

"Yeah, okay. Miss Delulu over here."

"I mean it, Nat. Nothing is going to happen between me and Travis. It… it's not."

"If you think you're going to be stuck in a car with that big beefy man candy for what—two to three days—and he's *not* going to do something about all that sexual tension that is literally *crackling* between you… you're crazy. *Straight delulu*, sis." Leaning back in the chair, Natalie stared at her knowingly.

Roxy rolled her eyes, but let the conversation drop. She didn't have the energy to argue with Natalie over this. Because *nothing* was going to happen.

Half an hour later, they had cried again, hugged for the millionth time, and finished their sandwiches when Travis messaged to let them know he was five minutes away. They stood, taking care of their trash and straightening the table, before walking inside the air-conditioned building again. Heading toward the back of the coffee shop, they hugged again.

"This is just a see you later," Roxy whispered into Natalie's ear, trying hard not to cry again. "I promise this isn't forever. Maybe once this is all blown over, I'll come back."

"Maybe I'll have to make a move to Michigan," Natalie countered, hugging her fiercely, then pushed her away. Tears glinted in her eyes. "Now get. You keep me posted the whole way, okay? Take care of you."

"Take care of you," Roxy whispered back, her lips wobbling slightly. "Love you, Nat."

"Love you, Roxy."

Natalie kept an eye on the front of the building as Roxy slid out the back door. Travis was already waiting for her just outside the door, the 4Runner still running. She dashed across the narrow back alley and climbed gingerly into the passenger seat and closed the door. He reached out a hand and helped to snap her buckle into place, noticing the wince of pain from her, and then his fingers drifted over hers, squeezing them gently. She stared over the console into his eyes, his gaze making a quick once over of her face, as if to make sure she was indeed alright. And then he smiled at her, that quick, mind numbing, brilliant smile of his, and they were off.

It wasn't long before he was turning them onto the interstate headed north. They had the back windows rolled down, letting the warm afternoon air rush through the car as he picked up speed until they were flying down the highway through midday traffic. She peeked over at him, watching him behind the dark lenses of her sunglasses as he drove.

He was relaxed, leaning back in the seat, his left hand draped loosely over the steering wheel, his right forearm resting on the console between them. Half of his long, light brown hair had been pulled up into a bun on the back of his head, the other half left loose around his shoulders, and the wind tousled it lightly. He had pulled on a pair of darkly tinted aviator sunglasses, which shaded his eyes from the glaring Texas sun. The breeze ripped at the cut edges of his shirt sleeves, making the material billow out slightly. Every once in a while, the way it shifted gave her an unrestricted view of his rippling pecks. That deeply tanned, heavily tattooed and muscled arm was bare from shoulder to wrist.

"Want to find us something to listen to?" he asked over to her, over the roar of the wind from the open back windows.

"I can queue up my Spotify list?" she asked.

He shook his head, turning to look at her, though she couldn't see his eyes behind the dark tint of his sunglasses. She could however, see her own reflection in them, and grimaced at the sight of her too pale face and those dark bruises that peeked out from behind her own sunglasses.

"I'd prefer the radio, that way the forecast will come on if there's any change in the weather," he said, explaining. She nodded; it made sense. Leaning forward to fiddle with the stereo before settling on her favorite country music station. As they drove, they would have to find different stations as they moved out of range.

He notched his chin toward the backseat behind them. "I put your pillow, blanket, and one of my hoodies back there for you if you get tired or cold. The tote behind my seat has all our chargers, extra bottles of water, and the Tylenol, if you need any for your head." She smiled over at him, and he continued, saying, "And I let Freeman know we had hit the road. I'd like to make it as far as Des Moines tonight; though it will be a long day, and we probably won't get in until late. Don't think you have to stay up to keep me company. If you get tired, you can close your eyes and rest."

Reaching her hand out, she placed it on his tattooed, muscled forearm, where it rested on the console. His skin was warm beneath her fingers, and electricity that had nothing to do with static cling zapped through her. She squeezed lightly, not even bothering to fight against the tripping and tumbling of her heart in her chest. "Thank you, Travis."

He glanced over at her, letting his lips tip up in another smile. "Anytime, baby girl."

They settled into companionable silence as the miles disappeared behind them.

TWENTY-SEVEN

Roxy jolted awake, sitting straight up in her seat. Shit. She must have fallen asleep. Blinking rapidly, she rubbed at her eyes carefully, yawning broadly.

"Hi there, sleepyhead," Travis teased from the driver's seat. He patted her knee, and she realized he must have reached behind them at some point to drag her blanket forward, covering her. He'd also rolled the back windows up.

She let the blanket slide down into her lap as she yawned again, stretching as much as she could in the passenger seat, then looked out the windows around her. The sky out the windshield in front of them was ominous looking; dark rain clouds rushed toward them from the horizon. Another hour and they'd be in the middle of that mess.

"Sounds like we're headed straight into a storm. We're too far North to try and go East, unless we take all backroads, which I don't necessarily want to do. We just passed into Kansas," he said. She reached for a bottled water, offering it to him first, but he shook his head. "No, thank you, I'm fine." She uncapped it, taking several long pulls. Her head was aching. "I'm hoping it blows over."

It did not. The further North they traveled, the darker and more ominous looking the skyline in front of them became. And then the rain started, pelting the windshield brutally, and Travis had the windshield wipers turned up to full speed. Lightning flashed, thunder cracking loudly, too close for comfort. Roxy sat up straighter in the seat, eyes straining to see through the damn near wall of water that was pelting the vehicle. Travis's hands were tight around the steering wheel, the only clue she had that he wasn't as unaffected by the storm as she thought.

He cursed when the wind buffeted them sideways for a third time. He had slowed the car drastically in deference to the conditions. Tuning the radio again and turning the volume up, they listened as the weatherman announced that there was a widespread tornado watch, though luckily none had been sighted yet.

"I've got to pull us off the highway, I can't see ten feet in front of me, let alone trying to drive at highway speeds," he muttered. "Might be a good time to stop for dinner."

Pulling up her GPS app, she noted that they were out in the middle of nowhere Kansas. They'd already passed one exit that had food and lodging, and the next one wasn't for another twenty miles. She relayed the information and he cursed again, scrubbing his hand over his beard and mouth.

"Dammit," he sighed, then shook his head. "That'll have to do if there's no where else to pull off."

The wind picked up fiercely around them, buffeting them back and forth, and the rain continued to lash at the vehicle harshly. Twenty tense miles later, he flipped the blinker on and slowed down for the exit, then laughed dryly when they realize the nearest town was another five miles away. They headed in the direction the GPS indicated, the sky growing steadily darker, the storm around them not lightening in the slightest.

Three miles away from their destination, a faint pop sounded through the vehicle, and then a wobbling rumble started. She turned to look at him with her mouth dropped open, eyes wide. "Oh my god. Is that—"

Travis pulled them off to the side of the road carefully, turning the hazard lights on to flashing, then put the car in park. He shook his head, laughing, then turned to look at her. "A flat tire? Sure is, baby girl."

"I'm so sorry," she whispered, twisting in her seat. He just grinned over at her, shrugging those impossibly wide shoulders, then reached out a hand and slid his palm over the back of her neck, squeezing lightly. She shivered at the contact.

He blew out a breath, looking around the darkened sky beyond. "What do you think the chances are of getting a tow way out here?"

She picked up her phone and wrinkled her nose, turning the phone to face him. "There's no service, Travis. Maybe a car will come by and see us?"

"We can only hope," he chuckled, then sighed again. "Well, shit."

"I'm really sorry," she whispered again.

He squeezed her neck, letting his fingers strum along the curves of her neck, just below her hairline. "It wouldn't be a cross-country road trip without a little adventure, huh?"

"Oh yes, this is exactly the kind of adventure I'm sure you were hoping for when you so gallantly volunteered to drive me across the country, Travis," she deadpanned. He laughed, grinning over at her. God he was so handsome when he smiled like that. It did wonderful, awful things to her middle. And her heart. But she wouldn't think about that right now.

He twisted in his seat, then unbuckled. "I'm going to hop out and see what the damage is, you stay here."

And then he was ducking out of the driver's door, slamming it shut as he was immediately pelted with the torrential rain. She watched through the rain slicked windows as he jogged around to the rear passenger tire, and then he disappeared from view. She twisted around to try and see him in the passenger side mirror, but the rain was so impenetrable and heavy, and the sky had darkened so much that she couldn't make out his form.

She squinted at the dark spot that she thought might be Travis, but then she startled with a jump when the driver's door opened and he slid back into the seat. His hair was soaked, clinging wetly to his face, neck, and shoulders. Rain droplets rolled down his bare arms, and his t-shirt and jeans were drenched, clinging to his skin. She didn't miss the way that wet t-shirt clung to every ridge and muscle of his shoulders, chest, and abdomen, her mouth going dry.

"Looks like we picked up some sort of metal spike; it's stuck in there good," he said, wiping his hands over his face to clear the water that still dripped down his brow, nose, and cheeks. He glanced behind them and his eyes widened. "There's a car coming. Stay here."

"Travis—"

But again, he was sliding out of the driver's door as soon as the car got close, and Roxy sighed in relief as it slowed, pulling up behind them, also putting their hazards on. She watched again as Travis cautiously stepped up toward the other vehicle, just barely able to see his outline through the downpour. He came trotting back, and then climbed back in. The poor guy was soaked clear to the bone now. The car's hazards turned off, blinker coming on to guide them back onto the road, and then they watched as the red glow of the taillights faded in front of them.

"They're going to go down the way and send a tow truck back for us. We can only hope someone close by has the right sized tire, though with the way our luck is going right now, everything is going to be closed for the night."

"I really am so sorry, Travis—"

He turned to look at her through the semi-darkness of the

vehicle, his gaze sliding over her face, to linger on her lips. She swallowed hard. His eyes slowly rose back to hers, and he rasped, "Roxy, I would drag this damn trip out for weeks if I could, just so I don't have to say good-bye to you in a few days. I'll take every extra second I can get with you."

TWENTY-EIGHT

He wanted to lean across the damn console that separated them and kiss her. The way her eyes widened at his words, the way her lips parted in a stunned, silent gasp. He wanted to taste that awe on her mouth, to shock her a little further by tangling his tongue with hers. Wanted to haul her over to him and bury his fingers in her hair, hold her to him until they melded together.

But he didn't, of course. Because the truth of the matter was that they didn't have weeks left. They had days. Mere days until they would part for good. And he knew if he let himself have her now, he would never want to let go. She had burrowed under his skin like it was her own, weaving her way into his very soul. And he hated it. Hated the ticking clock that was counting down the hours and minutes that he had left with her.

Leaving her was going to be the hardest thing he'd ever done, second only to saying good-bye to his mother, and that was without the added emotional damage of finally having her, feeling her everywhere. He needed her to stop looking at him with those damn expectant eyes. They were his kryptonite.

"Don't look at me like that, Red," he whispered through the

grayish gloom, the only sound in the vehicle the pounding of the rain on the roof and their breathing as they stared at each other.

"Why not?" she asked, licking her lips again. He nearly groaned with the effort of holding himself back, not giving in and giving her what she was damn near begging for with those eyes.

"Because I don't have the strength to tell you no."

A yellow glow lighted on the side of her face, growing brighter as the seconds passed, and he forced his eyes away from her face, looking out the windshield. A set of headlights moved toward them, and then the orange running lights on the top of the trucks cab signaled that the tow truck had arrived. It passed them, pulling over so that it was directly behind the 4Runner.

Escaping the tension and need that was running unchecked in the cab of that car, Travis climbed out and into the rain for a third time, meeting the tow truck driver by the shoulder of the road.

"Thanks for coming to get us," he called over the roar of the wind and sleeting rain. "We picked up a scrap of metal in the rear passenger tire."

The driver nodded, then gestured to Roxy, still in the passenger seat. "You get your lady and climb into the back of the truck, I'll get this all hooked up, and then we can get y'all into town and dried off!"

Travis nodded, then jogged over to Roxy's door. He opened it and held out his hand to her, assisting her out. They ran through the pelting rain to the tow truck, and after Travis opened the back door of the extended cab, he spanned his hands around the small of her waist and lifted her up into the backseat. She slid over on the bench seat in the back until she sat behind the driver's seat, and then Travis climbed in after her, closing the door behind him.

Once ensconced in the dim interior of the truck, they watched out the back window as the driver quickly hooked Roxy's 4Runner up, and within minutes they were on their way down the road.

The truck rumbled down the road, and from his peripheral he saw Roxy shiver from the rain and the AC that was running full blast through the trucks cab to fight the heat of the summer storm. He shifted over on the bench seat, draping his left arm around her shoulders and tugging her against his side. She shivered again as his wet skin and clothes made contact with her, but then she was leaning into him, and he felt her shoulders rise and fall with a sigh.

He rubbed his palm up and down her bare arm, doing his best to warm her. All it did was turn his own blood to boiling, his heart stammering in his chest and his cock hardening behind the fly of his jeans. The rain mixed with the perfume of her skin and the scent of her citrusy shampoo, and he breathed her in, letting his cheek rest on the top of her head for just the briefest of heartbeats.

Lights outside the truck came into view on either side of the street, and then they were pulling into a small, ancient looking car repair shop parking lot.

"I hate to tell ya that Grady's is closed for the night, but we can leave the car here and they'll get right at it in the morning," the driver said to them over his shoulder as he pulled in and parked alongside the faded blue building. "I can get this unhooked, if y'all need anything from it, I suggest you grab it now. I'll drop ya off at the motel just down the way. Right 'cross the street is Bertie's, they got good food. Y'all like to dance? It's Thursday, so it'll be full o' fancy feet."

"Which suitcase?" Travis asked, leaning close to Roxy so he could ask directly in her ear. She shivered again, her breath hitching in her throat, and he bit back a groan. Fuck this trip was going to be the death of him.

"The smaller one, and our chargers," she said, looking up at him through the dim interior. The lights from the dash illuminated the left side of her face. She'd long ago stuck the dark tinted sunglasses on the top of her head, and those bruises were on full display now. He ached to run his fingers over them, to erase them from her mind. Kiss each one, gently, so gently she could forget they were there. "Thank you, Travis."

He squeezed her upper arm where his hand was still rubbing gently. And then, because he was weak and unable to fight it any longer, he dipped his head and pressed a swift, chaste kiss to her lips. Heat zapped him straight to his soul. "I'll be right back."

Ducking out of the back seat of the tow truck, he hurried to the back of the 4Runner, grabbing her suitcase and then his duffel bag, along with his sweatshirt and their chargers from the backseat. He was back minutes later, tossing their bags into the front passenger seat, and then he climbed back in with her. The rain had lessened, if only slightly, but he was soaked through again. It helped to cool his body from the heat raging through him. Once settled on the bench seat, he handed her his sweatshirt, and she took it with a grateful smile.

He watched as she pulled it on over her head, adjusting it over herself. She swam in it, it was huge on her, the sleeves at least six inches too long, and he knew when she stood, it would hit low on her thighs. She pulled the collar up around her, burying her nose in the material. His cock groaned in agony against the fly of his jeans.

"Thank you. I was freezing."

"I know," he said, angling his body toward hers. He was rapidly losing the fight to stay away from her, against all of his better judgement. All of his self-control was fraying, all of his arguments against why he shouldn't fading away. If this was all the time he had left with her, he didn't want to waste anymore of it pretending there wasn't something here. Because there was, dammit.

Her face was still half hidden by the collar, the hood falling down her back. Her fingers clutched the material close. When she spoke, her words were muffled. "It smells good."

He laughed. "I'm glad it doesn't stink."

The driver climbed back into the driver's seat in front of them. "We're all set. I'll drop you off down at the motel. Call this number—" he said, twisting his body in the seat to hand Travis a business card with a scrawled number on it, "—in the morning, and they'll get ya all squared away. Tell 'em Harry dropped it off."

Minutes later, they pulled up in front of a neon motel sign that glowed red through the rain still pelting the truck. He pulled them up as close to the front door as he could, and he even helped carry their things inside the small, out of date motel lobby. They thanked him profusely, and then he was off.

Travis stepped forward to the lobby desk, where a young woman waited. Her eyes were wide as they took him in. He knew he could be intimidating looking, so he softened his features, smiling kindly as he approached. Gesturing toward Roxy, he said, "Our car popped a tire, so we're in need of a room for the night. Harry said you might have something available."

She nodded silently, then turned to an old, box style computer on the desk in front of her. "Umm. One room?"

"Yes," he said without hesitation, before Roxy could object or ask otherwise. Though he highly doubted Neal would have followed them, or would be able to find them here, he wasn't taking any chances, either. She would be with him every second.

The girl nodded, finalizing their check in, and then turned to a wall of vintage looking diamond shaped room tags. Plucking one off the peg, she handed it over to him, the orange plastic tag dangling from the silver key attached to it. "You'll be in room 210. Out the doors, turn to your left and it's about halfway down."

"Thank you," he said, taking the key and tucking it into his pocket, then turned to Roxy, grabbing her suitcase from her hand. "Shall we?"

She nodded, and though he could see frustration in those hazel eyes, she knew it was for the best. They exited the front door and took an immediate left. A wide sidewalk was covered by a metal roof that ran the whole length of the motel, which he was thankful for. It shielded them from the brunt of the rain, though the wind did whip drizzles at them as they made their way down to their room.

"I hope you at least got us two beds," she grumbled, though he could sense there was no real fight in her words. Fuck, he hoped they *hadn't* gotten two beds.

Pausing at the door that had a peeling placard with the numbers 210 on it, he dug the key out of his pocket. They stepped inside and he reached for a light switch along the wall, flicking it, and then he heard her sharp intake of breath.

"Well, Red, looks like we're sharing a bed."

Twenty-Nine

Oh god.

One bed. One king sized bed took up the majority of the floor space in the small room. This was bad. So, so bad.

Travis walked further into the room and she closed the door behind them, the soft snick of the latch sounding like a fucking bomb in her head. The room smelled faintly like moth balls, but it looked clean and well kept, if a little outdated. The room was stifling hot though, and she reached out to switch the AC unit on. It rumbled to life, then whirred quietly as cool air began to circulate through the room. It would be a while before it had cooled enough to be comfortable.

She watched as Travis checked the bathroom, then came back and flipped the covers of the bed, checking everything. He straightened, looking over at her. His clothes were still drenched, though his hair had started to dry, curling slightly. How in the hell was she supposed to survive a night sleeping in the same bed as him?

"It looks good, and we should be back on the road tomorrow. Why don't we get out of these wet clothes and head over to that bar Harry mentioned? Are you hungry? How's your head?"

"I could eat," she said, her words coming out on a rasp. "I took some Tylenol while we were waiting for the tow-truck, so it's fine." She gestured to him. "You're wetter than I am—"

His light brown brows rose, those golden eyes lighting with mischief, and she squeezed her eyes shut for a half a second, pulling her lips in between her teeth in mortification.

"We can remedy that, Red," he murmured gruffly, rounding the foot of the bed and coming toward her, slowly, so slowly. Like a predator after his prey.

"Travis—"

"Are you going to tell me you haven't thought about what could happen in that bed later, baby girl?" he asked, his voice husky and dark, sending shivers down her body. He stopped a foot away, and she had to lean her head back to look up at him he was so close. "Because I sure as fuck have."

A whoosh of breath escaped her, her lips falling open. "This is a bad idea, Travis."

"The worst," he agreed on a whisper, his eyes traveling across her face, stopping on her mouth.

"We should definitely go get dinner," she whispered, nodding.

"Right." His eyes found hers. "Dinner."

She took a deep, steadying breath in, then stepped back from him. He looked like he wanted to say more, to reach out for her, but he didn't, those honey gold eyes bouncing between hers. He finally turned away, reaching for his duffel that he had left on the floor by the door, and she breathed a little easier not having him quite so close. Though, she hated to admit, that she very deeply wanted to know what it would feel like for his mouth to settle on hers, for it to open for her, to taste him for the first time. He'd kissed her twice now, just a mere touching of their lips, and each time had turned her into a puddle.

Travis set the duffel on the edge of the bed, rifling through the contents until he found what he was looking for, and then he disappeared into the bathroom. She heard the shower turn on and blushed deeply, imagining him naked mere feet away from her. She knew what his body looked like; had seen him in nothing but gym shorts so many times she knew it like the back of her own hand. But there was so much more she wanted to see, to touch, to taste.

While he was in the shower, she pulled her own suitcase onto the bed, searching through until she found a pair of cutoff jean shorts and a simple black tank top with thin straps. It was miserably hot in the room, the outside temperature not much better. She decided to go sans bra, her body already sticky with sweat from the humidity. She found her favorite pair of teal cowgirl ankle boots at the bottom of the suitcase and set them aside to put on in place of her sneakers. She sank to the edge of the bed, scrolling through her phone now that they had service once again.

Ten minutes later he emerged, steam billowing out of the tiny motel bathroom. A white towel was slung around his hips and her mouth dropped open of its own accord, her eyes going wide. She jumped to her feet and spun around, giving him her back. She heard his low chuckle from where he still stood and she glared at the door in front of her because she'd be damned if she was going to turn around while he was still practically naked. Heart doing triple time in her chest, she heard his soft footsteps as he approached the other side of the bed.

"Bathroom is all yours, Red," he said gruffly, his voice mere feet away.

She nodded stiffly, then grabbed her clothes off the foot of the bed and nearly ran to the bathroom, closing the door behind her with a snap. It smelled like him, like his bodywash and shampoo; a heady mix of sandalwood and citrus, and it made her head spin.

She stripped, stepping into the shower just long enough to rinse her body and wet her hair down. Climbing out, she towel dried hastily, then dressed in the tiny room. Her legs were still damp, so pulling the jean shorts up her thighs was a struggle, but she finally managed to get them up over her hips and buttoned with a lot of huffing and puffing. Pulling the tank top over her head, the stretchy fabric molded to her breasts, the cut of the neckline dipping low across her chest.

Exiting the bathroom, she stood in front of the mirror and combed through her curls, raking a curl cream through them and then letting them dry around her head. She studiously avoided looking at Travis, who lounged on the bed, back propped against the headboard, his booted feet crossed at the ankles. A dry pair of jeans covered his legs, and his usual cutoff tee had been replaced with a white t-shirt—sleeves intact—and the material clung to his magnificently muscled upper body. That same cowboy hat that he'd worn to Lawless that day he'd come to see her at work sat on the bed next to him. His hair was left down, nearly dry already. When she realized she was staring at him through the mirror, she shook herself.

Using the tiniest amount of concealer she could stand, she covered the worst of the bruises on her face, then swiped her lashes with mascara, if just to make her eyes pop a little. Then, she turned away from the mirror, flipping the light switch off. Tucking her feet into the boots, she dug into her purse. Her ID and some cash was all she was taking with her, and she tucked both into the back pocket of her shorts.

"Ready?" he asked, raising his eyes to hers from where he still lounged on the bed.

She nodded, licking her lips, her eyes darting over him once more before flitting away. He rolled into a sitting position, throwing his legs over the side of the bed, then stood. Swiping the cowboy hat off the bed, he placed it on his head. He grinned down her.

Dammit was he good looking. And he fucking knew it, too, the bastard.

He gestured to the door. "The rain has slowed; it's just drizzling now. We shouldn't get too *wet* walking across to the bar." She glared up at him for his teasing, and he winked down at her. "Come on. I'm hungry. And I could use a drink."

He tucked the key to their room back into his front pocket, then guided her toward the door. He locked it, double checking it, and then they made their way across the mostly deserted parking lot and across the narrow two-lane road that separated the motel from the bar. This parking lot was fuller, and they could hear 90's country music playing as they approached the doors.

Walking in, it felt like they'd stepped into the past, and Roxy had never felt more at home anywhere in her life. She laughed out loud, a wide grin splitting her face. It was much like Lawless, if her old work hadn't been updated in thirty years. It was wonderful and nostalgic. Wood beams covered the entirety of the building; the floor, the walls, the ceiling. The only concession to the times was the dance floor that was lit with colorful spotlights that rotated above the throng of people line dancing to *Alan Jackson's* 'Chattahoochee'.

Travis's hand at her back, he guided her forward, finding them two empty seats at the long, wide wooden bar. A bartender found them moments later, leaning forward to ask them what he could get them.

"Margarita and a shot of reposado tequila, whatever you have is fine," Roxy called over the bar.

"Salt and lime?" the bartender asked.

"Salt rim on the margarita, a slice of orange and a dash of cinnamon for the shot, please," she called back, smiling.

Travis's eyebrows shot up, nodding when the bartender turned to him. "Tall PBR and the same for a shot, please."

When the bartender had turned away, Roxy smiled over at him, where he'd settled into one of the barstools next to her. He was angled toward her, his knees spread wide, one boot heel hooked on the rung of the stool, his knee bent. She angled toward, unable to stay away, situating her legs between his knees. "Have you had cinnamon on an orange with tequila before?" When he shook his head, she grinned, leaning forward slightly. "It's fucking delicious. You'll never go back."

When their drinks arrived, Travis asked for menus, which showed up seconds later. Roxy took a pull of her margarita, scanning the menu. The bartender was quick to take their order, and then Travis turned toward her.

He took a drink of his beer, then lifted the shooter of gold tequila in one hand, holding the slice of orange with a dusting of cinnamon in the other. Roxy grinned, reaching for her own. Clinking her shot glass against his, she lifted it to her mouth, tossing the tequila back at the same time Travis did. They both lifted the orange slices to their mouths, biting off the sweet citrus.

When he had swallowed, Roxy beamed. "Well?"

He nodded, his brows going up in surprise. "Fucking delicious. Although—" he muttered, shifting forward in his seat, clasping her around the back of the neck with one large hand, "—I'd much rather taste it off your tongue, Red." His eyes searched hers, her mouth dropping open in shock. They were mere inches apart. "I told you I'm going to kiss you. And I'm tired of fighting this, baby girl."

A jostling shove at her back by another bar patron had her falling forward, and with his hand still clasping the nape of her neck, he guided her mouth to his. They pressed, light and tentative, before he opened his mouth and beckoned for her to do the same.

He rubbed his open lips across hers, once, twice, before she opened her own, inviting him in. They shared breaths for a moment, neither one of them daring to move, and then his mouth slanted over hers, pressing. At the first taste of his tongue on hers, she knew nothing would ever be this good. He tasted of orange and cinnamon and tequila and she moaned into his mouth, drinking him in as she kissed him back. Her hands cradled his bearded jaw, her fingernails scratching lightly at the trimmed facial hair that covered his cheeks and jaw, and he growled into her mouth. His kiss deepened, tongue swiping through her mouth over and over again. Fuck. She felt his kiss all the way to her toes.

She didn't want to stop, but a wolf whistle sounded and they broke apart, grinning against each other's mouths. He pecked another kiss to her lips, then pulled back, leaning back in his seat. She was so wet she was aching, and when he adjusted himself in his jeans, she blushed. Allowing her gaze to drop to his lap, she licked her lips, imagining what lay behind that zipper. She could see the outline of him, hard and straining against the material of his jeans.

He tilted her face up with a finger under her chin. His eyes were hot on hers. "I swear to god if you lick your lips like that again while staring at my dick, we're not going to make it through dinner, baby girl."

THIRTY

er breath left her in a whoosh as she stared at him. Travis groaned, shaking his head. "Dammit, Roxy."

He was seconds away from throwing her over his shoulder and carrying her out of the bar and back to their motel room when the bartender showed back up with their food. Fuck, he wanted her so bad it hurt. But he wanted her for more than just tonight; he wanted her for so much longer than just tonight. He reminded himself how bad of an idea it was to start something with her now, now that they only had days left… but when she looked up at him with those gold and jade eyes, he knew the fight was over. He had lost. Had possibly never even stood a chance against this bombshell before him.

They ate, shoulder to shoulder, much like they had that morning at her kitchen counter. It felt like a lifetime ago, when it had only been hours. So much had changed in those hours since. He knew he would never be the same, not after her. She was like a tornado; she had ripped through his life and tossed all of the neatly compartmentalized pieces of his existence into complete and utter chaos. And he didn't care. He didn't want to go back to that life. He would follow her, wherever she decided to go. He was irretrievably caught in her gravitational pull. Sucked right in and powerless to get out.

When Roxy pushed her mostly empty plate away and requested a second shot, he ordered one, too. They didn't kiss after this one, though he very strongly considered it. A light flush had crept up her chest and cheeks, from the alcohol and the temperature in the crowded bar, he was sure. When she'd come out of that motel bathroom in the tight as sin tank top with no fucking bra on, he'd had to adjust himself in his jeans. Her nipples had poked through the material while they'd stood in the room, the AC having cooled the room enough to not be wholly stifling. It had taken all of his considerable will-power not to drag the neckline of the tank top down and feast on her right then.

Cole Swindell's 'Flatliner' started, booming over the sound system, and Roxy grinned, taking his hand in her own. "Dance with me."

He laughed out loud, but let her pull him out of his chair and out to the crowded dance floor. They found an empty spot, and Roxy caught up with the steps with ease. Her boot heels stomped and clacked, her fiery curls bouncing around her shoulders as she moved. Her wide, unrestrained smile was everything, and he was once again powerless against her. His gaze followed every move she made, and when she laughed, it cracked something in his chest wide open. *Alan Jackson's* 'Good Time' began, and the steps picked up in pace. He liked best when they faced the same direction, he thoroughly enjoyed watching her ass in front of him as she moved. Dropping into a crouch on one beat, she bounced back up in the next, kicking her feet out one at a time before spinning to face the next wall.

Josh Turner's 'Be Your Man' queued up, the deep bass of the singer's voice reverberating around them. Dancers on either side of them partnered up. A cowboy with a black hat and graying horseshoe mustache stepped toward Roxy, but Travis glared at the ballsy cowboy and hauled Roxy into his arms, until their chests were pressed close. She smiled up at him, those gold and jade eyes flashing with laughter and joy.

She grinned up at him, then reached up with one hand, pulling his cowboy hat off his head. Placing it on her own head, she winked up at him in challenge.

"You know what that means, don't you?" he asked roughly, his mouth grazing over the shell of her ear. "Wearing my hat?"

She licked her lips, staring up at him and then nodded, whispering breathlessly, "Yes, Travis."

He growled low in his throat, banding one arm around her waist, bringing her body flush with his. His mouth found her throat, just for a heartbeat, and then he pushed her away, turning her to face forward. She glanced at him over her shoulder, from beneath the brim of *his* fucking cowboy hat on her head, the hat that now claimed her as *his*. She settled into his embrace, and the next second they were moving around the dance floor along with the other couples.

Their movements together were effortless; Roxy moved with a grace that never ceased to leave him in awe as her hand found his once again as they made another circle around the dance floor. She was admittedly much better than he was, but you didn't spend a large chunk of your adult life in Texas and not know a few line dancing basics. She grinned over at him and bit her lip, the silent question in her eyes. He nodded, and then she spun under his arm and away, their fingers linked and arms outstretched. He snatched the hat off her head, replacing it on his own as she did a little shimmy, and he laughed out loud.

He pulled her back into him then, flush against his own body as his arm slid around her waist, hand splayed wide between her shoulder blades, supporting her as he dipped her low. Time seemed to slow, the blaring music fading around them, the noise of so many other people dancing around them disappearing altogether, until it was just the two of them. As if no one else existed in the room in that moment.

Her leg that was not pressed against his lap lifted and without a conscious thought, his hand was sliding down the curve of her hip and along the expanse of bare thigh below the short cutoff jean shorts. His fingers curled into the groove at the back of her knee, lifting it nearly to his waist, his heart hammering like a drum in his chest, and he stared down at her as she let her head tip back with the dip. Her fiery curls cascaded over her shoulders toward the floor. He tracked the way her eyes closed, the carefree, wide smile that pulled at her lips, the arch of her throat.

The low-cut tank top did little to hide the swell of her breasts and he was transfixed by a dot of sweat that rolled down between them, disappearing beneath the fabric. His cock ached painfully behind the fly of his jeans and he wanted nothing more than to follow that bead of sweat with his tongue.

In the next second, time sped up again, pulling him from the intimate moment as she lowered her leg back to the floor, her body straightening as she came back up from the low dip. His mouth tracked along the curve of her throat and the underside of her jaw as she came up, which caused her to suck in a tremulous breath, and he was done for. The sound of that little gasp ricocheted through his brain like a gunshot.

She spun away, doing two rapid turns on her boot heels before returning to his arms, but her eyes were wide, her lips parted with short, staccato breaths that went straight to his dick. Pressing his palm between her shoulder blades, he urged her closer, feet still moving them around the dance floor. His other hand disappeared into the hair at the back of her head, fingers sliding through the curls. Their eyes locked, and he was incapable of looking away from those green and gold depths. In the semi-darkness of the dance hall, with only the occasional flash of a revolving stage light to break up the shadows, it was easy to pretend they were alone in the crowded hall.

But then she was spinning away again, though their hands remained entwined as they continued moving around the floor. The song ended and Travis clasped her hand in his firmly, guiding them off the dance floor. Roxy didn't protest, following him as he led them back toward the bar, where he tossed a handful of bills onto the bar, and then pulled her out the doors and into the night. The rain had started again, the torrential downpour pelting them as they ran through the parking lot and across the road to the motel. The red neon sign glowed through the driving rain, guiding them as they ran.

Roxy was laughing freely by the time they made it to the shelter of the overhang that ran the length of the motel, and he couldn't help the answering chuckle that escaped him at the sound of her laughter. It was so carefree and husky, and the sound of it wound around his heart like a vice. He knew he would never escape her. She was as much a part of him as his own heartbeats now.

A few more steps brought them to the door of their room and he dug the key out of his pocket, the orange tag dangling between his fingers.

Drenched completely for the second time that night, their clothes clung to their bodies, and Roxy's curls had flattened against her head and around her shoulders. Her mascara had smudged slightly beneath her eyes from the rain. Half laughing, half panting from their sprint through the downpour, Roxy looked up at him, her lips still pulled into a wide smile that he could just make out in the shadows that surrounded them like a cloak. The roar of the rain was a cacophony as it pelted the ground, the metal roof that sheltered them, and the cars parked along the length of the motel, blocking everything else out around them.

Travis stared down at her smiling face, rain soaked, mascara smudged, and still sporting that bruise beneath her eye…and couldn't remember a time that he'd ever seen a more beautiful sight than the woman standing in front of him.

"*Roxy*," he breathed low as her eyes dropped to his mouth, and then she was moving, launching herself up to wrap her arms around his neck. One arm banded around her waist, the other curving beneath her ass as their mouths crashed together. He lifted her, groaning when her legs wrapped around his hips, ankles locking at the small of his back as they kissed with a ferocity that stole his breath. Striding forward, he somehow managed to slide the key into the lock, swinging the door open. It banged against the wall loudly before he shoved it closed behind them, plunging them into near total darkness. "Fuck, Roxy."

Travis dropped the key onto the tiny table by the door, the jangle of the single key clattering to the table the only sound in the room other than their harsh breathing and quiet moans. Lowering her back to her feet, their hands immediately began tearing at their wet clothes. She knocked his hat off his head, sending it thudding to the floor behind him. His hands gripped the hem of her tank top, yanking it up and over her head, dropping the sodden article to the floor.

Her breasts heaved with every breath she gulped in, a smattering of goosebumps breaking out over her flesh from the chill of the AC on her still wet skin. Her nipples peaked from the chill in the room and he growled low in his throat, ducking his head swiftly and taking one tight bud into his mouth. Laving it with his tongue, he hummed in appreciation when she let out a low moan, her hands sliding into his hair to hold him to her.

He straightened, covering both breasts with his palms and pushed them together, his thumbs stroking over each nipple. Her back arched, pushing them into his hands harder, and he groaned gutturally as he stared down at the soft flesh that he held. The striking difference of her pale skin and his rough, tattooed hands was enough to make him feral. Nothing had ever looked so goddamn perfect.

"Oh fuck," she groaned, covering his hands with her own, at the same time leaning up to capture his mouth with hers.

He was achingly hard, his cock pressing painfully against the zipper of his jeans, and those low, husky sounds she was making in the back of her throat were tipping him closer to the edge.

She reached for his drenched shirt, shoving it up his chest and over his head. She licked her lips and he fought to hold onto his rapidly fraying will. He bent at the waist, grabbing first one of the cowgirl boots on her feet and then the other, tossing them away. He toed off his own boots, then reached for her again.

Unsnapping her jean shorts, he groaned when the backs of his knuckles grazed against the skin of her stomach as he lowered the zipper, but he was long gone, done wasting time. Shoving his palms into the ass of her shorts, he peeled them down her thighs, the wet material clinging to her. He knelt, pushing the shorts down her calves until she could step out of them, and then he pressed his mouth to the flat plane of her stomach as he hitched his thumbs into the band of her panties. Those too, went the way of the rest of her clothes until she stood completely naked before him.

Her fingers slid up through his hair as he pressed hot, open-mouthed kisses to her stomach, to the sexy indent at each hip. His lips grazed the soft, trimmed tuft of curls at the apex of her thighs and she gasped, the sound cutting through the room like a gunshot. "I'm going to taste this, Roxy. When I'm done fucking you, I'm going to feel you come on my tongue."

He stood then, capturing her stunned face between his massive hands. Smoothing his thumb over her cheeks, he kissed her fiercely, his tongue snaking into her mouth to taste all of her. Tequila and oranges and cinnamon.

Her fingers scrabbled at his waist, fumbling the snap of his jeans and then the zipper lowered. She shoved the jeans down just enough to pull his cock free of his boxer briefs, her fingers wrapping around him. He growled into her mouth, his hips thrusting into her hand. The pad of her thumb grazed over the tip and he groaned on a breathless sigh at the pleasure of it. He knew by the slickness of her thumb across the head, he was already leaking.

"Roxy," he breathed, pulling his mouth from hers. Forcing her eyes up to his, he panted, "Fuck you make me so hard. I didn't want to want you… but fuck I can't stop. I'm fucking powerless against you."

Kissing her again fiercely, he lowered his hands from her face and dug his wallet out of his back pocket. Tossing it onto the table alongside the discarded room key, he tore open a foil condom packet with his teeth and then rolled it on. Her head was bowed, watching, and he could hear the tremor in her breaths.

"Travis…" she whimpered breathily, and he grinned from above her.

"You can take it all, baby girl," he whispered gravelly and she shivered as she raised her eyes to his. "Yes?"

She nodded, her breaths sawing in and out of her. Her breasts trembled with the tremulous breaths she pulled in. "Yes. Don't stop."

He kissed her again, her mouth opening to his as he slid his hands, palms flat, along the backside of her thighs, gripping firmly. Lifting her, she once again wrapped her legs around his waist. Spreading her wide and holding her away from his body, he panted raggedly, "Line me up, Red."

Her eyes were hooded and seductive, her face pale in the darkness that shrouded them, and then her hand disappeared between their bodies to grip his cock, angling the tip up and against her entrance. He clenched his teeth at the feel of her fingers wrapped around him, the heat that radiated from her core where he pressed up and in. With his arms supporting her, he lowered her onto his shaft, fighting the urge to thrust up and sink all the way in in one go. She squeezed him tightly as her body adjusted to his intrusion, and her head tipped back, her throat arching with each inch of him that she swallowed with her tightness.

Travis took two steps forward, pressing her bare back against the wall. With one arm, he held her up, his hips pinned flush against the apex of her thighs, all of him sheathed inside her as deeply as he could go. With his other hand free, he bracketed her jaw between his fingers and thumb, turning her face to his to kiss her again deeply as he gave her body time to adjust to his.

When she writhed her hips in a circular motion against him, he groaned gutturally and bit her lower lip sharply between his teeth, making her gasp. The back of her head thudded against the wall behind her, but her eyes never left his. He pulled back and thrust upward, hard. Her eyes rolled into the back of her head and he exalted in it, growing impossibly harder inside her. Repeating the move, he groaned as he watched her breasts bounce with the force of his thrust. They panted together in the darkness. Fuck she felt so good. So fucking *right*. Right, in a way that he hadn't experienced before.

"Fuck, I don't want to hurt you," he groaned, dropping his mouth to her throat and pressing hot, open-mouthed kisses to the tender flesh there. Her hands scrabbled at his shoulders, sliding up through his hair and holding tight. Her head rolled from side to side against the wall. "*Roxy*."

"I'm not…not made of glass, Travis. Don't hold back—" she panted breathlessly, her eyes searching his, and that was all it took to send him over the edge. Pressing his mouth to hers in a bruising, fierce kiss, he used his strength to hold her against the wall as his hips began to move in hard, deep thrusts. Her mouth opened beneath his in a silent cry and he slowed, his heart hammering in his chest. He didn't want to hurt her; she'd been hurt enough. But she nipped at his lip with her teeth and sobbed, "Oh, fuck, don't stop, don't stop. *Please*—"

Spinning them away from the wall, he bounced her on his dick, reveling in the way her head tilted back. He could feel her tightening, quickening around him and he breathed out another groan. "Goddamn, Red. *Fuck.* You're going to come already, aren't you, baby girl? I can feel this pussy squeezing me—"

On the next thrust, her head fell forward, her forehead thumping onto his shoulder as her entire body tensed and he swore she stopped breathing. Two more deep thrusts and he felt her detonate; a scream tearing from her throat, muffled against his skin. Her pussy closed around his cock like a fist, spasms clenching her inner walls so tightly he had to fight not to come right then and there. Her thighs shook where they were wrapped around his waist, her abdominals spasming wildly. It was the sexiest thing he'd ever witnessed, watching this woman fall apart in his arms.

"Fuck, yes, just like that," he groaned, his thrusts slowing but not stopping entirely, prolonging her orgasm. He exalted in the way her body trembled in his arms. "That was so good, Red. So good. You take my cock so well. You came so hard, baby girl."

"Travis," she whimpered weakly against the skin of his throat, aftershocks pulsing through her and around his cock. "*Ohmygod.*"

"Catch your breath, we're not done yet," he rasped, stepping back toward the wall and pressing her against it again. His hands released her altogether, his hips pinning her to the wall, his cock buried to the hilt inside her. Smoothing her still damp curls away from her face, he kissed her thoroughly, then pressed his forehead against hers, letting her take deep, shuddering breaths in. "You're so fucking perfect, Roxy. So beautiful."

"You don't have to say that," she whispered breathlessly, rolling the back of her head against the wall. "I know what this is, Travis. You don't have to lie to me about—"

Growling darkly, he pinned her face between his hands, forcing her to look at him. "And what is this, Roxy?"

"Just sex. A distraction while on a long, boring road trip with someone you didn't want to be stuck with— someone that's— that's broken like me—"

"Keep telling lies like that, Red, and I'll turn your ass pink," he warned roughly, his mouth moving against hers, but not quite kissing. "That's not what this is, and you fucking know it."

Bracing his hands beneath the curves of her ass again, he pushed away from the wall, striding over to the bed and lowering her to her back. He followed, sliding back inside all the way to the hilt, which made her gasp and reach for him.

Levering himself up on his hands over her, he retreated all the way to the tip and then slammed back in. Roxy tossed her head, her lower lip clamped between her teeth. Her fingers fisted in the bedding beneath them, her chest heaving as he continued to pound into her, over and over again. Blood roared in his ears, his heart hammered in his chest, and sweat beaded down his back. She was so beautiful it hurt.

"I will exorcise those thoughts out of your head. *You are not broken, Roxy,*" he panted from above her, wishing more than anything to make her believe him. Leaning down, bracing himself on his elbows on either side of her, he pinned her head between his hands, fingers tangled in her hair. Whispering directly against her mouth, he breathed, "You are incredible, Red. Don't you dare let him make you think otherwise. Do you hear me?" She nodded frantically; her head still bracketed by his hands. He continued to move inside her, hard, deep thrusts that took him to the brink of her. He wanted to come so badly, but wanted to feel her come again first. Kissing her ardently, he then growled into her mouth harshly, "Now get that son of a bitch out of your head while I'm inside you. You're going to come on *my cock*, Roxy. You're going to call *my name*. You are here with *me*, baby girl. *I've* got you. Always."

"Oh, fuck, *Travis*—" she mewled, her body tightening around his as he hit deeper, shifting his hips to drive into her at a different angle, and he could tell by the way her thighs were shaking violently that he was hitting that special spot deep inside.

"Yes, just like that," he murmured raggedly, grinning against her mouth. "That's it, Roxy. Let go, baby girl. Give me one more."

Tremors built, and he knew she was seconds away. He hammered inside, angling his hips in to hit that spot over and over, and then her body curled in on itself as she came. He groaned fiercely as she clenched around his dick so tightly it set off a series of fireworks in his body, barreling him toward his own release. He covered her mouth with his to stifle the cry that erupted from her, drinking in her pleasure and spurring on his own. His movements stuttered as his orgasm hit like a tidal wave and he came hard, spurt after spurt filling the condom as he slammed in deep once more, burying himself in her as they came together.

As they came down from the high, the fierce, hard kisses turned into slow, deep, languid ones. Sipping kisses across lips, cheeks, and throats. Her fingers danced along his back, light, tentative touches that sent shivers across his bare skin. He levered himself over her, making sure not to let his weight crush her into the mattress, and he untangled one hand from her hair to stroke the now haphazardly drying curls away from her forehead and cheeks. He kissed along her cheekbone, over the bridge of her nose smattered in freckles, to the other cheek, darkened with that damn bruise. Just like he'd been craving to.

She would never have to worry about that again. He would make sure of it. Because he'd done the stupidest thing he could… he'd gone and fallen in love with the firecracker beneath him.

Thirty-One

The metallic thrumming of the rain on the tin roof just outside their motel door roused her from sleep. The sky beyond the curtains that they'd pulled closed the night before was tinged with dark gray, as if the sun rising behind the continuous rain clouds could barely break through.

Her head rested on Travis's chest, the steady cadence of his heartbeat a soothing balm to her system. Her body ached in ways that it hadn't in far too long, and it would be a long while before she could forget what had happened between them the night before. They were insatiable and had been up until late in the night, wrapped in each other. Travis had made her come so many times and in so many different ways, using his fingers, his tongue, his dick. He was always thorough and unselfish in the pleasure he gave.

Pressing her body closer to his beneath the sheets, Roxy turned her head and pressed her lips to his chest, where her cheek had just rested. Her fingers traced along the myriad tattoos that covered every inch of his warm skin. His breath stirred her hair and she stilled her hand, flattening her palm against his abdomen. His right hand captured hers lightly, rubbing his thumb over the back of her hand. The heart beneath her ear was pounding, an erratic, deep thudding rhythm that she was sure matched her own. He pulled her hand with his beneath the sheet, and when her fingers encountered his hardness, she wrapped him in her fingers. His breath released against her hair in a puff, a groan rumbling in his chest beneath her ear as she stroked him from root to tip and back. His hand covered her own where it was wrapped around his shaft, guiding her, tightening her grip on the downstroke.

"Fuck," he groaned, thrusting his hips upward into their hands. His left arm curled around her shoulders, holding her tightly against his side before drifting down over the curves of her ass, slipping between her cheeks and finding her already wet. She shifted, allowing his hand access to her, and he slid a finger along her aching channel, before pushing two fingers inside. "Christ, Roxy."

Shoving off the sheets, she pushed herself onto her knees beside him, never slowing the pumping of her hand on him. And then she slid one knee over his hips so that she straddled him, her knees pressing into the mattress on either side of his hips. Travis grasped her hips in his large hands, his thumbs pressing into the groove of her hipbones, his fingers digging into the fleshy part of her ass as he guided her up. Her fingers only relinquished their hold on his steely hardness when the head was notched at her entrance, and she used the muscles in her legs to slowly, so slowly, lower herself onto him.

His fingers tightened almost painfully on her hips, but she exalted in it, in the way his throat arched, head thrown back slightly. His chest rose and fell like a bellows, holding himself back as she set the pace above him, until she had settled against him, taking him all the way to the hilt. Until their bodies were pressed so close together, and she was so full of him she'd never be without him imprinted on her. His eyes burned into hers, that razing heat searing her from the inside out.

"Roxy—"

She began to move, rising up on her thighs before dropping back down again. She repeated it, over and over, and below her she watched as he gritted his teeth tightly together, a low growl rumbling from his chest and out between those clenched teeth. He surged upward into her, rocking his hips hard as she dropped back down, and she gasped on a sharp moan.

Raising her hands, she cupped her own breasts, pinching the nipples between her fingers hard enough to cause a sharp twinge of pain, and in the next second he was feral beneath her. His hands slipped up from her hips to the narrowest part of her waist, spanning wide. He hauled her upper body down toward him, banding one arm around her waist as he drove his hips up again and again like a damn piston, slamming in and then drawing out nearly to the tip, just to do it again.

Bracing herself on her hands on either side of his head, she pushed up just enough to be able to look down at him, into that handsome and fierce face that she couldn't deny that she was rapidly falling for. His hips slapped into hers harshly, driving in as deep as she could take him, nearly to the point of pain, but she took every thick, glorious inch, every brutal, pounding stroke he gave her. He hit that magic spot deep inside at just the right angle, the head of his cock stroking it with every deep thrust. Her thighs shook as her orgasm raced toward her, her heart hammering, breath stalling.

"Travis. Travis, *please*—"

"I know you're close, Red. Come on," he ground out through those tightly clenched teeth. "Let me feel you come on my cock, Roxy. Fucking hell I love feeling you come on my cock—"

Burying her face in the crook of his neck, she muffled her sharp cry against his skin as she came hard, her abdominal muscles seizing with the force of her climax. Lights flashed behind her tightly closed eyelids, her thighs shaking violently as her inner muscles spasmed around his hammering cock, squeezing tightly. He groaned fiercely beneath her, his arm tightening around her waist, holding her still as he shifted his legs to allow him to fuck her harder, rougher.

"That's it, Red," he growled gutturally, and she both felt it rumble through her chest pressed tightly to his, and heard it as he pressed his mouth to her ear. "Such a good fucking girl, coming on my cock." His breath hitched as she continued to spasm around him, and his other hand buried itself in her hair at the back of her neck.

She was still coming, her entire body convulsing with the force of it... no, she was careening headfirst into another one. This time she screamed, biting down hard on his shoulder as the second orgasm ripped her apart. He grunted beneath her at the pain and then she sobbed as she felt him come inside her in hot bursts that filled her. His answering growl in her ear was deep and primal.

Her teeth released the flesh of his shoulder and she kissed it gently, positive she'd caused him pain and hated it. He clasped her close as he rasped breathlessly, "It's okay, Red, mark me up. Make me yours. Fuck, Roxy. *I'm all yours.*"

As their breathing slowed and their hearts returned to a normal pace in their chests, Roxy leaned up on one hand, trailing the other through his hair and down over his bearded cheek. She leaned down, kissing him slowly, thoroughly, lingeringly, his body still nestled inside hers.

Rolling them to their sides, he pulled out of her, and she groaned, realizing their mistake as their combined releases dripped down her thighs. "Sorry. I guess I got carried away," she whispered, laughing. "I'm clean, I promise. And I'm on birth control."

Her eyes tracked his as he reached out a hand, tucking a sweat dampened curl behind her ear, and then he leaned forward to kiss her sweetly. "I'm clean, too. I usually have a very strict rule about condoms, but I seem to be breaking all of my rules where you're concerned."

Reaching between them, she blushed when his fingers slid through the wetness between her thighs, collecting it and then pushing his fingers deeply inside her. Pushing it back in. "Travis—"

"That's so fucking hot," he whispered against her mouth, his fingers still stroking, gathering that wetness and pushing it back in. His fingers flicked against that spot deep inside, making her eyes roll into the back of her head and her body curl in on itself even as her inner muscles clamped around his fingers tightly. He groaned, kissing his way down her throat. His beard and long hair tickled her as his head moved over her, trailing kisses where he went. "I can't get enough of you, of this."

"Oh good *lord*," she breathed on a moan, her fingers fisting in his hair, holding him to her even as his fingers continued to flick deep inside. "I—oh fuck—*the feeling is mutual*."

He chuckled darkly against her throat and it sent shivers down her entire body. "Are you going to come again, Red?"

She nodded frantically above him, her hips gyrating and writhing against his hand. Her chest heaved with panting breaths as each flick of his fingers brought her closer and closer to that precipice. "Yes, yes, *yes*—"

"God dammit you come so fucking pretty," he breathed against her skin, then ducked his head and clamped his lips and teeth around her nipple. She bowed off the bed on a sharp, mewling cry as fireworks zinged through her, lighting her up from the inside out. His teeth nipped sharply at that sensitive bud again, and she was hurled over that edge. He groaned around her nipple, "Yes, Roxy."

"*Travis!*" she sobbed brokenly as she came around his fingers, her hands clutching at his shoulders, his back, his hair as he used his fingers to fuck her through the orgasm.

A growl rumbled through his chest and into hers, and when her thighs fell open as she crested that peak, he rose above her. Collaring her throat with his other hand, he tilted her face toward his so he could kiss her fiercely, voraciously. "That's right, Red. My name is the only one I ever want to hear come off your lips."

Panting against his lips, she smiled weakly, nodding. "Yes."

"Good girl."

Her eyelids fluttered closed as he squeezed her neck lightly, fingers and thumb constricting for a heartbeat before releasing completely. He rolled to her side, and she rolled with him, her gaze dropping to the steely length pressed against her hip. She grinned, a coy, feline smile, and slid down his body.

Taking him in her hand, she smiled up the length of his body at him as she took him in her mouth. He fisted her hair in his hands, gathering it away from her face. She hummed with approval as it was her name that fell off his lips in a chant as he came on her tongue.

THIRTY-TWO

"We should probably get out of bed and check on the status of my car," Roxy murmured from where she was draped over Travis's naked chest. His fingers stroked idly up and down her spine, and he reveled in the way her body responded to him. He glanced over at the clock, then nodded, pressing a kiss to the top of her fiery curls.

He could hear the rain as it continued outside, though it didn't sound like it was raining as hard as it was when they had awoken earlier. Reaching over to the bedside table, he grabbed his cellphone and his wallet, pulling out the card Harry the tow truck driver had given him the night before. Dialing the number, he pressed the phone to his ear, curling his arm around Roxy's shoulders as she made to slide away from him. He growled down at her to remain where she was. She did, curling herself against his side again.

It rang several times, then a gruff voice answered. "Grady's."

"Good morning, Harry dropped off our car last night with a flat tire—"

"The Toyota?"

"Yes, sir," Travis said, continuing to stroke Roxy's back with his free hand. "That's the one."

"You picked up one helluva piece of shrapnel, son." The man's gruff voice was gravelly and rough, like he'd been a three pack a day smoker for fifty years. "Afraid I don't have that particular tire in shop. But my brother does, he's on his way with it now."

"About how long should we anticipate that taking, sir?" Travis asked.

"Meh. Depends if he stops for lunch on the way or not. Maybe a few hours. We should have you back on the road by tonight. You got somewhere you gotta be quick like?"

"No, that works just fine. Is there a taxi service we can call to get a ride over to you when it's ready?"

"Oh, no taxi's here, son. We'll pop on down to collect ya when it's ready. This a good number to call?" the man asked. Travis confirmed, then the man said, "We right in assuming you're down at the motel?"

"Yes, sir, we are."

"We'll be down to get ya later then," he said, and then the call ended. Travis chuckled, dropping the phone back to the bedside table, then relayed the conversation to Roxy. "Sounds like we should be good to get back on the road by this evening."

Roxy propped herself up on her elbow, cheek in her hand, and she idly drew circles on his abs and around his belly button. He sucked in his breath when it tickled. "Do we really want to wait until tonight to start driving again?"

Rolling to face her, propping his own cheek in his hand, up on his elbow, he pushed the fingers of his other hand through her hair, cupping the back of her head. "What do you have in mind?"

She shrugged, her eyes trailing slowly over his face, gaze lingering on his mouth. "I think it's silly to wait until late to start driving for the night is all."

"I'm gonna need you to spell it out for me, Red," he rasped, clasping the nape of her neck and angling her face toward his.

"Can we stay? Tonight, I mean. I don't want to leave this… not yet," she whispered, gold and green eyes bouncing between his.

Leaning forward, he pressed his mouth to hers. "We can stay tonight, baby girl. I'm not ready to leave this yet, either."

THIRTY-THREE

"The rain finally stopped," he murmured, his lips moving against Roxy's temple. They were wrapped tightly around each other, their naked bodies intertwined completely beneath the sheet. Her back expanded beneath his arms as she took a deep breath in before letting it out slowly, her face pressed into his throat. He could feel her lips moving against his neck and then up to his jaw.

"I wondered why it was so quiet when I woke up," she whispered. "I got used to the sound on the tin roof outside the door…"

Grady had come down to collect them from the motel around three in the afternoon the day before. Travis had paid for the new tire, as well as the tow bill, which prompted a lot of arguing from Roxy. He had called in a to go order from Bertie's across the street, and they had brought their food back to the motel room, sitting half naked in the bed together as they ate and watched old episodes of Law & Order on one of the only channels the motel got on the ancient box TV in the room. They hadn't left the bed since, exploring each other's bodies thoroughly, fucking until they were both damn near dehydrated. Falling asleep with her wrapped in his arms, her body curled against his was almost as blissful as waking with her still there.

"We should keep driving now that the rain has stopped," he said, pressing a kiss to her forehead. He was loathe to leave the bed, to lose the closeness of her body against his. "I don't want to give that bastard any chance of finding you, baby girl."

She nodded, her head moving under his chin, but her arms tightened around him and he closed his eyes to revel in the moment. "Travis…"

"Hmm?" he asked, keeping his eyes closed.

"I wish we had met differently. I would have liked to have more time with you, I think," she whispered quietly, her lips pressing to his ribs just below his left pectoral.

"I would have liked to have had more time with you, Roxy," he admitted just as quietly, speaking directly into her hair.

Leaning up on her elbow, she looked at him. "Can we maybe take the long way north?"

Pushing her fiery red curls away from her sleep flushed face, he cupped her jaw in both hands, letting his fingers slide through her hair beneath her ears as his gaze traveled over her features. The bruise had started to fade from the angry black and blue to a muted purple, tinged with a garish looking green at the edges.

"I suppose we could go straight north through Wisconsin and take the long way around the Upper Peninsula and back down. I doubt he'd expect us to take that route, come to think of it," he murmured, smoothing his thumb over that hateful bruise and the smattering of freckles that shone through.

"I don't think he'd follow us, Travis," she said softly, propping her chin on his chest. "And he doesn't know where Free and Jodi live, other than a general 'somewhere in Michigan'."

Smoothing his palm over her curls to the back of her head, he furrowed his brows and let his lips thin. "I don't trust him not to figure it out. I'll stay a few days once we get there, just to make sure. And you'll be safe. Free seems like a good guy."

She smiled warmly, nodding. "He's the best. You'll like him."

"I have no doubts," he chuckled, nodding, too. "Do you have an actual address for where we're headed?"

"Of course," she scoffed. "I have it written down and safely tucked into the console of the 4Runner, and I have it saved in my phone, just in case. Jodi's family owns an equestrian boarding ranch, and they're going to let me stay in the loft in the barn until I can find something more permanent. Funny story, that same loft used to be Free's, back before he and Jodi got together. He moved back into it for like an hour when he officially moved back north. He had to grovel to Jodi a bit before she invited him to move in with her."

"What did he need to grovel for?" he asked, laughing.

Roxy made a face, her nose wrinkling. And then she sighed, letting her forehead fall onto his chest for a moment. She spoke directly against his skin, her words muffled. "Promise you won't judge me? Or him?"

Travis cupped the back of her head, rubbing gently. "I will never judge you, Red. Of all people, you never have to worry about judgement from me. I promise."

She exhaled heavily against his naked chest, then raised her head again. "Free lived in Michigan with Jodi's family, working on her father's ranch after his mom died. He's… significantly older than Jodi, and when he realized he had started having feelings for his buddy's teenage daughter… he left. Moved back to Texas and stayed there for like, seven years or something. I met Freeman the first week he was back in Texas, almost a decade ago. I was young and jaded from being on my own since I was sixteen. Met this hot, emotionally stunted cowboy and we…" She stopped, shrugging, dipping her head to tuck her curls back behind her ears again. "We had an *arrangement*, of sorts. No strings, no emotional attachment sex. Strictly sex, and that was it. We became 'best friends with benefits' or so another friend called us. I knew early on that Free had left someone in Michigan and his heart was always going to belong to her, and I never had those kinds of feelings for him like that anyway. It was maintenance sex when one of us needed it." Travis spread her curls out around her shoulders. She sighed again. "Anyway. I met Neal and mine and Free's 'arrangement' ended. It never picked up after that again, even after I broke things off with Neal after… well. Because of reasons." Gesturing to her face, he understood and nodded, though he wanted to rip this bastards' throat out all over again for putting his hands on her. "I moved into Free's place—my house in Melody Hills—and we just co-existed for a while. He's my best friend, but that part of our relationship was over, and we were both fine with it. He had to make a trip north for his brother's wedding, and while he was there, he went and fell all over again for his buddy's daughter, who had apparently been in love with him this whole time he'd been gone."

"And this is Jodi? His wife?" Travis asked. She nodded.

"Mmhmm. And she's *wonderful.* Just the sweetest. So, while he was home—well, in Michigan—he got into a fistfight with her ex-husband and got thrown in jail for a weekend." She laughed when his eyebrows shot up, nodding. "Oh yes, he was defending Jodi and the douchebag got him arrested for assault. Charges were dropped later, but that's another story," she said, waving her hand as if to re-center herself in her story telling. "At the same time that he was sitting in jail, Neal came back. He was waiting at mine and Free's house when I got home from work one night, and it started out with him begging for me to take him back, begging for me to come home. When I said no… he got violent. He was pissed because I was living with Free, even though nothing was going on with us anymore, but he knew about our past and was sure that we had picked up where we had left off.

Or, rather, that I had never stopped sleeping with Free while we were together." She swallowed, gesturing to that jagged white scar that bisected her lip. "He beat me into a bloody mess and then left me in the kitchen. I was in the hospital for a couple days. He broke three ribs, fractured my pelvic bone, broke my nose—it's much prettier now than it used to be, believe it or not, thanks to the fabulous plastic surgeon Dr. Landon—umm, fractured my skull in two places, and damaged my left eye. When I got discharged from the hospital, I was terrified he was going to come back for me, and when I couldn't get a hold of Free via phone, I did the only thing I could; I flew straight to northern Michigan and tracked him down at Jodi's." She smiled wryly then. "I'm sure I scared the hell out of her, showing up on her porch looking like I did. And then she found out that Free and I had been… well, Free and I. He was worried about me, terrified of leaving her again, and he didn't handle it all that great; like I said, emotionally stunted idiot that he was back then. He left with me that night to make sure I was okay back at home in Texas. Idiot didn't even bother saying anything to her for a month, just showed up with a fucking U-Haul at her parent's house and groveled for her to give him another chance." She shrugged. "The rest is history. They're sickeningly in love and so obnoxiously perfect for each other."

He curled his arms around her waist, pulling her up and angling her across his body. Collaring her throat with one hand, he drew her mouth to his, kissing her gently, sweetly. Brushing his lips over the scar on her lip first, he then brushed his mouth over her left eye, then the new bruises, and across her nose. "Thank you for trusting me with all that, Roxy. I understand more, now. Although I certainly hate Neal more than I did before. I will never let him hurt you again, Red. I promise you that."

She smiled, brushing her lips across his. "I haven't told anyone that full story other than Natalie, and obviously Freeman.

I don't know what prompted me to spill all that. It's an awfully heavy topic. I'm sorry."

He shook his head though. "Don't ever be sorry for telling me your truths, Roxy. And I will never judge you, you have my word on that. I know that our pasts can shape us in ways we never would have expected, probably better than anyone. I have not been dishonest when I tell you I am a monster, baby girl."

She pursed her lips, leaning forward to kiss him again, at the same time splaying her palm wide over his left pectoral, where his heart beat a steady cadence. "You're not a monster, Travis. This heart is too good for you to ever be a monster."

THIRTY-FOUR

After a quick breakfast at a truck-stop diner along the interstate, they were back on the road. Windows down, the wind whipped through the vehicle, the sun bright in the rich blue of the sky. Music blasted through the speakers, and they sang along as the miles disappeared behind them.

Travis's left hand was kept firmly on the wheel, but his right hand never strayed far from her. Either holding her hand in his, or clasping her bare knee, or strumming his fingers along the sensitive skin on the insides of her thighs. He touched her constantly, turned to look at her through the darkly tinted Aviator sunglasses back on his face, shielding his eyes from the bright sunlight as they drove.

Kansas disappeared behind them, then a short jaunt through the northwestern corner of Missouri, and up into Iowa. They had just crossed into Wisconsin, and they were trying to make it as far as Madison before stopping for the night, but Roxy would have been fine if they'd taken their time, too.

"Want to find us a hotel and somewhere to stop for dinner?" Travis asked, squeezing her knee lightly. He had to know what every single touch did to her, sending lightning zapping through her, straight to her core. She'd been painfully turned on all day, with every touch of his fingers against her skin.

"Already on it," she said, scrolling through her phone. "There's a Best Western that's not too expensive."

"Find us somewhere that will have the fluffy white hotel robes."

"Travis, I can't afford one of those fancy hotels," Roxy muttered dryly, rolling her eyes at him as he drove, that left hand of his draped loosely over the wheel. Peeking at him through her lashes, she did very much like the idea of seeing him lounging in nothing but a big fluffy hotel robe.

"Find one, Red," he murmured darkly, slicing his gaze over to her. He had tossed the sunglasses onto the dashboard, now that the sun had descended just beyond the horizon. "I'm not asking."

Huffing out a heavy, beleaguered sigh, she tried to keep the corners of her mouth from tipping up in a smile as she mumbled, "Fine."

Routing them to one of the city's five-star hotels, Travis pulled up to the valet parking and hopped out, stretching, before pulling first his duffel and then her suitcase out of the back. With his duffel slung over his left shoulder, and her suitcase held in his left hand, he clasped her hand with his right. Together, they walked into the fancy atrium and up to the long granite faced concierge desk.

"Checking in for Hayes."

It didn't take long to get them checked in, and then they were in the elevator. As the doors slid shut soundlessly, Travis backed her up against the polished mirrored wall of the elevator, spanning his hand across her throat and tilting her face up to his. He merely hovered his lips over hers, brushing his mouth back and forth, teasing her while keeping her trapped against the wall of the elevator.

"I can't decide if I want to order up room service, take a shower, or fuck you first."

"Umm. Yes?"

He chuckled, low and dark, and the sound sent fissures of pleasure down her spine, his breath ghosting over her lips. She shivered. The elevator dinged as it arrived on their floor, whooshing open almost silently. He backed up, removing his hand from her throat. Clasping her hand in his once more, they walked down the hallway to their room.

Her entire body was on fire, lit up from the inside out. Little fireworks continued to go off in her belly, sending butterflies flitting around crazily. Damn this man was driving her insane with want.

Pushing the door open, he let her enter ahead of him, flipping on the lights. The room was lavish and opulent. Roxy crossed the lush, carpeted floor to wide windows, peering through the gossamer curtains and across a lake that sat directly in the center of the city.

Travis deposited their bags by the door and then did his usual check of the room, though Roxy thought it was totally unnecessary in a hotel as nice as this. She meandered into the spacious bathroom. There was a double shower wide enough for two people to comfortably stand in with a floor to ceiling glass door, but Roxy was damn near gleeful over the oversized jacuzzi tub that sat in the corner. Two fluffy, starched white hotel robes sat folded on the tubs edge.

They would definitely be utilizing that tonight, if only to soothe her aching muscles. Her body was still sore from Neal's attack, and sitting in the car for the last two days hadn't helped much to alleviate the aches.

Travis walked in behind her and she whirled, throwing her arms around his shoulders. His hands settled heavily on the curves of her waist, holding her against him, at the same time lowering his head to take her mouth with a fervent, fevered kiss.

"I want to take a bath," she murmured against his mouth when he pulled away enough for her to breathe. "Will you join me?"

"Why don't you start the water and I'll order up some room service," he suggested, pecking another kiss to her lips. "What sounds good?"

"Breakfast," she laughed, leaning back against his arms that held her around the waist.

"That does seem to be our thing," he chuckled, smiling down at her. She loved it when he smiled. His eyes crinkled at the corners, and those honey gold depths seem to shine in a way that she hadn't noticed before, all those months ago. She was angry at herself for not taking a leap of faith earlier, to capitalize on the time that they could have had... time that now seemed so painfully short. "Pancakes? Waffles? French Toast?"

"Hmmm," Roxy hummed, pursing her lips and narrowing her eyes in thought. "Waffles. Strawberries. Lots of whipped cream."

Travis grinned down at her. "I like the way you think, woman."

"I've been known to have good ideas on occasion," she laughed, rocking side to side.

He slapped a hand to her ass once, a sharp, stinging slap that made her gasp and her inner muscles clench up tightly in response. "Turn on the water. Get naked. Get in. I'll get food ordered and then I'll join you."

Fifteen minutes later, the jacuzzi tub was filled to the brim with warm water. She turned the jets on, which sent the water to frothing bubbly. Setting the lights overhead to dim, it lent an intimacy to the room. Stripping, she let her clothes fall where they lay, then stepped gingerly into the warm water, sinking up to her neck and leaning against one of the sloped sides. The jets massaged her aching muscles, and she closed her eyes, leaning her head back.

Travis stepped back into the bathroom, eyes finding her where she was reclined in the tub. She watched him as he stripped, first his shirt up over his head, revealing the wall of tattooed muscle that was his chest and abdomen. And then his jeans, shoving them down his thighs and off his feet. His boxer briefs came next, and then he stood, fully naked, half hard before her. He stepped forward, then said gruffly, "Food will be here in half an hour. Lean forward, baby girl."

She did as he asked, sitting up and moving forward so he could slide in behind her, and then his arms closed around her, pulling her back flush against his chest in the warm water. The jets whooshed around them, keeping the water's surface a roiling, frothy bank.

His tattooed knees poked out of the water on either side of her, and she traced the black and gray shaded markings along his skin. "Did they hurt?"

"On my knees? Like a bitch," he laughed, and she loved the honesty she heard in his voice. He was always honest with her. "The backs of my knees were rough, too. That skin is so sensitive. I think the worst to cover was the scar tissue, though."

Leaning her head back against his chest, she looked up and back at him. "Scar tissue?"

He nodded, though she sensed him tense behind her. He swirled the frothy bubbles along the surface of the water around with his hands. "I was stabbed sixteen times. A very long time ago. I had them covered so I wouldn't have to see them. At least, not as easily as before."

Sitting up, she spun in the water slowly so that she faced him, her eyes wide and mouth dropped open in horror. "You were stabbed *sixteen times*?" When he nodded, she let out a soft, sad exhale. "*Travis.*"

"It was a very long time ago," he murmured quietly, taking her hands in his and bringing them to his mouth. He pressed a kiss to her knuckles, but his eyes were wary over the tops of them. "I was never the same after that night. And for a long time I was a bitter, angry shell of a man. It took me years to find my way out of that darkness."

Licking her lips, she inched forward until she knelt between his thighs. "Can I see them?"

Without answering, he lowered her hand to his chest, guiding her fingers over his skin, until she gasped, tears stinging her nose and eyes when she felt the first one. Raised and smooth, it was nearly invisible to the eye beneath the ink; but she could feel it. He silently guided her hand along the left side of his body, allowing her to touch all of them. Some were wide and short, others long and thin. Along his ribs, his chest, his arm, even his thigh.

She blinked as the tears spilled over her lids. His eyes were gentle as he sat forward, bracing his wet, warm hands on either side of her face, drawing her to him. He kissed her, light, chaste brushes of his lips against hers. Sweet and gentle.

"The—the man you killed. Did he do these?" she asked on a whisper, her lips barely moving against his. He nodded slowly. "Then he deserved whatever you did, Travis."

"I didn't do what I did for me, Roxy. I was blind with rage, with grief when I killed him. I'm no better than he is." His tortured whisper nearly broke her. "I still have nightmares of that night. Not because of what happened to *me*. Not because of what I *did*... I'd do it again. Without a moment's hesitation, without remorse, without regard to what would happen to me all over again... I'd do it all again if it meant I wasn't *too late*."

Sliding into his lap, legs braced on either side of his hips, she curled her arms around his neck. He'd pulled his long hair up into a bun on the back of his head before getting into the jacuzzi with her. His arms banded around her waist, holding her as close as she could get, his head resting against her chest as she stroked his hair gently.

And it was then that she knew without a doubt that she had fallen in love with him. With every beautiful, gentle, broken part of him. Because she recognized herself in all those pieces of him.

THIRTY-FIVE

Travis had turned Roxy back to face forward, putting her back to his chest again. He'd unloaded a lot of himself with that conversation, though he'd still kept some of it to himself, not quite ready to share everything just yet. She had held him so tightly, so gently, he'd known he would never be the same. Knew it in his bones that there was no way he was going to be able to say good-bye to her in a few days. He'd rather cut out his beating heart and hand it over to her. It already belonged to her.

But that was a conversation for another day, this had been heavy enough for one night. So he nibbled on the soft skin at the crook of her neck where it met her shoulder, biting lightly, scraping with his teeth, before loosening. She moaned, dropping her head to the side to grant him better access. Fuck she was so receptive, so trusting, so willing to follow his lead.

"You seemed very excited to see this jacuzzi tub," he murmured against her neck. His hands ran along her waist, fingers strumming along her abs, before sliding up to cup her breasts in his palms.

"I love taking baths," she admitted breathily, pushing her chest out, filling his hands with her tits. He squeezed them gently.

They fit his palms perfectly. So soft, so round. Not too big. He fucking loved these tits. "I used to take them every night after work. But I hadn't in a while."

"Why not?" he asked, running his nose under her ear. He scraped his teeth along her neck again, making her moan and shiver. His cock was hard as steel at her back, he knew she could feel it, because she kept rubbing against him.

She stilled, just for a heartbeat, and he stopped, too.

One hand released her breast and rose out of the water to collar her throat, turning her head up and back to look at him. "Why not, Roxy?"

She swallowed, and he could feel her throat shift beneath his palm. He wasn't squeezing, just holding. He'd never hurt her. "I fell asleep one night, in the bathtub after work." He growled low in his throat, and she rolled her eyes, muttering, "Yeah, yeah, I know. I was exhausted, and listening to an audiobook with my earpods in. When I got out, I realized that... that Neal had been inside. While I was asleep." Every muscle in his body went taut, fear and rage battling for supremacy within him. Her hand came up and covered the back of his, where he was still collaring her throat. Her touch was gentle, a grounding. "I don't know how long he was inside, if he'd been watching me in the bath... but it scared me enough that I wasn't comfortable taking baths anymore. I stopped sleeping well at night after that. Worried he'd come back. But I didn't know for sure it was even him. I thought I was losing my mind."

"God dammit, Roxy," he growled low, shaking his head. "I'd love nothing more than to kill this motherfucker." He tipped his head back, lost in thought for a moment. "The day I yelled at you for not paying attention at class..."

She shrugged, water lapping at the sides of the jacuzzi with the movement. "It had happened the week before. Like I said, I wasn't sleeping. And then the notes started showing up... You read me like a book, even then Travis. You saw everything, somehow."

"I'm never letting you out of my goddamn sight," he muttered darkly, that primal, possessive, protective instinct taking hold deep inside him and holding on like gangbusters. He'd known something was wrong and he'd damn near let her push him away. Dropping his forehead to her shoulder, he tempered his raging fury and whispered, "I don't know what I'd do if something happened to you, Roxy."

"I'm fine, Travis," she murmured, twisting her head to press her lips to his cheek. "I'm here."

"I've got you," he whispered back gruffly, emotion clogging his throat. "I've got you, always, Red."

She murmured something beneath her breath that he didn't quite catch, but then she wiggled her hips back against him, notching her ass against his still hard dick, and a groan rumbled out of his chest. His other hand splayed, fingers wide, palm flat against the lower part of her abdomen, pressing her back against him more firmly. Her breath stuttered in and out in breathy, ragged pants.

"I don't want to talk about any of that anymore, please," she whispered, again twisting her head to search for his mouth with her own. "I want you, Travis. I want you inside me. Please. I've been waiting all day."

Anger still boiled just beneath the surface, but he pushed it down, focusing his attention on the woman in his arms. Sliding his hand down between her thighs, he cupped her sex, fingers rubbing that bundle of nerves at the apex of her thighs until she was writhing against his hand. Only then did he slide two fingers in between those folds, sinking them in deep, all the way to the knuckle. She bowed, head tossing back against his shoulder as she moaned throatily. Fuck he was so hard. He had to be leaking at the tip.

"Fucking hell, Red," he groaned, scraping his teeth over that spot on her neck that drove her fucking wild, and she bucked against his hand. "If I fuck you in this tub, we're going to have one helluva mess to clean up. Let's go."

Standing, water sluiced down his body, and he reached for her, drawing her up on shaking legs. Grabbing a towel, he hastily scrubbed at first her body, then his own, getting just enough water off of them to not leave standing water as he carried her out of the bathroom and into the bedroom. He dropped her onto the mattress and she laughed, bouncing on her back. He had just knelt on the bed when a knock sounded on the door, then a quietly called, "Room Service."

"Fucking Christ," Travis groaned miserably, glancing toward the door. He was so hard it fucking hurt.

Roxy laughed, bouncing up off the bed and dashing into the bathroom. Half a heartbeat later, she was back, pulling on one of the fluffy white robes over her naked body. She tossed him the other one and began tying the sash around her waist, then pulled her rioting curls out from the back so that it draped down her back. The deep V of the folds of the robe did little to hide her cleavage and he growled savagely as she padded toward the door.

She laughed again, shushing him. "If you answer the door like that, you'll scare them off, and then we'll be without dinner." Pausing at the door, she turned and whispered, "And I have plans for that whipped cream."

Travis bit his lower lip to stifle the groan that erupted from him as she pulled the door open. He slung the robe over his arms, tying the sash around his own waist. It did little to conceal the raging hard-on he was still sporting, but he didn't give a fuck. As she backed into the room, the door shut with a click. She turned, carrying the tray of silver domed food items toward the bedside table. And as soon as she set it down, he was hauling her back into his arms and she shrieked with laughter before clamping a hand over her own mouth to stifle the sound.

"Food can wait," he growled, tearing at the sash at her waist and pushing the sides of her robe aside. He sat on the bed as she ripped at his own robe, and then she was crawling onto the bed, her knees digging into the mattress on either side of his hips. Chest to chest, mouth to mouth, he sank his teeth into her full lower lip as she straddled him. Fumbling hands between their bodies lined him up against her, and then she was sinking down onto him in one long, slow movement. Her hands came to his shoulders, using them as leverage as she rode him. His hands spanned her waist, holding tightly to the still damp, fevered skin beneath the folds of the robe. Head tossed back, she ground onto him, circling her hips. He knew that move, knew it meant she was taking him deep, hitting that special spot. He loved it, loved watching her take her pleasure from him.

"Mmhmm," he hummed in approval when she shimmied again. "Is that where you need me, Red? Such a greedy fucking girl."

Reaching between them, he circled her clit with his fingers, making her thighs shake. "Just like that, Travis," she panted, eyes pinched shut tight as she continued to bounce and swirl on him. He could feel her quivering, right on the edge. Her movements stuttered, her fingers clamping down tight on his shoulders, and then—

"Oh fuck!" he snarled, his hips snapping up to meet hers as she came so hard she nearly pushed him back out. He came without warning, pulsing and emptying into her with a ferocity that left him drained. Panting against the skin of her throat as she sagged against him, he breathed, "Goddamn, woman."

She laughed breathlessly, and the movement did wonderful, awful things to her inside muscles, which contracted around his length still buried inside her. Groaning, he pulled her off of him.

"Shower, then food."

"I don't have the energy to stand in the shower, Travis," she laughed, swaying on her feet. She made a face then, and he knew their mixed releases were sliding down the insides of her thighs. He loved the thought of her being pumped so full of him that she couldn't hold it all. Some age old, primal instinct had kicked in and rewired his fucking brain, apparently. Pouting, she sighed. "Okay. Quick shower. Then food."

They padded back into the bathroom, turning on the double shower heads on opposite ends of the glass walled shower. Showering quickly, they couldn't help but laugh as they watched each other from opposite sides, though only about three feet separated them. Washing their hair hurriedly, Travis was transfixed watching her rinse the shampoo and conditioner from her hair, and then she ran a washcloth over her body and between her thighs, and damn if he wasn't growing hard again.

She pointed at him and laughed. "No. I want food first, dammit."

He chuckled, rinsing his body off, too, though he did allow his own hand to stroke his thickening cock from root to tip. He thoroughly enjoyed watching her eyes follow the movement of his hand, the way her eyes darkened, mouth parting slightly with quick, panting breaths.

"Food first, baby girl," he teased, and she glared up at him as she turned her water off. Reaching around his hip, she yanked the hot water off and he bellowed with mock outrage when the water turned frigid a moment later. She danced out of the shower stall, shrieking when he followed. He caught her around the waist, hauling her back against him, curving his body around hers so he could growl in her ear, "You naughty fucking thing."

"I'm sorry, I'm sorry!" she cried on a laugh, but he knew she wasn't sorry.

When he caught their reflection in the mirror, he stopped

them, turning her attention to it as well. Naked and wet, his arms banded around her waist, chin nearly touching her shoulder, their cheeks pressed together…it felt like home. *She* felt like home.

Breaths falling from slightly parted lips, her cheeks flushed rosily, those green and gold eyes sparkling, and that brilliant smile that pulled at her lips? Fuck, that smile was his undoing.

THIRTY-SIX

"So, are we trying to make it all the way to Petoskey today?" he asked, pulling them away from the valet parking, where they'd just loaded their bags into the 4Runner.

"GPS says it's a 7 hour drive… so it's doable, if we want," she said from the passenger seat, scrolling through the cellphone in her hand.

"Is that what you want to do?" he asked gently, flipping on the blinker to get them turned in the right direction to get them back to the interstate headed north toward the Upper Peninsula of Michigan. They would drive along US-2 around the bottom edge of the state's Upper Peninsula, then take the Mackinaw Bridge south toward the lakefront city of Petoskey.

"It seems silly to pay for another night of hotel when we're so close…" she murmured, staring down at the phone screen. Stupid tears pricked her nose and she blinked them away rapidly. "But I don't want this to be over yet."

"Who says it has to?" he asked quietly, taking her hand in his. When she just stared at him, he continued, "I don't want this to be over yet, either. Let's get you there and settled. I already told you I'm not leaving right away."

She didn't want him to leave, *ever.* That was the problem. She wanted to ask him—fuck, *she'd beg him*—to stay if she needed to. She didn't want to say good-bye. Didn't want to lose him, not now that they'd finally come together.

By the time they had crossed the border into Michigan's Upper Peninsula and started heading east along the shoreline of Lake Michigan, Roxy was exhausted. As badly as she didn't want this to end, she was so ready to not be in the car any longer. When the massive, five-mile-long suspension bridge came into view, Roxy gasped, sitting up straighter in her seat. "Holy shit, we have to drive across that?!"

"We'll be fine," Travis chuckled.

His tone changed once they got onto the bridge nicknamed the Mighty Mac. His fingers were white knuckled around the steering wheel as he drove, slower than the posted speed limit. There were only two lane options; the outside lane, which was solid concrete beneath their tires, but far too close to the much too short metal guardrail in Roxy's opinion… or the middle lane, which was a metal grate that they could see straight through to the water that ran below the bridge, and Roxy hated that even more.

"Who the fuck designed this deathtrap?" he grumbled through clenched teeth, eyes straight ahead as they made it to the halfway point of the Mackinaw Bridge.

"You afraid of heights, big guy?" Roxy teased breathlessly, her own throat tight with fear, too. She shivered when she looked out over the expanse of water far below. The view would have been beautiful, if not for how terrifying it was.

"Yes," he admitted, laughing. "I don't much like the idea of plummeting over the side of this thing."

Once they'd made it to solid ground again, his knuckles unfurled from the death grip he'd had on the steering wheel, and he blew out a long exhale. Scrubbing one hand down his face, he rasped, "I don't even smoke and I need a cigarette after that."

Deciding to stop in the tiny town of Mackinaw City to stretch their legs and unwind from that treacherous drive, they wandered the streets, hand in hand. Early June in Michigan was stunning, Roxy admitted to herself as they walked. Lilac trees in varying shades of purple and white were in full bloom, the soft, heady scent filling her nose. After she'd stopped to smell every single lilac tree they passed, Travis plucked his switchblade out of his pocket and sliced off several small branches, handing them to her. She thanked him with a grin, and then he leaned down to kiss her swiftly.

"I'm sure Jodi has a vase we can put those in, when we get you home," he murmured, taking her hand in his once again as they continued back toward the car. "How much farther?"

"Looks like little more than half an hour." Her heart tripped in her chest. *She didn't want this to be over!*

Setting the fragrant blooms in the back seat carefully, she stepped toward Travis, wrapping her arms around his waist, fisting her fingers in the shirt at his back.

"Please stay," she whispered, not daring to look up into his eyes. It had taken all of her courage to force the words out of her mouth.

His arms banded around her tightly, his head dropping to force her own up. He kissed her, and this kiss was long and fraught with so much emotion that tears stung her eyes. When he lifted his lips from hers, he breathed against them, "I'd follow you anywhere, Roxy."

Smiling through the tears that clouded her vision, she clung to him. This wasn't how she'd imagined their trip ending. How drastically different her life was from a week ago, she marveled as she stared up into those honey gold eyes that she had fallen so deeply in love with.

Climbing back into the 4Runner, they made their last short leg of the journey toward Blue Haven, Jodi's parents ranch, and her new home. Roxy had let Free know they were almost there, and when Travis pulled them down the long, white picket fenced driveway, Jodi, Free, and Jodi's parents were there waiting for them when they arrived.

She hadn't even had time to open the door when Free swung it open, and she stepped out of the car and was immediately enclosed in his arms. His citrus and cedar scent hit her as he hauled her close. Burying her face in his neck and wrapping her arms around his waist, she let herself cry, all the fear and pain and exhaustion escaping her.

"This is the last time you're allowed to scare me like this," he muttered darkly into her hair, kissing the top of her head. She laughed through her tears, then pulled back, swiping at her face. She'd missed that Texas drawl.

"It's good to see you, too, Free," she deadpanned, rolling her eyes. God it was good to see him. He tilted her face up so he could assess the damage to her face, his lips thinning and those intense aquamarine eyes narrowing dangerously. "I'm okay."

Travis had alighted from the driver's side and stepped around the hood of the car. Roxy stepped back from Free, holding a hand out to Travis, who took it.

"Free, this is Travis. Travis, this is Freeman," she introduced, and the two men shook hands.

"Thanks for getting her here safely," Free murmured softly, though his eyes hadn't missed the way their fingers had intertwined. Clearing his throat, he turned, gesturing behind him. "Travis, my wife Jodi, and her parents, Serenity and Levi Kendall."

Jodi stepped up, launching herself at Roxy, who caught the pregnant woman around the waist and hugged her with one arm, her other hand still twined with Travis's. The shorter, dark haired beauty's shoulders shook with tears, and Roxy laughed.

"I'm sorry," Jodi hiccupped, leaning away and swiping at her own face. "These stupid hormones have been awful."

"She cried because a hummingbird came to the feeder today before she had refilled it," Free muttered out of the corner of his mouth, and Roxy laughed again. Travis grinned.

"What if it thought I abandoned it, Freeman!" Jodi cried, waving her arms as more tears fell. Free pulled her into his arms and rocked her there gently, smoothing a large, tanned hand over her flyaway curls, and pressed a kiss to her forehead. He grinned over her head at Roxy and Travis, shaking his head lightly.

Serenity and Levi, Jodi's parents, stepped forward then. Levi was a tall bear of a man, with broad shoulders, a wide chest, and dark hair that was streaked heavily with silver. Sapphire blue eyes that matched his daughters were kind, though shrewd. Seren was a petite thing, her dark hair twisted up into a loose French twist at the back of her head. Roxy had always liked Jodi's parents; they had welcomed her into their family like she'd always belonged.

"We're glad you made the trip safely," Seren said softly, stepping forward to hug Roxy. Turning to Travis, she asked, "And who is this handsome thing?"

Roxy smiled. God it was good to be here. "Thank you for opening your doors for me when I needed it. And, this is Travis Hayes. He taught the kickboxing class I was taking, and when everything happened, he railroaded his way into driving me here." He shook his head with a chuckle, rolling his eyes down at her.

Seren extended her arms, wrapping him in a welcoming hug, which he accepted with another grin. "It's nice to meet you all."

Levi stepped forward, shaking Travis's hand firmly before ducking and dropping a kiss to the top of Roxy's head. "Welcome home, kiddo."

Seren threaded her fingers together, holding them just below her chin as she turned from one person to the next, addressing them all at once. "We'll let you two get settled in; Travis, I do assume you're staying for a while?" Without waiting for confirmation or denial, she continued, "We're having a little welcome bonfire tonight, but feel free to relax for a bit. Levi's brother Micah—Roxy, you remember Micah and my sister, Summer—are grilling up some steaks and burgers. We'll have lots of food and drinks." She pointed toward the back of the big house. "Come on out when you're ready." Seren dug a key out of her pocket, handing it over to Roxy with a smile. "Welcome home."

Free tugged Jodi along with him, calling over his shoulder, "See you in a bit."

Once left alone again, Roxy turned to Travis. "Is it bad that I just want to take a nap?"

He chuckled, wrapping her in his arms again. They swayed that way for a long moment, and Roxy just breathed him in, that now familiar scent of him filling her, calming her. "Let's get these bags carried in, and then we'll nap."

It only took two trips to carry everything up the external flight of stairs that led to the door of the loft above the barn. They merely set everything down by the door and then fell onto the queen-sized bed that took up most of the floor space in the tiny open concept bedroom. An older looking, though surprisingly comfortable sofa sat along one wall with a coffee table in front of it, and a small, flat screen tv was attached to the opposite wall. There was a full, though small, kitchenette with a tiny table and two chairs. The kitchenette was stocked with everything she could need; all the small appliances, a full refrigerator, a small stove and oven, a microwave. The bathroom was much smaller than she was used to, just a narrow standing shower, a toilet, and a sink, but everything was clean and well maintained. A compact, stacked washer and dryer were tucked into a closet.

It was small, and not at all what she would have chosen for

herself, but it was homey and smelled like lemon Pine-Sol. And, she was safe here.

Tucked against Travis's side, her head on his chest, it didn't take long for them both to drift off into sleep.

THIRTY-SEVEN

When Travis woke, the sky outside the small window across the room was darkening, dusk filtering into the small apartment, casting everything in hues of blue. Stretching, he smiled, pulling Roxy closer against him. She groaned, stretching too, and then sighed, remaining where she was, as if she was just as content as he was to continue holding each other.

Out the window that they had left propped open to allow a breeze to come through the apartment, the sounds of country music on a speaker, laughing voices, and chatter drifted to them. The scent of bonfire smoke was just beginning to make its way toward them.

"I suppose we should probably go out and mingle with my new landlords," she mumbled around a yawn, tightening her arm around his waist.

Travis swallowed hard, running his hands up and down her arms, her back. "Our new landlords."

She propped herself up on her elbow, looking up at him with wide eyes. "You mean you actually want to stay?"

He nodded slowly, letting his fingers drift through the curls that were a flyaway mess around her head. "Wherever you are, that's where I want to be, Red."

"But you have a life in Texas—"

Travis braced his hand on the back of her neck, his thumb beneath her jaw. His chest felt like an elephant was sitting on it, emotion tightening it. Or maybe that was anxiety, as he whispered, "I have a job, one that my buddy will understand if I have to leave it. I have a house that sits mostly empty, because it's never felt like home. I have spent the last twenty years just going through the motions of life. I don't want that anymore, Roxy. You came into that gym and rocked my entire being. I'm so fucking tired of fighting it, baby girl. I want whatever this is, with you. For however long we can have it. I can lay my head anywhere, as long as it's next to you. You asked me to stay… I'm saying yes, if that's what you still want."

"You'd move, just like that? For me?" she asked, her brows furrowing over her eyes in wonder. He swept his thumb over her bottom lip.

"Just like that," he whispered earnestly, staring at her. He continued to sweep his thumb over her lips, her mouth parting slightly.

"We're going to need to find somewhere else to live," she laughed, shaking her head. "This is just temporary, anyway."

"And we will, but we can take our time, too. I'm in no rush."

She scoffed, rolling her eyes. "What about any of this *isn't* rushing, Travis?"

He shrugged, sweeping her hair over her shoulder and down her back. "Does it feel rushed?"

"No," Roxy admitted, her eyes dancing in the deepening twilight that seeped into the room.

"To me either," he said, then sat up, taking her with him. "If we stay in this bed any longer, I'm going to fuck you until neither one of us can move, and that would be rude considering we have a party we're missing."

She groaned, pouting, and he laughed as he stood from the bed, bending down to kiss her smackingly on the mouth. "Come on, Red. They're waiting for us. You're going to want to change into some pants before we go out. You'll probably be cold out by the fire."

"Hardy-har," she deadpanned. "Big guy thinks he knows me."

"I do know you. You'll be a popsicle in ten minutes if you go out in shorts and a tank top, even if it is seventy degrees out." He was rifling through his duffel bag, then pulled the hoodie out of it, throwing it at her.

She shivered in revulsion. "It's only seventy out?"

Travis laughed out loud, shaking his head. "You poor, spoiled thing. Get dressed before they come and drag us out."

Ten minutes later, hand in hand, Travis led her through the deepening twilight across the expansive yard toward where the fire had been built. Cheers of welcome and more hugs—this family was a hugging family, apparently—greeted them as they stopped at the chairs that circled the ten-foot-wide fire ring. Hand crafted Adirondack chairs were scattered around, some taken, others still empty. A long, wide picnic table sat just to the side, lit by the firelight, and masses of food trays covered the top.

Roxy was pulled away by Jodi and Serenity toward the table, and Travis's eyes followed, as if taking his gaze off of her was impossible. There they were met by a taller version of Jodi, their hair the same dark brunette curls, though this woman's hair was pulled into a loose French braid that fell over her shoulder. Sisters, if he had to guess by the similarities between the two. A Carhardt hoodie was pulled tight over a rounding stomach, just a touch rounder than Jodi's.

Free walked up to him then, holding out a bottle of beer. Travis took it with a smile. "Thank you."

"No, thank you," Free said, notching his chin toward the redhead across from them. The taller pregnant woman was handing Roxy a mixed drink of some kind, and Free shook his head. "Christ, don't let Shaun make too many of those for Roxy. Shaun doesn't know what a light pour is."

Travis laughed, grinning. "That your wife's sister?"

"Yeah," Free chuckled, nodding. "That's Shauntelle. Her husband is, ahh—" Free stepped aside as another figure joined them where they stood. He was tall, blonde, with storm cloud blue eyes. Travis stared for a long minute, trying to place where he recognized the man from. "This is my cousin, Kasey. Kasey is Shaun's husband, they just got married what, two months ago?"

The tall blonde extended a hand to Travis, and he shook it firmly. "Almost two months, yeah."

"And both sisters are pregnant?" Travis asked, gesturing to both women's rounding stomachs. Free laughed out loud, and the blonde, Kasey, groaned.

"Due four weeks apart," Kasey muttered, shaking his head. "God help us. We're due with twins in September."

Travis's eyebrows shot up. "Wow, congratulations."

"So how do you know my cousin?" Kasey asked, notching his chin toward Roxy. Raising a bottle of beer to his mouth, he took a long pull, those gray-blue eyes laser focused on Travis.

"Uhh, I teach a kickboxing class that she was in. Roxy is your cousin, too?" Travis asked. He glanced between Free and Kasey, then to Roxy. "Doesn't that make Roxy your cousin, Free?"

"Nah, Kasey is my cousin on my mom's side of the family, and Kasey and Roxy are like fourth cousins by marriage on his dad's side or something," Free laughed. His striking aquamarine eyes came to Travis then, understanding lighting in those eyes. "I'm assuming she told you?"

Travis didn't have to ask what he meant. He nodded. The man

standing in front of him was good looking, his dark hair worn slightly longer than was fashionable, and a dark, closely trimmed beard darkened the lower half of his face. Despite the assurance from Roxy that their relationship had never been more than sex purely for maintenance purposes, he couldn't help the flash of jealousy that coursed through him, knowing this man had been with her. "She did."

"Good, I'm glad she did," Free said quietly, looking over toward the redhead.

The hoodie that Travis had given her was huge on her, hanging down below the curves of her ass, and the too long sleeves had been pushed to her wrists. The sight of her in his clothing was enough to make him feral; she was *his*.

"I hope you understand that I love Roxy with my whole heart," Free said. "She's my best friend, aside from Jodi—" Kasey made a disgruntled sound at that, and Free rolled his eyes before continuing quietly, "—and that part of our history is just that; ancient history. She knew before I did that my heart belonged up here with that little thing—" He smiled lovingly over at Jodi, who was talking animatedly to the other three women, who were laughing. Travis watched as her hand dipped to cradle the swell of her belly, and he turned to witness the love radiating from the other man's eyes as he watched. The aching tightness in his chest eased slightly, that feral possessiveness tempering just a little. Freeman turned his attention back to Travis, who took another long pull of the beer clutched tightly in his fingers, waiting. "I'm in your debt for getting her here safely. I'm glad there were no issues."

"Fuck, me too," Travis chuffed roughly, rubbing the back of his neck with his empty hand. "After that blown tire in Kansas, I was sure that bastard was going to catch up with us."

"It took two days for that tire to get fixed?" Kasey asked, and Travis's attention was brought back to the tall guy with movie star good looks that stood with them. He still couldn't place his face, but damn did he look familiar.

"Uhh, yeah. We had to stay an extra night," Travis mumbled around another drink of his beer. Shit, would these two try and kick his ass for sleeping with their friend?

"Mmhmm," Free hummed, chuckling, grinning knowingly. Turning to Kasey, he asked, "How long did it take you and Shaun to leave the bedroom after—"

"She hightailed it all the way from Colorado back home the morning after. And like you're one to talk, fucker," Kasey grunted, shifting on his feet. "Pretty sure you and Jodi were shacked up for like a week before either of you made a public appearance—"

"Was not a week," Free protested, but he was grinning. "And my lady didn't run away from me. Maybe you didn't know what you were doing—"

An arm banded around Freeman's neck in a chokehold, but the two men were laughing. "If I didn't know what I was doing, how'd I knock her up that first fucking night, asshole? How long did it take you?"

Free's hands were clutching the forearm around his neck. Travis watched on, a shocked grin tugging at his mouth. The women had stopped chatting and were now watching the two men as they struggled. "We weren't actively *trying* until after the wedding, you jackass, and it only took—"

"Welcome to the chaos," Roxy muttered as she sidled up to him, sliding her hand in his. He turned to look at her, though she was watching the two men as they continued to grumble at each other. "I see you've met Kasey. He's taking a hiatus this upcoming season to be here for Shaun and the babies."

"A hiatus from what?"

She glanced up at him. "K.C. Corcoran? Nascar driver? Number 33?"

"Shit, I knew he looked familiar, just couldn't place the face," Travis muttered, shaking his head. "K.C. Corcoran is your cousin?"

Roxy shrugged, lifting the red solo cup to her lips. "I think his dad's uncle's kid married my mom's second cousin or something. It's confusing. I'd have to draw it out to explain it better. We didn't even know about the connection until after I'd met Freeman—who is Kasey's first cousin on their mom's sides—it's weird." She turned then. "Travis, this is Shaun, Jodi's sister and Kasey's wife."

Refusing to let go of her hand, he simply nodded at the woman that stepped up beside her. "Nice to meet you."

Shaun knocked her shoulder into Roxy's and grinned up at him. "Hello, handsome."

"*Woman*—" Kasey's dark growl cut through the air and he finally relinquished his chokehold on Freeman, straightening.

Shaun rolled dark, sapphire blue eyes, still grinning widely. "Oh please, do you not have eyes? Good lord, Roxy, please tell me you've—"

Kasey's menacing growl turned feral and then she was being swept up in her husband's arms and carted off, her barking laugh bouncing around them. As Kasey hauled her away, Travis heard him growl at her, "I'll turn this ass pink, *wife*."

"Promises, promises, *husband*," she purred back as he set her down on the opposite side of the fire, looping her arms around his neck and pressing her rounded belly against his abdomen. Travis swallowed and looked away. This family was certifiably insane.

It was amazing.

Having grown up the way he did, the life he'd lived, he didn't have any experience with a big, loud family such as the Kendall's. It was bizarre and overwhelming, but damn was it entertaining, and the love and caring he could sense pouring out of all of them for each other was a welcome change from the solitary life he'd always led. And they had just absorbed Roxy into it, no questions asked, as if she'd been part of it forever.

"Shauntelle and Kasey, we have company," Serenity's voice cut through, chastising lightly, but the two just laughed. "You'll scare poor Travis off."

"I doubt that," Roxy laughed, looking up at him. "If I haven't scared him off yet, I don't think it's possible."

"I don't scare easily," he responded, winking down at her. She shivered, curling her fingers into the long sleeves of his hoodie and holding the red solo cup between her material clad hands. Draping his arm over her shoulders, he pulled her against his side. "Are you cold?"

"A little," she admitted, but lifted her hands—swathed completely in the long sleeves—and took a drink from her cup. "I'll just move closer to the fire. Are you hungry?"

"Starving," he murmured quietly against the shell of her ear, and when he felt her shiver against him, he knew it wasn't from the cold. His cock jumped in his jeans. Fuck. Groaning into her ear, he husked, "We're surrounded by your family and all I can think about is how badly I want to eat this pussy as my meal."

"*Travis*," Roxy hissed under her breath, but her eyes met his and he recognized the hunger in them. It matched his own.

A hard slap to his back startled him, and he looked over to find Levi Kendall had sidled up to the both of them, his blue eyes twinkling in the firelight. He leaned down close to both of them and rumbled roughly, "Didn't anyone ever teach you kids to eat your dinner first, and then dessert?"

THIRTY-EIGHT

By the time eleven o'clock rolled around, Roxy was an icicle, despite sitting as close to the fire as possible without being physically in it. Travis sat next to her in one of the handcrafted Adirondack chairs that she knew Levi himself had built. She'd tucked her feet up on the chair she sat in, pulling her knees to her chest and then sliding the extra-large hoodie over them clear to her feet so she was a big ball inside the hoodie itself.

"Are you ready to go in for the night?" Travis asked from beside her, and she shook her head. He was in jeans and his usual cutoff t-shirt, but he seemed perfectly comfortable. The other men were dressed similarly in jeans and t-shirts, though Levi had on a long sleeved Carhartt with the sleeves pushed to his forearms. Serenity and Shaun had gone inside, while Jodi had fallen asleep curled in Free's lap.

Travis's thumb stroked across the backs of her knuckles. He had been deep in conversation with Levi and Kasey, but his hand held hers captive where they rested together on the armrest between them. He'd hardly let her go throughout the evening. If anyone had doubts of what was going on between them before, there were none now.

"No, I like being out here with everyone. I'm just chilled."

"Do you want me to go grab a blanket from the house?" Free asked from where he sat with Jodi curled in his lap in another chair.

"No, don't get up," Roxy said, indicating the sleeping Jodi on his chest.

Travis unfurled his fingers from around hers. "I'll go get it."

"No, Travis, you're in the middle of a conversation. I can walk across the yard to get a blanket," she muttered dryly, pulling her legs from beneath the hoodie. Leaning over to him, she pecked a quick kiss to his bearded cheek. "You got me here safely, Travis. Neal isn't here to hurt me."

He nodded, though those honey brown eyes searched hers for a long heartbeat. They looked almost golden in the firelight, so beautiful it sent an ache deep into her chest. This gentle, kind, beautiful man had stolen every single piece of her heart, she knew it without doubt.

She loved Travis Hayes.

"I'll be right back," she whispered, her throat closing with emotion that threatened to suffocate her. She was going to say those words that were on the very tip of her tongue, blurt them out right here and now. But she didn't want to do that, she wanted to tell him later, when it was just the two of them. Because it had always been just the two of them, hadn't it? From the moment they'd met…it had been inevitable.

They had been inevitable. A fight that neither one of them could win. Or, maybe in this, they were both the winners.

Slipping away from the fire, she hurried across the darkened yard toward the barn and their new loft apartment several hundred yards away. Pulling the hoodie around her more securely, she shivered, but for the first time, she felt safe. She glanced around her, not to check for an unwelcome stare, but to appreciate the space around her. The gentle summer breeze that drifted across the property, carrying more of that heady, fragrant lilac scent with it. Roxy remembered the pretty purple blossoms that Travis had cut for her earlier and rushed up the steps, eager to find a vase or even just a cup to place them in.

Up the steps and into the small apartment, Roxy flipped the light switch on and crossed to the line of cupboards next to the fridge, opening several until she found a tall crystal water glass. Filling it with water from the sink, she then fluffed the blossoms they'd left sitting on the tiny table, placing the stems in the water. Centering it on the table, she smiled, then leaned forward and inhaled deeply. That deep anxiety that she had lived with for the last several months lifted, leaving behind space for joy and peace and love in its wake. Tears pricked her eyes and stung her nose.

Spinning slowly on her sneakered feet, she surveyed the tiny apartment. Travis's duffel was perched on the edge of the bed, opened and clothes half strewn out of it from when he'd been digging for his hoodie to give her. Always looking out for her, protecting her. She wouldn't have to worry, not anymore. She was safe. Safe with Travis. And that meant that it was time for her gun to find a new home, packed away, because she didn't need it anymore. Not with Travis at her side.

Crossing the room to her purse, she stopped, nearly stumbling. The neon orange hit her first, and then her hand shook violently, fear and dread and panic warring inside her so brutally she thought she might throw up. The neon orange post it note sat gently atop her purse where she'd left it when they'd got in, that damning, hateful, familiar scrawl a cruel reminder that she was in fact never going to be safe. Never going to be free of him.

You can't run from me, Rox.
And I'll kill him for touching you.

. . .

HER VISION DARKENED AS HER BREATH WAS STOLEN OUT OF HER lungs by vicious claws, anxiety so potent she feared she may pass out. Shoving the note off her purse, her hands shook as she pried the purse open, digging through it. A sob broke out of her throat when her fingers closed around nothing where the small handgun should have been. *No. No no no no.*

Fingers closing around another scrap of paper, tears sprang to her eyes when she removed it and read the words written on a second neon orange post it.

Did you really think you could keep a gun hidden from me!

FOOTSTEPS ON THE STAIRS BEHIND HER MADE HER JUMP, HER heart kicking viciously in her chest. Snatching both notes in her hand, she crumpled them, shoving her hands into the front pocket of the hoodie just as Travis opened the door, stepping inside. Her heart broke at the gentle smile that tipped up his mouth, those golden eyes that saw every single broken piece of her.

She schooled her features as best she could, smiling up at him as he closed the door and crossed toward her. Catching her by the shoulders, he rubbed his hands up and down her arms, as if to warm her.

"You didn't have to come find me," she whispered, her voice breaking. His brows drew together, but she smiled up at him. "I was just putting our flowers in some water so they don't die."

"Free just left with Jodi, and Kasey said he needed to get Shaun home and to bed before she turned into a gremlin or something," he chuckled lightly, shaking his head. "And I couldn't stand one more second away from you."

That crack that had begun in her chest widened. This was so unfair! And Neal's threat; she had no doubts he would kill Travis if he got the chance. She needed to make him leave, somehow. As soon as possible. If he had any inkling that Neal had found her, he wouldn't go, he would stay, and she couldn't stand the thought of him being hurt, of him dying— Her heart shattered in her chest, the ache nearly taking her to her knees.

His hands slid back up her arms, one going to the nape of her neck where he fisted his fingers into her hair, the other sliding to the front to collar her throat. It centered her, brought her back to him, as he tipped her chin up. Mouth descending on hers, he breathed, "I said our goodnights to everyone. Now, I want you naked, Red. I want you naked and on your back on the bed so I can eat this pretty pussy until you come all over my tongue."

He kissed her then, thoroughly, drinking in her moans as she arched against him. Pulling the hoodie up and over her head in one swift tug, he dropped it to the floor, then reached for her shirt. She was naked in moments, shoving the jeans down her legs and tossing her sneakers away as he divested himself of clothes. Until he stood as naked as she was, every delicious, muscled, tattooed inch of him on display for her.

The light in the tiny kitchen illuminated just enough of the bedroom for them to see each other. She wanted to see all of him, wanted to imprint him on her mind, on her body, like he was on her heart, her very soul. If this was the last night she would have with him, she was going to take everything, give every particle of herself to him. Even if he didn't know, and even if he would never understand in the morning.

She reached for him as he did for her, fingers frantic as she touched everywhere, following with her lips, her tongue. Dropping to her knees in front of him, he growled from above her, fisting her hair in his hands again. "Roxy, I said get on the bed."

"I want this first," she whispered, fisting his hard length in her hand, pumping from root to tip and back. His head tipped back with a raspy groan as she took him in her mouth. Looking up the length of his hard, tattooed body, her core tightened. She was so wet she ached. Clenching her thighs together, she bobbed her head, taking him to the back of her throat again and again. His thighs bunched and flexed beneath the palm of her left hand, and when he began to thrust, meeting her, she moaned around his length. His hand stroked her cheek, tenderly, sweeping beneath her chin. Eyes watering, she stared up at him from beneath her lashes.

"Fuck," he snarled, clenching her hair tight enough to sting sharply, hauling her off of him. "Goddamn, Red. If you don't stop—"

"I didn't say to stop," she panted, licking her lips. She dropped her eyes to the steely length of him, which twitched. "I want to taste you."

Grasping the back of her neck with one hand and fisting his cock with the other, he guided the tip back to her mouth. She opened, greedy for him.

"Stick out your tongue," he rasped from above her, and she did, electricity zinging across her every nerve, lighting her up at his rough demand. "Show me where you want my cum, baby girl."

Roxy watched as he pumped his hand, and then his abs contracted, his thighs bunching. The hand at the back of her neck tightened, and then he groaned harshly as he came, painting her tongue with his release. His panting breaths heaved his chest like a bellows, but his eyes never left hers.

"So pretty," he breathed, releasing the nape of her neck and sweeping his fingers across her cheek, his thumb sliding over her bottom lip. "Fuck, Roxy. Get on that goddamn bed and spread those pretty legs for me."

Staggering to her feet, her knees ached, legs wobbling. He chuckled as she lowered herself to her back, and then he was on his knees before her. Spreading his hands wide on the inside of her thighs, he pushed her legs apart as he settled in, licking and suckling until she was a writhing, panting mess. Fingers fisted in his long hair, she bowed off the bed with a cry when she came, his tongue dancing wickedly around her clit. His approving hum thrummed through her and her legs shook where he'd laid them over his shoulders.

He rose from the floor, his gaze an inferno as he stared down at her nakedness. She expected him to climb over her, but he reached for her, flipping her over onto her stomach.

THIRTY-NINE

"On your hands and knees, woman," he rasped, letting his palm crack on one of her ass cheeks sharply. Redness bloomed there, and then he soothed it with his palm, rubbing and stroking as she did as she was told, rising onto her hands and knees on the mattress. Kneeling behind her, he used his knees to notch hers further apart, then gripped his aching cock in one hand, pumping it from root to tip several times. Feeling her come on his tongue, her hands in his hair, had gotten him hard again. He would never get enough of her.

Running the blunt head along her wet, glistening folds, he pushed in. Transfixed, he watched with hooded eyes as her body swallowed him whole, the sight of his hardness disappearing inside that tight pussy hot enough to make him see stars already. "You are so fucking perfect, Roxy. *Fuck.* Do you feel how well we fit together? You take all of me so fucking prettily."

Dropping his hands to the slope of her waist, he spanned his fingers wide across her hips as she moved, shifting forward and then throwing herself back against him. Her head dropped between her shoulders, arms outstretched and holding herself off the mattress. She repeated the movement, moaning sharply when he went deep.

"Yes, oh fuck. *Just like that*. Fuck yourself on my cock," he grunted, holding still as she continued to move on him, throwing her hips back as hard as she could, slamming him in as deep as she could take him, as deep as he could go. Over and over again, she rode him from in front. His mouth dropped open, brows drawing together into a deep V as he struggled to hold his orgasm at bay, fighting back the words that he ached to say. He loved her. He loved her. He loved her. He wanted to tell her, so that she knew how fucking important she was to him. She was everything. But he didn't want to tell her like this. When he said those three words for the first time, it needed to be perfect.

"*Goddamn*. Take what you want, baby girl. Take all of it," he whispered raggedly. "Take everything I have."

"Travis," she mewled, her back arching low, her round ass high. He grasped her hips hard in his hands and hammered into her, over and over again. She was quivering around him, tightening, and she sobbed, "I'm going to—*Travis*—"

Wrapping his hand around her throat, he hauled her up so that her back was flush against his chest, his other arm banding around her waist. Her head was thrown back against his shoulder, her eyes squeezed tightly shut, mouth dropping open in a silent scream as she came. Her abdomen contracted wildly, her thighs shook, her pussy squeezing the fucking life out of him as he continued to slam into her.

"Fucking *breathe*, Red," he rasped raggedly into her ear, because the fucking woman had stopped breathing as she came around him so hard it drew his own from him.

Harder, faster he thrust, until the tingle at the base of his spine ignited into sparks shooting through every one of his extremities. Vision tunneling, he came hard, emptying into her with long, hot bursts. Panting, chest heaving against her back pressed tightly to him with each breath, he held onto her as the world righted itself around them. She was trembling, whole body shaking violently with the force of her climax and the aftershocks, still upright, her back pressed fully to his chest.

Sobs shook her then, and she clutched at his forearm still banded around her middle with trembling fingers. He turned her face toward him, covering her mouth with his, kissing her with every ounce of hunger and possessiveness that coursed through him. Tears tracked down her cheeks, and he swiped at them with his fingers. Still they kissed, pouring everything into the other. All the words he ached to say, but wouldn't let himself. Not yet.

Gentle, sipping kisses replaced the fervent ones from before, but tears still trekked down her cheeks. "Roxy," he whispered against her mouth. "Breathe, my love."

A hiccupping sob escaped her, and then she was pulling away from him, turning in his arms. She threw her arms around his neck, burrowing her face in his throat as she clung to him. Her shoulders shook with her tears, and he hated it. It crushed his chest into dust.

"What's wrong?" he asked, smoothing his hands over her hair as they sank into a sitting position on the bed. He cradled her close, but she shook her head. Finally, the tears seemed to slow. "Was I too rough?"

"God no," Roxy laughed huskily, leaning away to swipe at her face with the heels of her hands. Leaning her cheek against his chest, directly over where his heart beat beneath it, she sighed, closing her eyes. "You're perfect, Travis. This is everything I've ever wanted."

Chest aching, throat burning to say the words, he swallowed them down. "Come on, baby girl. Let's get some sleep. I think it's been an emotional couple of days."

She nodded, allowing him to tuck her in. He padded into the tiny bathroom—they really would need to find something bigger soon, this loft was miniature in comparison to his bulk—and returned with a warm, wet washcloth. He cleaned her up, shushing her with a stern look when she protested, and then slid into the bed behind her, curving his arm around her waist and pulling her tight against his chest.

"Go to sleep, Roxy," he whispered, pressing his lips to the back of her neck. She snuggled into him, wrapping her arms around his arm that was banded around her. "I've got you. Always."

FORTY

Roxy waited until Travis's breath had slowed into deep, even breaths before she slid out from beneath his arm. Padding over to the door, she double and triple checked the lock. It seemed secure, but so had her house in Melody Hills.

Crossing quietly to the fridge, she opened it just a crack, not wanting the light to wake Travis. Pulling a bottled water out of the pre-stocked fridge—she was sure she had Jodi and Serenity to thank for that—she drank half of it while standing by the tiny kitchen table. Moonlight filtered through the small windows on the other side of the room, slices of silvery blue light arcing across the bed and the man that lay in it, the sheet barely covering his lower half, one leg thrust out from beneath it.

He looked peaceful as he slept and so beautiful she ached from loving him. It had crept up on her, stealthy and slow, and she had had no chance of fighting it. She had possibly fallen in love with him the day she'd woken in his lap after passing out. When he'd let her see the soft, quiet Travis behind the former MMA fighter 'The Reaper' that he let everyone else see. Or maybe it was the day he'd called her out on her bullshit, and then had still taken care of her even after she had acted like a temper tantrum throwing brat.

Or that night, when he'd confessed to being dazzled by her.

She'd been just as dazzled by him. His quiet grace, the beauty in his strength, the careful way he caged everyone else out. Everyone except for her. He had let her see all of his brokenness, all of his shadows, all of the scars that he carried both on his mind and his body.

He was everything she had never known she wanted, had never allowed herself even the thought to cross her mind that someone like Travis could be hers. That a love like Freeman had found with Jodi, like Kasey had found with Shauntelle, could ever belong to her, too.

Despair fairly choked her. Everything she'd fought so hard for, everything she'd run from… it had all been for nothing. Because he would always find her.

Her eyes burned from both exhaustion and from her tears, but she refused to let her eyes close. She couldn't sleep, despite the late hour. Not with Neal out there, probably watching, waiting for her to be vulnerable. She wouldn't let Travis get hurt because of her. She would rather cut out her own heart than to put him at risk.

Sinking into one corner of the couch, she flipped through Facebook, watched TikToks, and scrolled Instagram. Every creak and groan of the old barn around her made fear rachet her heart into her throat. Every shadow that drifted across the floor from the windows by the door caused her eyes to flash toward them, watching for him. The clock moved at an agonizingly slow pace, the minutes drawing out interminably. She tried to read on an ebook app for a while, but nothing held her attention, until her eyelids became too heavy to remain open. Checking the clock, she sighed. In another hour the sun would be up, and Travis would be waking.

And she would be forced to give up the best thing that's ever happened to her. If only to keep him safe, as he'd done for her.

Sliding back into the bed, she curled against his side, allowing herself this last little bit of time with him. In moments she was asleep.

FORTY-ONE

"Good morning," Roxy murmured as she stepped up onto the wide, covered front porch of the big house. Serenity sat in a hand-crafted Adirondack rocking chair, cup of coffee balanced on the armrest. She'd waved at Roxy from across the wide yard as soon as she'd stepped down the loft stairs.

"Good morning," Jodi's mother said with a wide, kind smile. These people, they were some of the best. Which meant Roxy would have to leave them, too, so none of them would be hurt by Neal. "There's coffee ready in the kitchen, feel free to help yourself. Fallon stayed at a friend's house for the weekend, and Levi and Freeman went out early to check a stretch of fence, so it's just us here. Jodi works this morning, but she'll probably come over around two this afternoon when she gets out. The guys should be back in about an hour."

Roxy nodded, stepping into the massive, beautiful home. She knew that Levi had made a name in the small northern Michigan town, that he simultaneously ran the largest equestrian boarding ranch in the area, as well as owning a successful construction company. The man was worth millions, easily, but you'd never tell by looking at the man. His jeans were always well worn and covered in a fine layer of dirt, his boots were scuffed, and his hands were callused from years of hard work right alongside his employees. Roxy adored the big, gruff guy, and the petite, gentle woman that was his counterpart.

She poured herself a cup of coffee and rejoined Seren out on the porch, lowering herself into a matching rocking chair beside the older woman. Travis had woken before her, and when she'd finally awoke after not enough sleep, the sound of the water running in the shower of the tiny bathroom had alerted her to where he was. She'd slipped out of the loft before he'd emerged from the bathroom, not entirely sure she was ready to face him yet, knowing what she had to do.

She had a plan, but executing it was going to be difficult and painful, for both of them. She hated it.

"Did you sleep alright?" Serenity asked from beside her, the woman's blue eyes on her, a slight V pushing her brows together in worry. "I know it's probably a lot smaller than you're used to—"

"Umm," Roxy hedged, but sighed. She didn't want to lie anymore to the woman than she needed to. "I didn't, actually. I think the last several days have finally caught up to me, and my mind just wouldn't shut off."

Seren reached out and squeezed her hand gently. "You've had a lot happen, Roxy. It's okay to not be okay right now. Lean on those that care about you; you're here now, so you don't have to do this alone."

Tears pricked her eyes and she blinked rapidly to fight them back. Seren tutted, waving her hands frantically.

"Oh, please don't cry," she whispered, leaning forward in her seat. Grabbing Roxy's shoulders, she had no choice but to sink into the embrace as the older woman wrapped her in a hug. The kind only a mother can give. "I'm a firm believer in no one cries alone, so if you cry, I cry, too."

Roxy laughed, taking a deep, steadying breath before letting it out. Squeezing the woman tightly for just a moment longer, she pulled back. "I can't thank you and your family enough for what you've done for me."

Serenity tucked a stray curl behind Roxy's ear and she smiled, those blue eyes that were so like her daughters' shining. "You're family now, too."

Roxy nodded, picking up her coffee as Seren leaned back into her chair. Taking a sip of the coffee, she scanned her eyes around the expansive ranch. "It really is so beautiful up here."

"Springtime has always been my favorite," Serenity laughed. Pointing toward a wall of purple and white along the far edge of the property, she said, "We bought this property simply because of that stand of lilac trees. They're stunning in full bloom, like now. They'll only last another week or so, but when the wind picks up just a little, you can smell them all the way over here. Levi usually brings me fresh sprigs every few days while they last."

"Travis cut me a few yesterday when we drove through— Mackinaw?" When Seren nodded, letting her know that her question was correct, she continued. "They're in a glass on the table now."

"I see the way he watches you," Serenity said softly. "It's like you're the sun, and he just gravitates around you. It's beautiful to see that kind of devotion."

Roxy swallowed around a knot in her throat, then picked at a chip in one of the Adirondack chairs with her nail. "It's not like that for us. He'll be leaving soon."

"Oh?" she asked, her brows raising. "It didn't seem like that was the plan."

"Umm, well it wasn't, entirely," she hedged, shrugging her shoulders. "But he has a life in Texas that I can't just expect him to walk away from."

The woman's blue eyes felt like lasers on her. She felt a blush crawling up her chest. "Yet, you were the one that pushed Freeman to leave Texas to follow where his heart was beating."

"That's different," Roxy whispered, her chest tight. "Free had been in love with Jodi for years, as had Jodi with him… It made sense for him, for them."

"And it doesn't make sense for you two?"

"Maybe if we had had more time… But this is asking too much of him. I can't do that."

"Does he feel like it's asking too much?" she asked quietly. "Because I don't think that's how he would see it."

"It's just not the right time," Roxy argued, tossing her curls over her shoulder as she took another drink of her coffee. "He needs to go back to Texas, to get away from all of this, to make sure he's not making a rash decision. Once he's back home, he'll see."

Out of the corner of her eye, Roxy watched as the woman leaned back in her chair, rocking slowly. After a few minutes of tense silence, she glanced over.

"Is there by any chance a computer or laptop I could use just for a few minutes? And a printer?" Roxy asked.

"Of course, in the office," Serenity said, pushing herself to stand. Roxy followed through the house to a spacious, bookshelf lined office. "Everything is wifi connected, so it's all ready for whatever you need."

"Thank you, I won't be long," Roxy said, nodding. When Serenity had left her alone, she sat down in the comfiest office chair she'd ever sat in, and got to work.

Forty-Two

Travis was alone in the loft when he emerged from his shower, towel wrapped around his waist. He walked over to the window and could just see Roxy sitting on the porch with Serenity. He smiled, watching them together. She would be okay here. Safe with this wonderful family. With him.

By the time he'd towel dried and dressed, the two women had disappeared from the porch. Down the loft steps, he was just glancing around when he heard hoofbeats. Turning, he grinned when Freeman and Levi rounded another large boarding barn, both on horseback.

They trotted closer to him, stopping several yards away, their horses prancing in place. Dust stirred at their feet. "Morning."

"Morning, to you," Free drawled, notching his chin toward the loft at Travis's back. "I know it's tiny, but we made sure the bed was comfortable."

"I do feel a little like a bull in a China shop in there," Travis laughed, rubbing the back of his neck with one hand. He'd pulled his hair up into a half bun on the back of his head. "But it's comfortable, thank you."

It felt like he had hardly slept, the time change messing with his internal clock something fierce. His body was screaming at him that it was only five-thirty in the morning, but the clock inside the loft read eight-thirty. It would take some getting used to.

"Want to come in for some coffee?" Levi asked, gesturing toward the big house. "We just have to settle these two in at the barn and we'll be done."

Travis nodded, rubbing the back of his neck. "Coffee sounds great."

Levi chuckled then. "The time difference takes some getting used to."

"Are you a transplant, too?" Travis asked. He walked alongside them as they turned the two horses toward the largest of the barns, then set off at a slow pace.

"Born and raised in Texas, then went to New Mexico for college. After my parents died, my brother and I came up here—our parents had moved here after retiring—to get their estate closed out. I met Serenity, and the rest was history. Been here almost twenty-five years, now."

Alighting from their steeds inside the massive barn, a ranch hand took over. Both men thanked the man, and then the three of them sauntered back out into the early morning sunshine. Everything was so green and lush here. Perfectly blue skies with fluffy white clouds.

The three of them made their way toward the big house, climbing the steps to the wide front porch. Several Adirondack chairs dotted the covered porch, but Levi led them inside. The house was stunning, and he admired it as they walked through toward the kitchen.

"Oh, good morning," Serenity murmured with a smile as they walked in. Levi skirted the massive white marble island in the center of the large space, his long strides eating up the distance between himself and his wife. He wrapped one arm around her middle, pulling her close as he swiped the dark brown cowboy hat off his head, setting it on the counter beside them. He ducked his head, kissing her thoroughly. When he pulled back, she whispered, "Levi Kendall, we have guests…"

"If I have to witness that one—" he muttered darkly, gesturing to Freeman over his shoulder, who was currently pouring three cups of coffee out of the carafe on the wide counter, "—kissing our daughter, then he can suffer through me saying hello to my wife."

"I'm just glad you got that out of your system after that punch," Free muttered, then grinned over at Travis.

Seren pushed her husband away with a roll of her eyes. "I still can't believe you hit him right before Shane's wedding. You're lucky Jodi could fix it with concealer, poor Cassie's photos would have looked like a trainwreck."

Levi harumphed something unintelligible, but accepted the cup of coffee Free extended toward him. Travis nodded in thanks as Free handed him one as well, watching the three of them with slightly raised eyebrows. Free chuckled, leaning his hips back against the marble countertop. "Levi didn't take well to the idea of me and Jodi, at first."

Taking a drink of his coffee, he nodded slowly, remembering the story that Roxy had told him. "You two have been friends for a long time, right?"

"My younger brother and I lost our mom when I was seventeen, and our dad was never in the picture. We bounced around family for a bit, but I was young and grieving. I decided to up and leave my aunt's house, and my little brother came with me. We managed to make it up here where we thought our dad had some family, but our car broke down and we were hungry and cold. Found this little half dilapidated shack back on some property. We started a fire and a little while later this big motherfucker showed up with a shotgun in hand, scared the piss out of both of us. Then this little dark-haired kid convinced him to let us stay. Levi and Seren took both myself and my brother in, gave us a place to live, gave me a job, gave my life a purpose again. Gave me a family, and the best friends a guy could ask for." He smiled over at Seren and Levi, and Travis watched on as Free continued. "About ten years later, that dark-haired kid that had convinced her dad to let me stay... I realized that she had become more to me. But she was still young, way too young for me. I kissed her, and then hated myself for it, because I never wanted to stop."

Travis glanced at Levi, who was staring at the floor between his scuffed boots. Seren had one hand splayed wide on his chest, rubbing gently.

"I left that night, didn't explain to anyone why, other than my brother. I went back to Texas, absolutely wrecked inside. My cousin—Kasey, who you met yesterday—convinced me to go out with him one night about a week after I'd gotten back, and I met Roxy. She knew as soon as she met me that I was a fucking mess. I loved Jodi, even back then, and nothing was going to change that. Came back for my brothers wedding what, seven years later?" When Seren nodded, he chuckled, shaking his head. "Jodi had me poleaxed within ten minutes of being back. Leaving her again was impossible. So I did what I had to do, and confessed everything to my best friend. He took the news well, considering I'd made out with his eighteen-year-old when I was twenty-seven—"

"Alright, enough," Levi grumbled, shooting the younger man a death glare. "I don't want to be reminded of that, you bastard. That punch was well-deserved, and you know it."

Travis and Free laughed, as Free nodded in agreement. "Never said it wasn't. Roxy was the one that convinced me to not give up on Jodi, even though I was fucking terrified. She's a good wing-man."

Travis laughed then, taking another drink of his coffee. "Speaking of Roxy, has anyone seen her this morning?"

Seren nodded, gesturing with her own coffee cup toward the hallway. "She's in the office, do you want me to show you the way?"

"Nah," he said, shaking his head. "I know she has a lot to arrange back in Texas still, I don't need to bother her."

"What is *your* plan?" Free asked, eyeing him shrewdly. Travis took another drink, contemplating how to respond, but it was Seren that responded first.

"I think she's feeling a little overwhelmed this morning," she said quietly. "Be gentle with her, both of you." Free gasped in feigned outrage, but Travis nodded solemnly. "A lot has changed for her in the last week, even just the last few days. Be patient with her, Travis. She's not used to having this kind of support system, and I know it can be jarring at first, when she's been so used to being self-sufficient for so long."

Travis swallowed, staring into the dark depths of his coffee. A soft hand touched his elbow and he looked up into the soft blue eyes of the woman in front of him, and she smiled gently. "Don't be upset if she tries to push you away out of fear, okay? And don't take it personally, if she does. It's a form of self-defense, self-preservation. I promise you, she'll come around, after she settles in."

He nodded, hoping like hell that wasn't the case, because he wasn't going anywhere.

FORTY-THREE

Thumping her head back against the wall of the hallway, Roxy swore fiercely in her head. *No, no no no. Don't tell him that. Don't give him hope when I have to break his fucking heart!*

Her plan was printed and folded neatly in her hand. It had to work.

Padding silently back toward the office door, she made a production of making sure they heard her coming this time. Smiling tightly at all of them, she raised her now empty coffee cup. "Thank you for the coffee, Seren, and for letting me use the computer." Daring a glance at Travis, she wished she hadn't. His eyes, those beautiful, golden eyes, lightened when they connected with her own. Heat spread through her, that now familiar warmth that only he could induce, as if just being near him, being seen by him, could make everything else disappear. She loved him so much she ached with it, and hated herself even more for what she was doing. Setting the empty cup in the sink, she murmured, "I'm gonna head back to the loft and shower."

She avoided Travis's gaze as she slipped out of the kitchen, walking quickly across the yard to the barn. Climbing the stairs, she hid in the bathroom, taking a longer than necessary shower before taking an obnoxious amount of time getting herself dressed. Combing through her mess of curls with curl cream, drying it with the diffuser, and then covering some of the bruising with concealer.

When she exited, she was surprised that Travis wasn't waiting for her, but one glance out the window showed that he was crossing the yard. Grabbing her purse, she slid it on over her shoulder and waited until he had climbed the stairs, pushing the door open to enter.

"Hey, good morning," he murmured quietly, stepping toward her. She smiled tightly, but managed to avoid his embrace. If he put his arms around her, if he held her, she would break.

"Morning," she whispered, beelining for the door. "I'm going to run to the store real quick for a few things. I'll be right back."

"Would you like me to go with you?" he asked, stepping back toward the door with her.

She shook her head vehemently, snapping out a harsh, "No!" He stopped, his light brown brows lowering over his eyes briefly. "I mean, no, I'll be fine. I just have to grab some umm, some— Some stuff."

His eyebrows rose, his eyes crinkling at the corners as he smiled. "Ahh. I understand."

He did?

"You don't have to be embarrassed around me, I hope you know that," he said, tucking his hands into his pockets. "I'm not afraid of a little blood."

Blood?

Oooohhhhh. He thought she'd started her period. She lowered her eyes to the floor, playing it off. "Uhh, right. Well, I'm just going to go get that *stuff*—"

"I'll be here when you get back. But if you want me to help—"

"No, I'm fine. Thank you." She bolted for the door, fairly flying down the stairs as she escaped. Her cheeks felt like they were on fire.

Only after she'd climbed in behind the wheel of her car and headed down the driveway did she question whether this was a good idea. Neal was watching her, she knew that. Knew that he knew where to find her. Then again, maybe this would make it easier. If she just disappeared—

But she made it to the small grocer down the road with no issues, grabbed a few random items, then doubled back to grab a box of tampons just for show—and was headed back to Blue Haven without having killed nearly enough time. She needed to avoid him for as long as possible, before she had to cleave what they'd started in two.

He wasn't in the loft when she got back, and the night of little to no sleep caught up with her. Sliding into the bed beneath the sheets, she pulled them up to her chin, closing her eyes.

When she woke, her back was curled against Travis's chest, his heavy, warm arm draped over her waist, holding her to him tightly. His deep, even breathing told her he was asleep, too. The days of driving and the time difference and the lack of sleep the night before had clearly drained them both.

Sliding out from under his arm, she sighed when he didn't wake up, and she disappeared into the bathroom. Washing her hands, she stepped out, surprised to see him awake and sitting up on the bed. "Are you feeling better?"

Nodding, she crossed to the fridge, pulling out a bottle of water. She drank half of it before capping it and setting it on the counter beside her. The paper was tucked into her back pocket for safe keeping, and it currently felt like it was burning her alive. "I think I'm going to go outside, get some fresh air—"

Travis's eyes were on her as she left, and she'd made it

halfway down the stairs when his footsteps sounded behind her. "Roxy—"

She didn't stop, continuing down the steps. Reaching the bottom, she looked around, unsure what to do. *She wasn't ready for this.* She wasn't ready for any of it. Panic clawed at her as she sensed him behind her.

"Okay, what is your problem?" Travis snapped, clamping one hand onto her elbow and twisting her around to face him. She yanked her arm away, not that it took much effort because he wasn't holding her tightly. Glaring up at him, she was stonily silent, her heart breaking wide open in her chest. He pointed toward the loft and ground out, "What the hell happened, Red? You've hardly said three words to me since we got up this morning, you won't look me in the eyes… So what happened between you coming on my face last night and this morning? Is this because of what I said last night?"

She flushed a brilliant shade of red and glanced around, grateful there was no one around to hear him. Memories of Travis's head between her thighs, his tongue doing deliciously wicked things to her clit and his fingers going deep to find that special spot… She swallowed hard and begged her body not to betray her, forcing her breathing to remain steady and wishing her heart wasn't pounding in her chest at the memory of how hard she'd come, or what had followed… the way she'd so desperately wanted exactly what he was offering, what he was asking for in return. She wanted it, all of it.

But even those passionately whispered words couldn't change what had already been put into motion, and she knew what she had to do. She needed Travis to go, to leave, to be safe, even if it killed her in the process. Her heart hammered in her throat, fear radiating through her being like a flash flood all over again. If Travis got hurt because of her… no. She wouldn't even think of it.

"Travis—"

He took one step toward her, towering over her. "Don't lie to me, Red. I can see it in your eyes, on your face. Don't lie to me. *What happened?*"

"You think you know me just from a few months of seeing me come into your gym or because I take your class? You think you know me because we were stuck in a car together? Or because we fucked like bunnies in a shitty highway motel? You don't know shit about me," she snapped, shaking her head. It killed her to do it. He was kind to her, gentle in a way that made her heart ache, and didn't deserve anything that she was about to say. He wouldn't know that it was all lies. He couldn't know. She gripped her thumbs inside her palms until it felt like her nails would break skin, forced herself to scoff, steeling her face into a sneer that she thought might just break her. "I'm a whore, Travis. Always have been, always will be. That's why Neal has been the way he is. I had an on again off again fuck agreement with Freeman, among others. He's jealous because I give him plenty of reason to be. So you happened to be a convenient fuck on a really long road trip, but don't mistake this for more than that. I'm sorry you became attached, and this was fun while it lasted, but it's done. I don't want you to stay."

Digging into her back pocket, she held out the piece of paper that she'd had printed out while she'd been at the big house. He opened it, those golden eyes flicking across the page. A boarding ticket, paid in full. Departing the small airport just north of Petoskey to Austin, TX, tonight. His eyes came back to hers, and she swallowed hard. A muscle ticked in Travis's jaw as he stared down at her. His chest rose and fell with his uneven breaths, but she didn't look away from his eyes. The setting sun made the honey brown color of them fairly glow as he stared at her, eyes squinting against the sunlight. She would miss his eyes, his smile, that dimple in his cheek hidden by his beard, the low rumble of his voice as he talked to her while her head rested against his chest. She needed him to walk away. For his own safety. And the safety of her heart.

"You're a shit liar," he whispered low and she let her eyes flick down for just a heartbeat. The paper crinkled as he fisted his fingers around the edge of it. "You rub your right thumbnail with the pad of your finger when you lie. Just like you're doing now."

She released the fists her hands were balled into, flattening her hands against the sides of her thighs. *Shit.*

"I just can't figure out why you're lying to me now, why you're pushing me away," he whispered, shaking his head. Holding up the piece of paper in his fist, he rasped, "And this? This is horseshit, Roxy. Less than twenty-four hours ago you were asking me to stay. So I'll ask again, what the fuck happened between last night and this morning?"

Her heart was trying to kill her, where it was beating so hard against her ribcage, she thought she might throw up. But, she squared her shoulders, pulling her spine straight and giving him an insolent stare. He had to go. He had to. He would never forgive her, but she was fine with that, as long as he was safe from Neal. "You said so yourself, it's been an emotional week."

He was shaking his head again, those damn eyes spearing into hers so acutely she feared he would see her truth. "I'm not fucking buying it, Red."

Shrugging, she raised her hands and let them fall back to her sides, palms slapping against her thighs. "What can I say, Travis? I've always been a slut; that hasn't changed. Maintenance sex is all I'm good for."

The growl that rumbled out of his chest made the hairs on the back of her neck stand up. Oh fuck. His expression was fierce as he bit out through gritted teeth, "If you ever talk about yourself like that again…"

"Or what, Travis?" she challenged, because she knew he

wouldn't do anything. He would never. "You'll do what? Hit me? Teach me a lesson?"

"Now you're just spouting off anything you possibly can to piss me off," he murmured darkly, his brows lowering over his eyes in a glare. "It's not going to work, Red. You're scared of something; I can fucking see it in your eyes. Why can't you just tell me instead of trying your damndest to shove me away? You know good and well I'd never lay a hand on you."

"I don't know shit," she sneered. Her chest was cleaving in two. She didn't want to do this, didn't want to hurt him or push him away. But he couldn't get hurt. She couldn't let Neal hurt him, and if she didn't give him a reason to leave, to go back to Melody Hills where he would be safe… Digging in and hating herself with every fiber of her being, she scoffed, "You've admitted to being a monster, Travis. Am I really supposed to believe you leave all that rage in the ring? That you've never hit a woman before? *You've admitted to killing someone.*"

Travis's head tipped back as though he'd been struck, but still those honey brown eyes never left hers. She shivered as he leaned down close, until his face was mere inches from hers. "I did. And I'd do it again, for you, Red. I took my father's life with my bare hands after he killed my mother. He was drunk and enraged, and he strangled her with a dish towel. I was nineteen and still living at home because I was too scared to leave her alone with him but she wouldn't leave. When I came in from work to him with that towel wrapped around her neck, he came at me with a butcher knife off the counter that she'd been using to cook his dinner. A dinner that cost her her life, Roxy. My tattoos cover the scars of that night. He stabbed me sixteen times before I managed to wrestle that knife from him, and then I beat him with my bare hands until there was nothing the paramedics could do when they arrived. Not one single part of me regrets it. And I'm okay if that makes me a monster, because I'd do it all again."

Roxy's mouth had fallen open, tears stinging her nose as he spoke. He straightened and backed away a step.

"You want to throw shit in my face, Red, at least make sure you have all the information first."

"Travis…"

He shook his head, holding one hand out as if to shush her. "You made your point, so you don't need to say anything else. I don't want your pity, now that you know. I just wanted you to trust me. I only ever wanted you to trust me, Red."

He turned and walked back up the stairs to the loft. She tried like hell to steady her breathing, to shove the tears down that were trying to escape. Her throat hurt from holding them in, her bottom lip trembling. In the distance, against the horizon, ominous storm clouds darkened the skyline. Seren had mentioned that morning that a storm would be coming.

Minutes—or maybe a lifetime—later, her heart cracked open wide when he emerged from the loft, duffel bag slung over one shoulder. As he descended the stairs, he draped the hoodie he'd let her wear the night before over either side of the strap. "Travis—"

"Don't," he said quietly, and the pained gruffness in his voice nearly killed her. "Don't say anything else, please, Red."

He stepped toward her and placed his hands on either side of her jaw, before dropping a kiss to the center of her forehead. His lips lingered there, his fingertips pressing into the space behind her ears beneath her hairline, his thumbs braced beneath her jaw. His lips moved, and she could just hear the words as he breathed, "I did what I said I would do, baby girl. I got you here. You'll be safe. But you're right, I did get attached, and dammit I know you did, too. If this is what you need to make it easier…" He pressed another kiss to her forehead, lingering for what felt like forever. "I'll let you make me the monster, Roxy."

Roxy squeezed her eyes shut as tears stung her nose and filled her eyes. A hiccupping sob threatened to escape her and she held her breath to fight it back. She couldn't let him know. Couldn't let him know how wrong he was.

He stepped back and tipped her head up, settling his mouth over hers. His lips were warm and soft and she so badly wanted to sink into the kiss, to beg him to forgive her, to beg him not to go… *She didn't mean it, she didn't mean it, she didn't mean it…*

His thumbs tracked along her cheeks, picking up the tears that slid down them. He broke the kiss, but whispered against her lips, "For what it's worth, there isn't anywhere I wouldn't have gone with you."

FORTY-FOUR

Forcing himself to walk away was the hardest thing he'd ever done.

Turning his back to Roxy and forcing his feet to move him away from her nearly killed him, damn near taking him to his fucking knees. Something was wrong, but he had no idea what, and if she wouldn't fucking talk to him…

The boarding pass and travel information printed on the paper clutched in his hand had felt like nails in his coffin. She was pushing him away. Sending him away. *It made no fucking sense!* Why, after everything they'd shared? After everything that they had said, everything he knew they both felt!

He heard her footsteps as she climbed the stairs behind him, then the sound of the loft door closing. He made his way toward the big house, where he could see Jodi, Free, Seren, and Levi all settled into the Adirondack chairs on the front porch.

He stopped at the foot of the stairs, and Free stood from his chair, crossing the planked porch, his aquamarine eyes bouncing from Travis's to the loft door. "What the fuck happened? Why are you packed? Did she kick you out?"

Travis glanced at Seren, the woman's blue eyes shining with

tears. "She needs some time, I think. I don't want to make this more difficult for her than it already is." Holding up the paper, he shrugged one wide shoulder. "She already bought the ticket." Sighing heavily, he scrubbed at the back of his neck again, massaging the tightness out of the muscles the best he could. "Would someone be able to give me a ride to the airport? If not, I can call an uber—"

"Uber's aren't really a thing up here," Jodi said softly, standing to cross the porch. Her lip wobbled as she gestured toward the barn. "I'm sorry, Travis."

He smiled gently up at her. She was the cutest thing he'd ever seen, and he would have liked to spend more time with them, get to know them, maybe become their friend. "It's okay. I'm not leaving for good. I have some things to figure out back home, and then I'll be back, whether she likes it or not. She's not getting rid of me that easily." He shrugged again, adjusting the duffel slung over his shoulder. He notched his chin toward the loft. "I left my pistol in the cupboard over the fridge, I won't be able to take it with me on the plane. I don't think she'll need it since she brought her own, but if you could let her know it's there…" Free nodded. Travis bobbed his head once, his lips pressing together before exhaling heavily. He would be back, soon. "Anyway, if someone wouldn't mind giving me a ride, that would be great."

"She'll come around," Seren said, stepping forward and down the steps to wrap him in a hug. She was tiny compared to his size, but he hugged her back. "Don't let her push you away."

"Like I said, she's not getting rid of me that easily," he murmured, clearing his throat of the emotion that clogged it. "Fuck, this sucks, I won't lie. But I'll be back. I promise."

"I'll drive you," Free said, digging his keys out of his pocket. "And then when I get back, I'll have a word with her—"

"Freeman Thorp, you will not badger her," Jodi said, crossing her arms over her chest and glaring up at him. She looked at

Travis then. "We'll get her to come around. You're stuck with us now, too."

"Sounds good," he laughed, though it sounded forced and sad to his own ears. She skipped down the few stairs to hug him hard around the middle. "I'll see you all soon."

Levi shook Travis's hand with a gruff thank you and farewell, and then Free was leading him toward a shiny, cobalt blue pickup truck with the Blue Haven logo on the doors.

He set his duffel in the back seat of the extended cab truck, then climbed into the passenger seat. Free was behind the wheel a moment later, the truck rumbling to life as he started the ignition. As he backed them out of the parking spot in front of the big house, Travis glanced over at the barn that sat roughly a hundred yards away and the door that stood closed to him.

"I'm sorry, man," Free said as they rumbled down the long gravel driveway. "She's the most stubborn, hard headed woman I know—and that's saying something with my sister-in-law being Shauntelle—but she'll come around. She doesn't do well with big emotions, so I'm sure this has been a lot for her to try and work through. She's crazy about you. All of us can see that."

Turning them onto the road, Free scrubbed a hand down his face, glancing in the rearview mirror.

"Anyway. We should be to the airport in about twenty minutes or so. I can't believe she just handed that ticket over—"

"Yeah, well, that's Red for ya," Travis mumbled, staring out the passenger window as the world passed by them. They were quiet for a while, the only sound the radio that played a country station filling the cab of the truck.

Free's phone buzzed in his pocket, and he dug it out, his dark brows sliding into a deep V before he answered it, putting it to his ear. "What's wrong?"

Travis could hear Levi's deep voice through the phone. "Oh, just your hormonal and overly emotional pregnant wife. She's been crying since you two left. You know I don't handle her tears well; it makes me feel helpless—so I offered to go get her some ice cream. She's requested a double Reeses Whiteout." Free laughed out loud, shaking his head. Travis couldn't help the smile that lifted the corners of his mouth. Poor thing. "I just wanted to call and let you know that I'm headed out, but Jodi is with Seren at the house. I'll be back with her ice cream as quick as I can."

"Thanks, Levi," Free chuckled again.

"Yeah, well, she's my baby girl, I can't let her cry like that," Levi grumbled. "You spoil her too much."

"*Me?*" Free exclaimed, glancing over at Travis with a wide, shit eating grin on his face. Travis rolled his eyes. "You spoiled her rotten for twenty-five years before I got to her. If anything, you laid the groundwork and got her accustomed to that!"

"I'm her dad, it's my job," Travis heard Levi argue. "Anyway, I just wanted to let you know."

"Thanks," Free said again, and then he hung up, sliding the phone into the cupholder in the console between them. He shook his head, blowing out a long breath. "This woman has both of us wrapped around her damn finger."

"That's how it's supposed to be," Travis chuckled. "You nervous?"

"To be a dad? Christ on a cracker, yes." Scrubbing his hand down his face again, he nodded. "Every new thing that happens makes me nervous as hell. There's so much that can go wrong in a pregnancy, man. So much that I didn't know before, and knowing any one of those things that could go wrong could take her and that baby away from me… And don't get me started on the fear of actually bringing that baby home. *What if I break it?*"

Travis grinned, elbowing Free gently over the console that separated them. "For some reason, I don't think that's a problem you're going to have. You'll be a great dad."

"Fuck, I hope so," he chuckled, blowing out a ragged breath, then turned them onto a larger highway, heading north. "You ever wanted kids?"

Travis shook his head. "It's never been something I've thought about, to be honest."

"Roxy always wanted to be a mom," Free said quietly, glancing over at him. "Her mom wasn't the greatest, never around much. She always said that if she got to be a mom, she'd do it right, be better than what she'd had growing up."

Free's phone began to ring, buzzing and rattling around in the cupholder between them. He sighed, lifting it to his ear as he answered it. His words were gentle as he murmured, "Hi, sweetheart. I know your dad is on his way to get you ice cream—"

"Free, I think something's wrong."

Travis went stock still in his seat as Freeman's entire body tensed. "The baby? Are you okay?"

"I'm fine," Jodi rushed to say. Free lowered the phone from his ear, tapping the speaker icon. Her voice filled the cab then. "Free, there's someone here. We didn't even see a car pull in, but when I looked over at the barn, there was a—a guy at Roxy's door."

Travis's heart stopped, then thundered back to life.

"What did he look like, Jodi?" Free asked, his voice low.

"I don't know, I barely got a glance at him before he was in the loft. Darkish hair? Kind of thin build. What do I do? Should Mom and I walk over there—"

"No!" both Travis and Free exclaimed at the same time. "Stay in the house. Don't fucking leave the house, Jodi!"

Travis dug his phone out of his pocket, calling Roxy's number. It rang and rang, then finally went to voicemail. He hung up, cursing, and called again, but still no response. He twisted in his seat, pulling his duffel bag up and into his lap, the hoodie he'd draped over it falling to the floorboard between his feet. A flash of orange caught his eye, and he bent down to pick up the crumpled mass of paper, and it felt like he was wading through quick sand, his mind slowing as it registered.

Unfurling the neon orange post it, his eyes scanned the two notes that had been crumpled together. Fear, rage, agony, terror all rolled through him at the words scrawled there.

Neal was here. He had found her. And he knew about her gun, possibly had taken her gun from her, leaving her completely at his mercy, completely unprotected…

"Turn around!" he bellowed, terror seizing his chest. He held up the note, his hand shaking. "*Fuck!* It's Neal. He's there. I fucking left her there, and the bastard found her fucking gun! She knew he found her and she made me fucking leave her unprotected!"

Free was already executing a very illegal U-turn, tires squealing on the pavement. "Jodi, do not fucking leave that house, do you understand me?" Free snarled through the phone. "No matter what you see, what you hear, do not leave that house. Lock the doors. Have your mom call the police, now."

Within heartbeats—though it felt like an eternity—they heard Seren's voice as she spoke with 911 dispatch. Seren called loud enough for them to hear, "Free, they're sending a deputy out. She says Deputy Beckett is only three minutes away, but Chase can't get here that quick—"

"We'll be there in ten," Free said calmly, far more calmly than Travis felt, pressing his foot down on the accelerator harder. The pavement flew beneath the tires. "We're on our way. Don't answer the door, don't go outside, please, sweeheart."

Travis hated that they were leaving Roxy alone with Neal, but he understood the fear radiating off of the other man, that innate need to protect his pregnant wife and mother-in-law.

"I'm coming, Roxy," Travis whispered, sending prayers up. Something he hadn't done since before his mother was killed.

FORTY-FIVE

Washing her face in the bathroom sink, Roxy stared at her puffy eyes in the mirror. The tears had been hard and brutal, the ache in her chest as she watched Travis leave killing her inside. She'd let herself cry, and then when she was able to calm herself enough, she'd gone into the bathroom to wash her face of the salty tears that had covered her cheeks. Her throat hurt from crying. She hated this.

Now that Free was gone, and she'd seen Levi leave shortly after, she had to go. She needed to re-pack her suitcase. She would only take the one bag, needing to get as far away as possible before Neal came for her. She needed to get away from Blue Haven, away from Jodi and Serenity and everyone here that was good and kind.

Leaving the bathroom, she had just crossed to the suitcase she'd left lying open on the couch when the door to the loft opened behind her. *Travis? Had he come back?* She whipped her head over her shoulder, but dread filled her like an icy bucket being dumped over her.

"Jesus, I thought he'd never get the hint."

Tears stung her nose, fear clogging her throat at the sound of his voice. The sunshine that had highlighted Travis as they'd stood outside as she'd pushed him away had disappeared, hidden by those dark, ominous storm clouds that had moved in rapidly. The wind whipped in through the open doorway that he remained standing in, the chill from the coming storm rippling up her spine. Or maybe that was just the bone deep fear settling in as those dark eyes tracked over her from head to toe and back again. He closed the door behind him, and Roxy attempted to steady her racing heart, to take deep, even breaths.

"You did good," Neal murmured gently as he stepped slowly toward her across the small space, his hands coming to rest on her shoulders. The feel of his fingers on her skin made her stomach revolt. How had she ever thought she could love him? How could he ever think she would love him after everything he'd done?

The pain in Travis's eyes as he'd walked away… he would never forgive her. But at least he was safe.

Her phone began to buzz where she'd left it on the counter, but she was too far away to answer it. She'd never get to it before Neal stopped her anyway.

"You did good, Rox," Neal said again near her ear, his breath making her shiver in revulsion. "He's still a dead man for putting his hands on you, but you did good. At least you don't have to see it happen this way."

Her heart fell into her stomach as fear and dread swamped her, making her vision blur. The tears slid down her cheeks, and she reached out grasping the front of his shirt as she shook her head vehemently. Her phone started ringing again, but she blocked out the buzzing sound, concentrating on Neal. Her voice wavered precariously as she pleaded, "No, Neal, I sent him away, you don't have to hurt him, please—"

Anger flashed in his eyes as his fingers clamped down on her wrists painfully. "I really do, Rox. Because even if you sent him away, you're still in love with him, and that's inexcusable. He touched you. *You let him*. You let him kiss you, and defile you… I can't let that go."

Tears slid down her cheeks and she shook her head. "No, please, Neal—"

His fingers tightened around her wrists until she cried out. "I told you what would happen if you ran, Rox. I warned you. And you didn't listen. I warned you what would happen if I had to find you."

"Neal, please—" Roxy begged, more tears slipping down her cheeks, over her lips. His grip on her wrists became painful, and she cried out again. "I'll go with you. I promise, I'll go. Just let him go, I'm sorry, baby—"

One hand released her wrist, and before she could blink, white hot pain exploded in her face. Slumping to her knees, she swayed, her vision tunneling before returning. He knelt in front of her, fisting her hair in his fingers tight enough to make her scream. Scrabbling at the punishing hold on her hair with her fingers, she sobbed.

She was going to die. She was going to die, and she had hurt Travis, and for nothing. All of it had been for nothing. Despair choked her as he forced her head back so that she was staring up at him.

"You lie," he snarled through clenched teeth. "You and I both know that's a lie, Rox. Don't fucking lie to me, you stupid whore. You spread these fucking legs for anyone, don't you? God, I should have fucking known better! You've always been like this. My love was never going to be enough for you, was it?!"

"Neal, please, you're hurting me—"

"We're just getting started, Rox. You've been extraordinarily bad, and it's going to take a lot for you to make up for everything you've done." Dragging her up to her feet by her hair, she screamed again, wrapping her fingers around his wrists to try and alleviate some of the sharp pain in her scalp. She was shaking, trembling so violently she could barely stand. "Fucking move. Out the door. *Now.*"

"No, please—"

Snapping her neck so hard it cracked, he whipped her face toward him, banding his free hand around her throat like a vice. "If you fight me, Rox, I will walk over to that house and shoot those two women I know are inside." A sob choked her.

"I won't fight," she whispered, pleading. "Just don't hurt them. Please. Neal."

"Let's go," he snarled, pushing her toward the door. The wind whipped around them, the sky dark, and rain began to pelt them. They had just made it to the bottom of the stairs when a car broke through the trees that lined the long gravel driveway, blue and red lights flashing.

Roxy sagged in relief. Oh, thank God—

The sheriff squad car came to a stop, and when the door opened, a tall, blonde deputy stepped out, hand already on his holster. Neal swore, moving them closer to her 4Runner, attempting to use it as a shield between them and the officer.

"Put your hands in the air!" the deputy shouted, and a heartbeat later his gun was drawn, aiming at them—no, aimed at Neal —but terror squeezed her chest tight enough to seize her breaths. The deputy remained standing behind the opened door of his squad car, gun drawn and aimed at them over the top of the window. "Let her go!"

Neal reached behind him, and when he pulled his hand back, her gun was gripped in his fingers, pointing back at the deputy. The man was incredibly tall, most of his torso rising above the ledge of the window frame.

"Drop the weapon!" the deputy shouted, but Roxy knew he wouldn't. Time seemed to slow to a crawl as Neal's finger depressed on the trigger, the noise of the blast screaming in her ear. Or maybe that was her own scream that echoed inside her head as the bullet connected with the deputy's chest, just to the left of his Kevlar vest. He went down, his head bouncing off the car as he fell backward, his body disappearing as he fell into the dirt.

Bucking wildly against the hold Neal still had on her, she managed to free herself, scrambling away a dozen feet before another shot rang out, a bullet ricocheting in the dirt to her right. She screamed, coming to a halt, her body folding in on itself as she stared at how close that bullet had come to hitting her. She was trembling violently as she turned slowly to face him.

His chest was heaving like a bellows, his arm outstretched, gun pointed directly at her. His face was a vicious mask of rage, dark eyes blazing with fury, mouth twisted in hate. "Look at what you made me do, Rox! *Are you happy now?*" he raged, his arm shaking with his wrath. She shook like a leaf where she stood. "I don't want to shoot you, Rox, but so fucking help me, I will."

FORTY-SIX

"I can see them, they just came out of the loft. Oh my god, he's got her by the hair, dragging her, Free, please let me—"

"No, Jodi! Don't leave that house!" Free snarled, careening around a corner.

Rain lashed at the windshield, the wipers wicking it away as quickly as it was coming down. They were almost there. Almost there. So fucking close. *Roxy. Roxy. Roxy*, Travis's mind and heart chanted. White hot fury raced through him at Jodi's words, at the fear Roxy must be feeling right now, at the hands of this fucking monster. And he'd let her push him away. Let her push him away, when she'd known all along that he'd found her. Neal had threatened his life, and Roxy had done what she thought was right, to save him, to protect him.

He was going to have one helluva talking to this woman, when this was all said and done. Because there was no other option for how this was going to end.

"I see the lights flashing, the deputy is in the driveway," Seren called, but relief was far from coming. He'd had Seren relay that Neal would most likely have Roxy's gun on him, he was armed, and he was incredibly dangerous.

A gasp from the other end of the line brought his head around and then the worst sound he'd ever heard made his gut clench tightly. The muffled sound of a shot ringing out. "Oh my god, the deputy, he's been shot! Run, Roxy!"

Pure, unadulterated panic choked him when the sound of a second shot rang out, muffled by distance and walls, and Jodi was sobbing. Seren was still on the line with the dispatch, now relaying that their officer had been shot. This couldn't be happening. *He couldn't fucking lose her!*

The driveway came into sight, the headlights lighting on it in the distance and Free took the corner far faster than was safe, the truck sliding sideways before he straightened it out. Gravel flew behind the tires as they sped down the long drive, and then he saw the flashes of blue and red painting the main house garishly. A sheriff's cruiser was parked in the drive, the lights flashing, but he didn't see an officer as they sped closer. Free reached between Travis's knees, popping open the glove box as they careened closer, skidding to a halt, gravel spraying. A handgun sat in the glovebox. "Take it. Go!"

Travis grabbed it, jumping out of the truck before it came to a complete stop. Rounding the hood of the truck, he saw Neal dragging Roxy, one arm wrapped around her neck in a chokehold, toward the other side of the barn. He had just slipped between the truck and sheriff's cruiser when he skidded to a stop.

"Holy shit," he breathed, dropping to his knees in the gravel next to the prone figure. Blood covered the officer's chest and left arm, pooling beneath him, a bullet wound cleaving open his shoulder. The rain mixed with the blood, sending it seeping in all directions in garish rivers through the gravel.

He was soaked in rain, his short, dirty blonde hair shorn close to his head and dripping wet. Gasping, choked breaths made Travis's own breath stall.

Free caught up to him then, skidding to a halt in the rain slick gravel. He shoved him. "Go! I've got him. Go, God dammit!"

"No," the deputy wheezed, lashing a hand out to catch Travis's wrist as he made to stand. "I c-can't le-let you g-g-go after th-them—" he coughed out. Blood seeped from the side of his mouth. Fucking hell. "B-backup. W-wait f-for backup."

"Graham, you listen to me," Free snarled, closing one hand over the bloody wound on his shoulder. The deputy hissed in pain. Free's other hand grasped the back of the deputy's neck. "Your only fucking job right now is to stay alive; do you hear me?"

The deputy nodded weakly, releasing Travis's wrist. Travis jumped to his feet, catapulting over the hood of the cruiser and taking off in the direction that he'd seen Neal take Roxy. Barreling through the rain, he ran as fast as he could, pumping his arms and legs as hard as he could manage, his legs eating up the distance. He was a hundred yards away from the corner of the big barn when the blast of a gun echoed, followed almost simultaneously by an agonized scream, and then the terror of pure silence.

"Roxy!" he bellowed, putting on a burst of speed. He only prayed he wasn't too late.

FORTY-SEVEN

Think, Roxy. Fucking think!

She had no idea where Neal was trying to take her, other than away. And now that they were far enough away from the house, that she didn't have to worry about Neal doubling back to make good on his threat to go back and hurt Jodi and Serenity, adrenaline and self-preservation instincts kicked into high gear.

After he'd fired off that warning shot at her feet, she'd allowed him to drag her toward the farthest barn with minimal fight from her, attempting to lull him into a false sense of victory. But she had no idea what his plan was for her; was his goal to get her away from Travis and back somewhere where he could have her for his own? Would he kill her? Her skin crawled with the realization that she'd rather die than go back with him.

Forcing her breaths to calm and her eyes to close for the smallest span of heartbeats, she assessed her situation. Her back pressed into his side, his arm around her neck, she focused on her breathing. And reminded herself to *think.*

Her gun was still clutched in his right hand, though it hung at his side, pointing toward the ground. There was a thick forest of trees that ran on the far side of the property, behind the barn they were headed toward. Maybe he had his car hidden somewhere. Maybe she could run through the trees.

No, that would let him head back to the main house, to Jodi and Serenity. She would have to disarm him, maim him somehow. Enough to keep him down until the deputy's backup could arrive.

As they rounded the corner of the barn, he glanced behind them, swearing viciously. She swung her head around, too, gasping as his arm tightened around her neck, but the sight that greeted her, in the split second she had… she would not go quietly.

Because the cobalt blue truck breaking through the tree lined driveway, headlights flashing through the pouring rain, gave her the smallest glimmer of hope.

Travis had come back for her.

So as Neal continued to drag her farther away, she knew what she had to do. She would fight like hell. Even if it cost her her life, she was going to fight to get back to Travis. Because he had come back for her, even after everything she'd said.

I am not going to die out here. I'm not. Fight, dammit!

"That stupid son of a bitch just can't take a fucking hint!" Neal seethed, yanking her forward again. She slipped in the wet grass, her knees buckling, and when his right hand swung forward to steady them both from falling, she struck.

With a primal shout, she shot her elbow back, sending it on an upward trajectory with all the force she could muster. His throat took the blow and he released her on instinct, clasping his now free hand to his throat as he choked from the power of her hit directly against his trachea.

Swinging her leg out, she used the roundhouse kick Travis had taught them in class to knock the gun out of his hand. It fell into the mucky grass several feet away, but he recovered quickly and lunged for it, beating her to it by half of a heartbeat. His arm swung out and she had only a fraction of a second to register before the blast rent the air around them.

The shot rang in her ears, so loud it made them buzz, and then the searing pain in her arm forced an agonized scream out of her throat. Her brain went foggy for several heartbeats, pain and fear paralyzing her. *No. She had to keep fighting. She had to get back to Travis!*

Her left arm was on fire. Kicking out, nothing but pure adrenaline fueling her, she fought with everything she had. Her kick sent the gun flying again. This time she lunged for it before he could scramble to his feet. Picking it up, she spun and pulled the trigger.

The kickback sent a wave of agony through her arm, the bullet connecting with his stomach. He pressed one hand to the wound as he grunted with the pain, then bared his teeth, nothing but pure, unadulterated evil pouring from those dark eyes.

"I'm going to fucking kill you, and I'm going to enjoy it," he snarled, taking another step forward, and she didn't hesitate as she squeezed the trigger once more.

FORTY-EIGHT

"Roxy!" Travis bellowed again, putting on a burst of speed. Twenty feet from the corner of the barn, a shot rang out, then another. He skidded around the barn, slipping on the rain slicked grass, catching himself by grabbing hold of the corner of the building. He raised his arm that still clutched Freeman's handgun, but he slammed to a stop, his heart hammering in his chest at the sight that met his eyes.

Neal lay flat on his back. A gasping, choked breath stuttered out of his mouth, and then he went completely still. His eyes open, but unseeing. Two bullet wounds pumped red blood, one from his stomach, the other from the side of his neck, where it had severed the carotid artery.

Roxy stood three feet away, splattered in mud and rain and blood, her hands clamped tightly around the butt of the handgun, still pointing directly at Neal's now lifeless body. She was soaked, her hair lying flat against her head and shoulders, clothes clinging wetly to her body. She was shaking, eyes wide and filled with horror, tears mixing with the rain sliding down her cheeks. A gash across her left bicep oozed blood, dripping down her arm and off the tip of her elbow. *The bastard had shot her!*

"Roxy," Travis whispered, stumbling forward. He flipped the safety on, then tucked Freeman's gun into the waistband of his jeans at his back.

When her eyes lifted to his, her hazel eyes were unfocused, faraway. She blinked away the rain, her eyes finally focusing on him, and she whispered, "Travis."

And then her face fell as soul deep sobs wracked her body. She cried wretchedly, the sound breaking him entirely. Tears filled his own eyes as the anguish exploding from deep inside enveloped her. Her arms lowered, the gun falling from her fingers to the mud at their feet.

He didn't waste another heartbeat, wrapping his arms around her so tightly he wished he could imprint her on his own body, burrow her under his skin to carry all of her pain. She cried miserably, her fingers clutching at the material of his shirt at his back, her face buried in his neck.

"Travis," she sobbed, great, hiccupping breaths leaving her as she clutched at him desperately.

"I've got you," he breathed, stroking her hair reverently. He pressed kisses to her forehead, to the top of her head, as he continued to chant, his voice raspy and broken. "I'm here, Red. I've got you. I've got you. I've got you…"

Picking her up beneath the knees and cradling her back in his other arm, he strode away from Neal's lifeless body. She wound her arms around his neck, as if holding on for dear life. He held her as tightly as he would allow himself, fear of hurting her, not knowing what Neal had done to her before they'd gotten to her… He tamped down the fear, striding around the barn and back toward the main part of the driveway. As they got closer, he heard the sirens, and then saw the lights flashing as two, then three police cars pulled down the driveway toward them all. An ambulance was right behind them.

Free was up then, running toward the ambulance as the doors

opened and two EMT's hopped out. They raced back to the deputy that had been shot as three officers approached the two of them as they crossed the yard. Their guns were drawn, aimed at their feet in precaution.

"They're with us!" Free shouted as he became aware of the situation. A tall, black-haired deputy with striking blue eyes glanced between Free and Travis, who still held Roxy cradled in his arms. "Chase, dammit, that's Roxy you're aiming your fucking gun at!"

"Who's he?" the deputy called back, not lowering his gun entirely.

"That's the guy that just drove her across the fucking country to get her here safe," Free hissed, stepping closer before another officer stopped him. "Oh, fuck off Cross. I'm not going to hurt Chase."

"And the suspect?" Chase called to Travis.

Travis tightened his arms around Roxy. Fear and anxiety swirled inside his chest. She had done everything she had to in self-defense… but that fear still ate at him. He would take the blame before he ever let her see the inside of a fucking jail cell.

"Deceased. Around the barn," Travis said loud enough for him to hear. Roxy's arms tightened around his neck at his words. He pressed a kiss to her forehead. "She's been shot. Looks superficial, but it will require stitches." Then he looked squarely at the first officer, the one Freeman seemed to be on a first name basis with. "I have a firearm at my back, the safety is on."

The dark-haired deputy notched his chin at the other officers around him. "You two take the weapon, then go check the suspect. I want to go—"

"You go with Beckett," the one Free had called Cross said. They all holstered their guns, stepping toward Travis and Roxy, still held in a bridal carry in his arms. "Sorry, it's just precaution.

Travis nodded stiffly as they lifted his shirt, pulling the gun out of his waistband. Anxiety was clawing at his chest, but he rasped, "I understand."

The deputy named Cross asked, "Does the firearm belong to you?"

Free spoke then. "It's mine. I gave it to him just before he went to find Roxy."

"How is the other deputy?" Travis asked then, glancing across the yard to where the ambulance was parked.

The EMT's were loading the wounded deputy into the back of the ambulance, and the dark-haired deputy jogged over to the back of it before they could close the doors. They spoke for just a minute, and then the doors closed, the lights and sirens coming on as they pulled out quickly. The officer in front of Travis shook his head. "Not sure." Pointing to the dark-haired deputy who stood staring after the ambulance, he continued, "That's his partner. I've never had a partner wounded like this before. It's got to be rough."

Travis adjusted Roxy in his arms and she hissed in pain, her breath sucking in through her teeth where her head was resting against his shoulder. "I'm sorry," he murmured, walking forward again. "Is there another ambulance coming or should I take her myself?"

"I don't need—"

"Shut up, woman," Travis growled, though there was no heat in his tone. Pressing his lips to her forehead again, he breathed, "You're going to get checked out this time whether you like it or not."

She nodded, just barely. Jodi, Seren, Levi, and Free waited nearby. It was going to be a long night of getting her checked out, lots of questioning, and documenting the scene. But he would be with her, wherever she was.

Her lips moved against his neck as he continued forward. "You came back for me."

His chest tightened; heart wrenching open inside his ribcage. "Always, Roxy."

FORTY-NINE

The next several hours passed in a blur for Roxy. Travis waited with her for a second ambulance, continuing to hold her in his arms, refusing to let her go. Free had stepped up close enough to catch her gaze, and then he was gone again, as if he simply needed to ascertain for himself that she was alright. In Travis's arms, she was.

Travis relinquished her to the EMT's once they arrived, climbing into the back of the ambulance and setting her down on the gurney. They wrapped her up in a silver blanket, her muscles locked from the trembling, the cool rain, and the shock. Travis refused to stay behind, insisting on riding with them to the hospital, but once there, the hospital staff wouldn't let him back with her until they'd completed their exam. She didn't remember most of what happened, the shock dulling everything. They numbed her arm and closed the bullet wound with eleven stitches.

When the police arrived later to document her portion of the incident, Travis had been forced to remain in the waiting room. She recounted the events of the night, skimming over the past incidents and the outstanding Protective Order she'd had filed against Neal in Texas. It would be a long road, but the conclusion was undoubtably that she'd acted in self-defense.

It was hours later that Travis was finally allowed back into the room with her, after they'd come in to tell her she was being discharged. Gathering her things into the plastic bag they'd given her, along with an overnight supply of pain meds and an ice pack for her newly battered cheek, she turned when the door opened. Travis strode in, his long hair a mess around his shoulders, as if he'd been shoving his fingers through it for hours.

His honey gold eyes were wild as they lit on her, up and out of bed, dressed. He looked like he wanted to say something, his mouth opening and closing several times. His shoulders were bunched tight, his chest rising and falling with deep, uneven breaths. Then he let out a long, slow breath, squeezing his eyes shut. Opening them, he held out his hand toward her.

"Come on, baby girl, let's get you home."

She placed her hand in his, those big, strong fingers closing around hers, and then they were out the door. He jangled a set of keys in his hand as they exited the Emergency Department doors. "Free and Levi brought your car down so we would have a way back when you were discharged."

She nodded, allowing him to help her up into the seat. He leaned in, pressing his forehead to hers for a long time before leaning away to buckle her in. Every time he touched her, it sent electric jolts through her. He remained quiet on the way back to Blue Haven, but his right hand never left hers.

The sun was just beginning to rise over the horizon when they pulled in. Gold and orange and pink tingeing the skyline in a stunning watercolor. He helped her out of the car, but she stopped, staring at the dazzling sky as the world began to wake. Last night, she'd fought for every heartbeat, terrified she'd never get another single minute away from Neal, let alone another day with Travis.

He made it several steps away before he stopped, too, his

back still to her. His shoulders slumped, his head falling forward until his chin nearly touched his chest. And then he was spinning toward her. Her eyes met his, that wild, fierce light in them back.

"Why didn't you tell me?" he demanded roughly, his voice breaking. "You put yourself in danger instead of telling me what was going on. Why?"

She shook her head, tears stinging her nose. "This wasn't your fight—"

"*Try again, Red*," he growled.

"I couldn't bear the thought of you getting hurt because of me," Roxy whispered through clenched teeth, her lower lip trembling. "He threatened to hurt you. I couldn't let him hurt you."

"Did you really have such little faith in me that I couldn't protect you, baby girl? That I couldn't take care of myself?" he asked, stepping forward until he towered over her. His long hair fell over his brow and down his shoulders as he stared down at her. His voice was rough, but his eyes were gentle.

"I didn't know what lengths he would go to, and—"

"Don't ever doubt my ability to protect myself, or you, Roxy. I have been a fighter my whole life, you know better than anyone that I'm perfectly capable of taking care of myself. Try again."

"You already know why," she whispered through clenched teeth, tears tracking down her cheeks.

"I'm going to need you to spell it out for me," he murmured, raising his hands to cradle her face in them. "I want to hear the words."

A sob caught in her throat, and she squeezed her eyes shut, then she gasped when she felt his lips brush across her cheeks, her lips.

"Because I fell in love with you, you big bully," she whispered miserably. "And I figured you would think I wasn't worth the trouble."

She felt his lips lift into a smile against hers, before he pulled away and she opened her eyes to find his.

"I never thought love was worth the fight. But when I found you, baby girl, I was ready for war." Those large hands, capable of inflicting so much damage when he wanted them to, were infinitely gentle as they cupped her cheeks. His thumb rubbed along her cheekbone, and his gold flecked eyes searched hers. "Do you understand what I'm telling you, Red?"

"I might need you to spell it out for me," she whispered, her voice cracking around the words as more tears stung her nose.

One corner of his mouth quirked up and she could see the indent of the dimple in his cheek as a chuckle rumbled out of him. She cupped the side of his jaw in her hand, running her finger over his bottom lip.

"You are worth everything, Roxy. I don't ever want you to think you have to fight alone," he murmured, leaning down to press his forehead against hers. "Where you go, I go. Your fight is mine." Trapping one of her hands in his, he pressed it to the left side of his chest, and she could feel his heart beating beneath her palm. "And this heart is more yours than mine. Because no matter how hard I fucking tried to fight it… losing my heart to you was one fight I was powerless against. I love you, Red."

"I love you," she breathed against his lips, tears steadily tracking down her cheeks. "I didn't want to. I tried not to…" Pressing soft, sipping kisses to his lips, she took a deep breath in and let it out slowly. "We were set on a collision course from the start. There was no stopping the free fall I was in, Travis. I love you so much."

Her hand still trapped beneath his, palm pressed to his chest, he stroked the back of her hand with the pad of his thumb. "Does this mean I can stay?"

"I never wanted you to go," she whispered, flexing her fingers against his chest. She reveled in the steady thrum of his heart beneath her palm. "I want to be wherever you are, Travis."

Curling his arms around her, she sighed when their bodies aligned, and she pressed her cheek to his chest. "Good. Because you're stuck with me now, Red."

Lifting her chin, she smiled up at him, and he kissed her forehead gently. "I can live with that."

EPILOGUE
ONE YEAR LATER

"Okay, y'all, we're going to start from the top all the way through!" Tapping her teal cowgirl boot on the hardwood floor, she called out, *"Five, six, seven, eight!"*

Boot heels tapped, laughs rang out over the music, as Roxy led the beginner line dancing class through an easy version of 'Copperhead Road'. By the end of the song, the group applauded and laughed, high fives ringing out amongst many of them. She grinned at the group around her.

"That was great you guys! You're really getting the hang of this one!" she said through the microphone. "Why don't y'all take a water break, and then we can give 'Freight Train another try from last week!"

There was a mix of hoots and hollers and groans at that announcement, and she laughed again. The hall was dimly lit by colorful, rotating dance lights attached to the rough wood beam ceiling. The Junction was a quaint little tavern nestled on the outskirts of Walloon Lake, about ten minutes away from Petoskey. She had gotten a job as a bartender, the old-timey tavern reminding her so much of Lawless back in Texas. It felt like home.

The community interest had been incredible, the lines forming out the door on lesson nights. Who would have thought the little northern Michigan town would have such a passion for line dancing?

The skill levels ranged from novice to pretty dang good, and Roxy had been impressed with the outpouring of support. She'd had to add extra lessons in different skill levels, and instead of just once a month, she had weekly classes.

A skintight, white bodysuit with thin straps sucked her in, keeping her breasts in place, and it was tucked into her short jean shorts. Her hair had been left wild and curly down her back, but she'd started sweating during *Shania Twain's* 'Any Man of Mine' routine.

Glancing around, she winked at Travis, who was leaning against one wall off to the side, manning the sound system, as always when she taught these lessons. She sidled over to him, and he handed her a bottle of water before leaning down to kiss her swiftly. His black cowboy hat sat low on his brow, and his long, light brown hair had been left loose around his shoulders. He wore an indecently well-fitted pair of jeans, the hems curled slightly over his black cowboy boots. A black Jack Daniels Whisky t-shirt stretched across his chest, the arms cut off as usual, revealing those beautiful, muscular, tattooed arms.

The nightmares that had started after that last night with Neal had been awful, to put it mildly. She'd awake, sweating and crying, terror squeezing her throat, dread a suffocating weight on her chest as she relived those moments. The kickback of the gun in her hands when she'd pulled the trigger, once, then twice. The spray of blood that had shot from Neal's neck with the second bullet piercing his neck. The wet, squishing *thunk* that his body had made on the rain-soaked ground as he'd fallen, dead before her.

Travis was always there, had been there through all of it, every nightmare and all the subsequent police interrogations, the brief—though terrifying—court proceeding. He'd been a rock beside her through it all.

He had convinced her to try therapy. It was helping. But more than anything, knowing he was there and knew exactly the torment that haunted her, despite the knowledge that she had acted in self-defense… that if she hadn't done what she'd done, she'd be the one dead… She had fought like hell to live.

Travis knew, better than anyone else in her life, what that felt like. They shared the same demons, now. He knew all the shattered, broken pieces of her; knew all the darkest moments that tortured her still. And yet, he loved her deeply, in spite of that brokenness. She'd never been more thankful to have him by her side.

Splaying one hand on his chest, she smiled up at him. She loved him so much. It was strange now, to think back on those times before Travis had come into her life, before his love had saved her, in more ways than one.

"Are you going to join me tonight or just be a fly on the wall?" she asked against his mouth. He banded one arm around her waist, hauling her against him and she smiled.

"What did you have in mind?" he murmured against her lips.

"'Freight Train' with our dip?" she asked, grinning. He groaned. It was a fast-paced song and definitely wasn't for beginners, but it was her favorite, and she knew Travis liked any excuse to put his hands on her while dancing.

"Anything for my girl," he sighed, shaking his head with a wink.

While the group took their five-minute water break, they could run through the dance as a reminder of the steps she'd taught them the week prior.

"Okay y'all! We're going to run through 'Freight Train', so feel free to just watch or join in if you're feeling ready!" she called, leading Travis out to the middle of the floor, their fingers linked together. Several women sighed as they passed, and Roxy grinned up at him. She knew they liked watching him as much as she did.

Travis used the remote to cue up the music, and then she spun so her back was to him. The fingers of their right hands were linked over her right shoulder, their left hands linked down at their sides. Counting out the start, they were off. Flying through the steps, Travis kept up with her easily, they'd practiced this one so many times. Out of her peripheral, she could see several other individuals and couples join them, but the majority of the group stayed on the outskirts of the dance floor, letting the more practiced dancers take the floor.

Spinning, she laughed up into Travis's face as he backed up, stomped, and then paced forward as she repeated the move he'd just made, backing up and stomping her boot heel. Reaching out, she snagged the hat off his head, plopping it onto her head with a wink.

When their hands linked again, moving them both forward, he leaned down and growled into her ear, "You know what that means, Roxy."

Butterflies took flight in her belly, like always when he used that gravelly, growly tone with her. Breathless, she glanced up at him from beneath the wide brim of his hat and nodded, smiling. "Of course I do, Travis."

He spun her under his arm twice, then hauled her close, her chest colliding with his as his arm banded around her waist, holding her as he dipped her low over his arm. His other hand slid down her hip, over the bare thigh that she lifted toward his waist, kicking her booted foot up to a round of raucous cheers from the attendees at the edge of the dance floor.

Pulling her back up, he let his fingers trail down the exposed skin of her chest, and goosebumps flashed across her skin despite the heat in the room and the sweat dancing along her skin. Then he was twirling her away and she spun once, twice, stomping as she came back around.

She startled when the entire room exploded with noise, screams and shouts and applause ringing out, nearly blocking out the music. Eyes wide, she spun around to face Travis, but stopped in her tracks, mouth falling open in shock.

Down on one knee in the middle of the dance floor, he grinned up at her, that perfectly white smile she loved so much pulling at his bearded cheeks. His honey gold eyes crinkled at the corners, lighting her up from the inside out. In his outstretched hand sat a tiny black box, a glittering diamond ring nestled inside.

The cheers from the group around them was deafening, and he continued grinning up at her. She was panting raggedly, out of breath and stunned speechless. God, she loved this man.

"If you're going to wear my hat, you're going to wear my ring, too, woman," he rasped, his eyes dancing. "Be my wife, Roxy. Please?"

Stepping forward so that she stood directly in front of him, she cupped his bearded jaw in her hands and leaned down to press her mouth to his in a searing, heated kiss. The roar of the crowd exploded around them again, and when she finally pulled back, she nodded against his lips.

"I'm gonna need you to spell it out for me, baby girl. I want the words."

She laughed then, rolling her eyes. "Yes, Travis. I will be your wife."

He grinned widely against her mouth before capturing her lips with his again. And then he was standing, holding her left hand in his as he slid the stunning ring onto her third finger as the crowd continued their cheers. Bringing her hand up to his lips, he pressed his lips to the sparkling diamond nestled safely on her finger. Tilting her face up with his other hand beneath her chin, he whispered, "To forever, my love."

And what a beautiful forever it would be.

Upcoming Novels in the Petoskey Stone Series!
Stay With Me – Coming Summer 2025!

Hard To Love
That One Night

Upcoming in the Holiday Romance Novella Collection!
Meet Me Under the Mistletoe- Coming Winter 2024!
Lucky In Love
A Saturday in June
Halloween Night
Midnight Kiss

Keep watch for announcements for the Multi-Author
Collaboration Series

SKY RIDGE HOTSHOTS

FEATURING A 3-BOOK SERIES WITH AUTHORS

Sloane St. James
Paisley Hope
Danielle Baker
all releasing December 2024!

About the Author

Danielle Baker, romance author of the *Petoskey Stone Series*, including *Love Unbound, Best Kept Secrets, A Heart So Wild*, and *When Hearts Collide*, and the *Holiday Romance Novella Collection*, including *Be Mine, Valentine* and *Birthday Wishes*, was born and raised in the beautiful city of Petoskey, nestled on the crystalline shores of Lake Michigan. She is married to the love of her life, Nicholas, and they have four children between them. Danielle's love of writing began while she was in high school. She wrote a slew of short stories and had written three novels by the time she graduated. Life got busy and writing was put on hold for many years while she started her family. At the urging of her mother, sister, and husband, Danielle was given the boost she needed to "get back in the saddle" and keep reaching for her life-long dream of becoming a published author. When Danielle isn't working, writing, or spending time with her family, she can be found with a cup of coffee in one hand and a book in the other.

**Meet Me Under
the Mistletoe
Coming November 2024 to the
Holiday Novella Collection!**

**featuring Noelle and Theo in a friends-to-lovers, unrequited
love,
sweet and spicy Christmas novella!**

ACKNOWLEDGMENTS

I truly cannot believe that we are here at the end of my sixth book already, and number four in the Petoskey Stone Series! What an adventure this has been, and I truly feel so blessed to be doing what I love! Thank you all for your continued love and support throughout this journey!

Mom, you were my first and always my biggest fan, and the best proofreader around. Without your love and support this wouldn't have been possible! You knew when I was fifteen that I would be here one day, even when I doubted it myself. On to book seven and eight (holy crap!) already with so many others on the way! I love you!

Nick my love, thank you for letting me hide away at my desk for hours—and sometimes days—on end. Thank you for messaging me that my breakfast, lunch, or dinner was waiting for me when I was ready for it, because you knew I wouldn't even think about eating (thank you, Chef). Thank you for your support, faith, and enthusiasm for this passion of mine. Without you and the love you give me, I wouldn't have started writing again. Without your support, I wouldn't be able to do this full-time. You are my favorite cheerleader, my love. You are my forever Prince Charming. I love you!

Kara, you have been such a champion in my corner, for your unwavering faith in these stories and in me! And THANK YOU for excitedly and willingly volunteering as tribute to come with me to all our author events! I can't wait to see what kind of trouble we can get into! Thank you for being one of the best friends a girl could ask for!

Sloane, *woman.* Thank you for being my friend and I am so so blessed to be on this journey with you and Paisley! This authoring thing can be intimidating and lonely at times, and I am so freaking thankful for your friendship!

Tatia with Miblart, thank you as always for the amazing and sexy model cover! I already love Graham's cover, and I can't wait to share it with everyone!

Melody with Aurora Publicity, thank you sooo much for the absolutely gorgeous discreet cover!

KG and Dustin, thank you for always being willing mentors and taking me under your wings! And a million 'thank you's' to KG for the stunning interior formatting, as always!

To all my favorite author friendly Facebook groups: **Bookish Sirens**, April and all the wonderful **Smut Sluts**, **The SmutHood**, and Courtney and Dorothy and all the **Michigan Booktok Babes**, THANK YOU for allowing me to be unapologetic in my shameless promotions and all of you that have recommended The *Petoskey Stone Series* and this *Holiday Romance Collection* to this absolutely voracious world of spicy romance readers!

To my amazing **Street Team** and **ARC Team**, THANK YOU for loving these crazy characters and their stories as much as I do! I hope you all love Roxy and Travis as much as I do! I love all of you! So many of you that enthusiastically beta read, ARC read, and shout about these books from the rooftops, *thank you!*

To all the people that are not named but have beta read, listened to me venting or joined in my excitement over each new milestone, and all those that have rooted for me in this scary and enthralling journey, thank you! I wouldn't be here without you!

Lastly, to all my readers, old and new, this has only been possible because of the love and support you've shown me and these characters. I hope you love reading their story as much as

I've loved writing it. Roxy and Travis sure took their sweet time coming to life, but man do I just adore these two so much! Thank you for all of your patience as their story kept being put on the back burner. I look forward to introducing you to MANY more in the future! Thank you!

Coming Soon

**Don't miss what's next in the
Petoskey Stone Series,
coming Summer 2025!**

STAY WITH ME

Ripping up the loose floorboard in the back of the tiny closet, her fingers fumbled the old coffee cannister as she pulled it out of hiding. It was despairingly light, but she didn't care; it would have to make do. She could live below her means; she'd done it most of her life, this would be nothing new.

Scrambling up from her knees, she tossed the cannister into the black trash bag sitting on her bed, then shoved armfuls of clothes into it. A handful of her favorite books went next, and the ache of leaving her small but prized collection of books behind cut her deeply. They were her escape from reality… but this escape was far more important. And she was running out of time.

She grabbed the pillow and a blanket off the bed and then took one last look around the room that had been hers for most of her life. She wouldn't be back, she couldn't. Not if she wanted to escape the life her father had dragged her into, even if his motives had been for the right reasons.

She didn't bother closing the door, just raced through the small house and into the kitchen, where she snatched up as much non-perishable food as she could hold; none of it was all that nutritious, but it was food and wouldn't go bad while traveling.

Backtracking through the living room, she grabbed the small, decorative urn from the TV stand. It was all she had left of her mother, and she'd be damned if she left her behind now. She would never get the chance to say good-bye to her father. He may have made bad choices in desperation, but he'd loved her. He'd loved them both, so much. So much that he'd risked his own life to keep her out of the hell he'd fallen into…

But it hadn't worked. They'd come for her. She'd escaped, barely. And now, she needed to *run*.

Even if she had no idea where she was going to run to.

Away. Away was all that she could think. As far away as possible.

In the distance, sirens sounded, and she forced the panic to the back of her mind. She needed to go, before they found her. She couldn't go to the police... not when the police were in the pockets of the LA mafia. No, she needed to go. Before they came for her.

Nearly tripping as she raced out of the house, she skipped down the concrete steps and threw everything into the backseat of her car, an older Ford Focus that she'd scraped every penny to buy the year before. She would have to ditch it, or try to sell it and get a little cash out of it, before she made it too far.

They would be looking for it.

She had immediately turned off her cellphone and would not be turning it back on, but leaving it behind was not an option. Not after what she'd managed to record… She wasn't sure if it could be used to track her, but it was the only thing that could possibly save her now.

Climbing behind the wheel, she turned the car on and glanced into the back seat of her car. She forced tears back as she stared at the pile of files and the zip-drive that lay on top. Documents and files and records that had gotten her father killed in front of her eyes. Documents that she was now in possession of. Documents that they would be looking for, desperate to get back, and they would know exactly who had taken them. They would come for her, she had no doubts. She wouldn't be here when they showed up.

Turning back around, she reached over and pulled a small manilla envelope from inside the glovebox. Opening it, her hands shook as she looked down at the fake ID she'd had made when her father had started working for Victor Alverez and the LA mafia. Something she had hoped to never have to use.

Fear squeezed her throat and tears stung her nose. She tucked the new ID into her wallet, tucking the old one into a small tear in the seat cushion.

Teresa Gonzalez was gone. She would disappear.

She only hoped it would work, and she could make a new life somewhere else—*anywhere else*—as Thea Morgan.